"AN IMAGINATIVE AND IMAGINATIONAL
RENDITION OF WHAT MIGHT HAVE BEEN."
The Sunday Oregonian

HARRY HERON: A crime reporter whose career
is over. Now he's involved in the biggest story
of his life—a web of beatings, arrests, murder, and kidnapping, and a nest full of un-
savory characters . . .

ROSS: A British Security Service agent, who continually turns up as Heron's rescuer, but only
so long as Harry is useful . . .

COMMANDER DEFOE: British war hero and now
head of the Caversham Foundation, who
hires Harry to deflate certain World War II
myths . . .

CHARLOTTE GORDON: Harry's elusive girlfriend,
who turns up in the oddest places and asks
maddening questions . . .

GLEN SELTZER: An agent in the U.S. Bureau of
Covert Operations, London Station, who can't
quite get used to the deviousness of British
security services . . .

ALEKSEI SHILENKO: Russian agent in London,
determined to take the Goering Testament
out of circulation permanently . . .

THE MAN WITH
THE GLASS EYE: His identity remains as secret
as the organization for which he works . . .

Also by George Markstein
Published by Ballantine Books:

CHANCE AWAKENING

The
Goering
Testament

George Markstein

BALLANTINE BOOKS • NEW YORK

Copyright © 1978 by George Markstein

All rights reserved under International and Pan-American Copyright Conventions. Published in the United States by Ballantine Books, a division of Random House, Inc., New York.

Library of Congress Catalog Card Number: 78-19628

ISBN 0-345-28047-4

Manufactured in the United States of America

First Edition: March 1979

Paperback format:
First Edition: January 1981

*To the girl who drove
a staff car and knew
the route*

Yesterday

The eleven men were due to be hanged in three hours' time, and over in the gym the new triple set of black gallows stood ready. Thirteen steps led up to each of the platforms, and the ropes swung expectantly from the crossbeams.

The Army executioner, a thickset master sergeant from Texas, had already made his final inspection. Working quietly in the silent gym, he had checked that the levers worked perfectly, the nooses were correctly knotted, the drops opened smoothly. He had hanged three hundred soldiers in his time, but none on such a fine, custom-built scaffold.

Everything else was ready, too: the screen behind which the doctor would pronounce each man dead and the stack of stretchers on which the corpses would be carried out.

The hangings were going to be quite a show. A

1

fatigue party had placed chairs and tables in the gym to give the spectators a good ringside view. And the colonel had laid on refreshments in the officers' mess.

The place even smelled right. Clean, antiseptic, businesslike. And it was much airier than the usual death shed.

The executioner looked at the list on his clipboard. He wondered how the order of precedence had been decided. It was not alphabetical and, since they were all guilty of the same thing, he couldn't see any particular logic in who had been picked to go first and who'd follow him. Not that he cared. He had their height and weight, and all his calculations had been made.

Orders were for each man to be manacled to a guard when the time came for the final walk to the gallows. After they had been hanged, they were to be photographed, once fully clothed, once naked. Each body would be placed inside a mattress cover, together with the rope that broke its neck, and then sealed in one of the coffins already lined up in neat rows.

The doors of the gym were pushed open, and one of the guards, a corporal, came in. He stopped when he saw the executioner.

"Hey, you're early," he said.

He gave a slightly nervous laugh. It covered his uneasiness in the presence of the hangman. Ever since he had arrived, like a VIP in a chauffeur-driven Army sedan, the G.I.'s had eyed the executioner with a kind of grisly fascination.

"Just making sure." The hangman smiled. He knew he intrigued the soldiers.

The corporal glanced up at the scaffold. "You all set now?"

"You bet," said the executioner genially.

He looked at his watch. The eleven men were eating their last meal in their cells, and he decided he might as well go to the mess hall. Nobody could do a good job on an empty stomach.

"What's for chow?" he asked.

"Fried chicken."

The executioner nodded at the guard.

"See you later."

"Take it easy," said the corporal, and watched him go.

The prison grounds were brightly lit. Time and date of the executions had been kept secret, but nothing was being left to chance. Maximum security had been ordered. Army engineers had rigged up extra lights. Military police cordoned the walls. Patrols prowled the neighborhood.

And a steady, relentless rain pelted down unceasingly, soaking the soldiers as they huddled in doorways, cowered in jeeps, sheltered in watchtowers.

The streets of Nuremberg, shiny with rain, were deserted. Any German civilian who broke curfew knew he was to be arrested on sight.

But, periodically, staff cars raced through the darkness, throwing up showers of spray. Staff cars with the silver-star plates of U.S. generals, the insignia of Soviet army brass, the emblems of British and French staff headquarters, all on their way to the prison.

In freshly pressed uniforms, the official witnesses were arriving to watch the eleven men die. They sat in the backs of their cars, listening to the regular click of the windshield wipers and the unbroken drumming of the rain on the roof. If they looked out of the windows, there was little to see. It was too dark and wet.

Not that the British officer in one of the cars cared. He leaned back, looking at the closely cropped head of his driver but not seeing him. He was a captain, and it would not be the first time he had seen men being killed. Anyway, he was here for a different reason.

As the car passed a row of bombed buildings, the driver turned to his passenger.

"We're almost there, sir," he said.

"Good," grunted the captain. He was still young, but the neat, trimmed moustache made him look older.

The white-helmeted MPs waved down the car at the prison entrance. "Captain Fennerman," said the driver, showing the special permit. They peered at the officer, gave him a salute, and waved the car through the gates.

In the condemned block the corridor lights had not been dimmed, as was normal at night. Instead, the harsh white glare that would not go out until it was all over made the usually dingy walkways brighter than an operating theater. But inside the eleven cells only a pale glow illuminated the occupants.

The guards had been doubled tonight, on this floor and the upper tier. Now both the men of C Company, Twenty-sixth Infantry, and their charges were waiting . . .

Although they were locked away behind iron bars and steel doors, they could all hear the rain steadily coming down.

The sergeant of the guard clattered down the steel steps from the upper tier.

"All quiet?" he asked the man posted at the death cells.

"Sure."

The sergeant's eyes swung around, looking at the cell doors and up and down the corridor as if he didn't quite believe it.

"Keep on your toes," he said, and stalked off.

The guard transferred his chewing gum to the other side of his mouth. Hell, he didn't blame the guy for being jittery. If anything went wrong tonight, heads would roll.

The guard clutched his night stick. Nothing could go wrong. Nothing here. Not tonight.

He slowly walked along the row of cells, his steps echoing. Everything echoed here—the stamping of feet, the clanging of doors, even the jangle of keys.

This time tomorrow the men behind those steel doors would all be dead. He wasn't sorry. Guarding them day and night had been a lousy, boring job. It wasn't like an ordinary military stockade. This place was already a living tomb.

Each cell door had a grillwork peephole with a sliding cover. The G.I. decided he'd take one final look at the eleven men he'd never see again.

They wouldn't get a funeral. Barracks talk was that they'd all be cremated and the ashes washed down some local sewer.

He came to cell No. 5. This one was first on the list. He'd lead the procession to the gym.

The guard peered through the grille. He saw a small, austere room, with a barred window set high in the wall opposite. There was a steel bed. A toilet and a washbasin with running water. A plain table and a straight-backed wooden chair.

There was no way for the man inside to escape the watchful eyes that peered at him through the door. Even if he sat on the lavatory, the guards could always see his legs and feet. If he lay on the bed, both his hands had to be outside the bedclothes at all times. They woke him any time they couldn't see the hands.

The man was sitting at the table, slightly hunched. Despite the dim light, he was writing. Even if he was aware of the eye staring at him through the grille, he didn't look up. He was too engrossed in what he was setting down on paper in quick, impatient hand-writing.

Goering had lost weight. The plain gray tunic he wore hung loosely on him. His face was less bloated, his features more clean-cut, his eyes bright. His hair, neatly trimmed, was brushed back. He looked healthier and younger.

You got to credit it, thought the guard; he doesn't seem worried for a guy who's going to be swinging from a rope in a couple of hours. Maybe he doesn't realize it's going to be so soon. Sure, he knows this is the night, but maybe he thinks they won't be coming for him until dawn. Or perhaps he doesn't care.

The guard took another squint. In front of Goering,

on the table, stood a couple of small photographs in miniature frames. The guard knew whose pictures they were: Emmy, his wife, and the daughter, Edda. He always had them facing him whenever the daily inspection of his cell was made.

Earlier on, the guards had made the final search. The mattress had been turned back, the blankets shaken, his clothes checked, the washbasin and the toilet examined, the floor and walls scrutinized; they even gave his tin mug the once-over. He had been made to strip, and by the time they were finished there was nothing left for them to probe.

The G.I. guard moved on. He didn't feel any sympathy for the bastard. His own outfit, the Black Eagles of the Twenty-sixth, had liberated Dachau, and he was in one of the first armored trucks to enter the concentration camp. What he saw that day he was still trying to forget. No, he wasn't wasting pity on any of these men.

Footsteps approached. It was the officer of the day on his rounds.

"Everything in order, soldier?" he asked.

"Yes, sir."

The lieutenant peered through the spy hole, nodded, and walked on.

The guard's chewing gum had lost its flavor, but he went on chomping it regardless. In the movies, he reflected, a death watch in the big house had looked different. The guards sat in the cell with Jimmy Cagney or Humphrey Bogart and played checkers or made small talk until Father Pat O'Brien came in. Then the padre would give the last rites just before the final walk.

It wasn't like that at all in here. The chaplain had even refused him the last sacrament. Not that it worried Goering.

Slowly the guard began his round of death row once more. He looked into each cell in turn. Scar-faced

Kaltenbrunner scowled at him. Keitel sat hunched on his bunk, sobbing quietly. Streicher, the Jew-baiter, crouched in a corner, his lips twitching, mouthing obscenities to himself. Ribbentrop, ashen, was praying by the side of his bed. Others lay quietly on their beds, staring at the ceiling.

Before dawn they would all be ash, swept by rain-water down the gutter. The guard was glad he wasn't part of the squad detailed to dispose of the corpses. It would be a cold, wet job in this weather. By that time his platoon, off duty, would be getting their shut-eye in the barracks.

He stopped suddenly. He thought he could hear something. It was some kind of strange noise. A half-moaning, half-choking sound. It came from cell No. 5.

He went over and peered into it. For a moment he stood gaping.

Then he yelled: "Sergeant! Sergeant of the guard!"

It was 10:44 P.M., October 15, 1946.

They found Hermann Goering, Reich Marshal, prisoner 31G 350013, lying on his bed, his mouth gaping open, his face a grimace of pain. He was in a pale-colored pajama jacket with blue spots and black silk trousers. His right hand hung down over the side of his bed, and he was dead.

He had taken cyanide, and the suicide capsule lay on the floor.

They flung back the blankets and placed him on the floor, trying to resuscitate him. But his face was already beginning to have a greenish hue, and there was nothing they could do.

It was the G.I. guard who spotted the letters. There were three of them, lying on the mattress under the blankets.

One was addressed to the colonel. It exonerated the commandant and his staff of negligence.

"None of those charged with searching me is to

be blamed, for it was practically impossible to find the capsule," wrote Goering.

The second note was a farewell message to his wife and daughter.

The third letter was the Goering Testament.

Today

1

Heron resented himself. He had overslept again, and it was already after eleven o'clock when he arrived to open up Fennerman's shop at the corner of the mews.

The little man who stood at the window of the tobacconist's next door, engrossed in studying the grubby cards, meant nothing to him then. The cards offered "Expert French Lessons," "Strict Discipline by Experienced Governess," and "Riding Tuition with Ex-Actress," among other services.

Heron took out the spare key Fennerman had left with him and unlocked the door. The shop had a distinctive smell to which he had never become quite accustomed, a kind of stale, musty aroma, like an attic that hasn't been cleared for years. It hit Heron as soon as he entered.

He raised the blind on the door to tell the world the shop was at last open for business, and picked up the mail. The envelopes lay on the worn-out mat, a couple of circulars and a bill. Fennerman would deal with those, and Heron put them on the shelf, next to the three German steel helmets ("£4 Each, Complete With Liners, a Bargain").

The first thing he needed was a cup of coffee. He walked through to the little room at the back where the gas ring was. The place was a mess as usual, a muddled bazaar of old weapons, bits of uniforms, bric-a-brac, military insignias, model soldiers, and faded pictures. It was one of Fennerman's tricks in trade; the chaos beguiled souvenir hunters.

The tin of powdered coffee was next to the kettle, but the milk had gone sour.

"Damn," said Heron. He hated drinking the instant stuff black. Fennerman could at least have made sure there was some fresh milk.

He heard the street door open and went back into the shop. It was the little man.

Heron registered the slicked-back hair, the pink shirt with the floppy bow tie, the gold bangle around his right wrist, the trendy suit, the crocodile-leather shoes.

Instinctively, he disliked the man. The whiff of perfume did not help.

"Yes?" he grunted.

"Madek," said the little man. "I am Madek." He smiled expectantly. "Mr. Fennerman? He is here?"

"Not today."

"But he said he would be. He knew I was coming." Madek pouted, like a small boy who's been cheated out of a treat.

He had a soft voice, and his accent was a melange of pseudo-American and Franz Lehar Viennese. Heron wondered what his nationality was.

"Is there anything I can do?" he asked.

"You work here?" Madek's eyes studied Heron. "I have not seen you before."

"I help out."

"And he has not told you Mr. Madek is coming today?"

"Afraid not."

"This is most inconvenient," said Madek reproachfully. The thick gold bangle on his wrist had cost plenty, Heron decided.

"Well, if you can tell me what it is about . . ."

Madek shook his head. "It is a private matter." Then he paused. "You are sure?"

"About what?" said Heron irritably. The man was annoying him.

"That you have nothing for Mr. Madek."

"I've told you, no." He soft-pedaled his irritation. "Your best bet is to come back when Mr. Fennerman is here. On Monday."

To his surprise, Madek nodded almost amiably. He strolled over to the other side of the shop and looked at a German officer's ceremonial sword and a framed print of a U-boat at sea.

He picked up the sword and examined it.

"Beautiful," he said. "Is it genuine?"

"Everything in the shop is genuine," lied Heron. Some of it actually was.

"And this?"

Madek tapped a glass case containing a white china statuette of a uniformed man leaning on a spade.

"Careful," called out Heron, "that's very expensive."

And it was genuine.

"I know," said Madek. "Real Allach. SS porcelain. Custom-made for the party elite. Very nice."

He glanced around the shop.

"You have very interesting things here," he commented. "Especially if one knows where to look for them."

He walked to the door, then looked back at Heron, who was still watching him.

"You tell Mr. Fennerman. I will be back. Tell him Madek will call again."

"I'll tell him," said Heron.

Madek closed the door. In the street outside, he smiled and gave a little wave. Then he walked off.

Curious son of a bitch, thought Heron. But the important thing right now was to get some fresh milk. He was dying for that cup of coffee.

By the time he came back from the dairy up the road, two green police buses were parked in the mews by the side of the shop. The policemen sat in them, looking bored. Some had their eyes shut, others were reading newspapers. They were waiting for what was going to happen later.

Heron had already seen the police signs posted at traffic lights in Ladbroke Grove: AVOID THIS AREA. DEMONSTRATION. Now, gradually, the supporting players were moving into their positions. White-helmeted police motorcyclists posted themselves at the road junctions, their radios chattering. Green buses dotted the district. Four troops of police horses pawed the cobbles in the back street; their riders had dismounted and were standing around, gossiping.

Business was slack in the shop. Heron looked up as an American couple came in, the man and woman in identical white raincoats. They could have been carrying a sign saying PACKAGE TOUR. They walked around, whispering to each other. Then Heron heard the woman say, "But it's only a load of junk . . ."

"Yeah, let's go, Francine," said the man.

Later a schoolboy, serious-faced, with glasses, asked to see "Rommel's goggles." For a moment Heron was baffled. Then he remembered the plastic motorcycle goggles "as worn by the Afrika Korps in the desert. Guaranteed German army issue." There were a dozen of them in a cardboard box, and Heron produced a pair.

"These look new," said the schoolboy doubtfully.

"They're surplus stock."

"Oh." The customer sounded suspicious. "I seen them advertised as Rommel's goggles."

That had been Fennerman's idea.

"Well, you don't expect them to be the ones he actually wore, do you? They're the same kind. Left over from the war."

Heron's sales talk came glibly enough. It was a throwback to the days when he could persuade grief-stricken mothers to let him have a snatch picture of their strangled, raped daughters "because she'd have loved to see it in the paper, wouldn't she?" Ridiculously, it usually worked.

"How much?" asked the schoolboy.

"Two pounds."

The boy hesitated, then, somewhat reluctantly, handed over the money.

"Got any more Afrika Korps gear?" he asked.

"We might be getting some in."

The schoolboy departed, and Heron thought he had made him work hard for a beggarly two quid.

It was bad for a Saturday. The flea market close by usually attracted the crowds and the shop benefited from the drifters strolling past. Today, though, Fennerman's militaria wasn't drawing many.

Heron sold a Hitler *Jugend* dagger to a leather-clad youth for fifteen pounds, which wasn't bad considering it had been made in Hong Kong and cost six pounds wholesale. A ragged woman staggered in, smelling of drink and offering to sell her husband's Burma Star, but Heron turned it down. Burma Stars just weren't worth it.

Fennerman rang at lunchtime.

"How goes it, Harry?" he asked.

"Slow. We've taken seventeen pounds."

"Oh, well. What else?"

"Nothing." Then Heron remembered. "A bloke came in for you. Said you were expecting him. Seemed a bit put out you weren't here. I think his name's Madek. Mean anything to you?"

There was silence at the other end.

"Colin? Are you there?"

"What did you tell him?" Fennerman's voice had suddenly become less friendly.

"Told him to come back when you're here. Monday."

Another pause. Then: "Harry, why don't you close up the shop for today?"

"What? *Now*?"

"You said there's nothing doing. You might as well."

"Thought Saturday was your best day."

"Forget it. Push off." Fennerman's tone was clear. It wasn't a suggestion, it was an order. "Take your money out of the petty cash and call it a day."

"You sure?"

"Just do as I say. Okay?"

"All right," said Heron.

"Oh, and listen, Harry. If Madek shows up again, you don't know anything."

"But I don't, anyway."

"Exactly," said Fennerman, and rang off.

In the back room, Heron took the petty-cash tin out of the drawer and started to unlock it with the key from the empty jam jar. Then he stopped. He pocketed the morning's takings instead. "You don't mind, Colin, do you?" said Heron. "I'll pay you back sometime."

He put the metal box away, switched off the light, and locked the shop.

Across the road, another police riot van had drawn into position. The Indian grocer was boarding up the front of his shop, hammering in the nails. He took no notice of the freshly daubed slogan on the nearby wall: SEND THE NIGGERS HOME.

2

He stopped at a phone kiosk, waited until the two giggling girls came out, and dialed.

"Miss Gordon, please."

"One moment."

There was a click, and a man's voice said, "News desk."

They should have put him through to her extension. He didn't want to talk to the desk.

"Is Miss Gordon there?" he asked.

"Who wants her?"

"It's personal," said Heron.

"She's out on a job."

"How long will she be?"

"No idea."

"Thank you," said Heron, and hung up.

He knew he should go and sit down at his typewriter. "The Police and Corruption" had a long way to go. "Ex-crime reporter tells all. The truth behind the Scotland Yard scandals." He could see the headlines in his mind's eye, but on paper he had only fifteen pages, and they had taken three months.

He looked at himself in the phone-booth mirror.

"You need a drink, Harry," he told his reflection. "To help you think creatively."

It was noisy in the pub, and crowded. As Heron made his way to the bar, a burly man, his huge hands clutching two pint glasses of beer, bumped into him.

"Sorry, mate," said the burly man amiably. They were a good-humored bunch, sporting their party lapel

15

badges, standing in little clusters, talking loudly. Occasionally one of the groups would erupt in loud guffaws at some funny story one of them had told.

"Scotch," said Heron to the harassed barmaid. He might as well start the way he intended to finish.

Then the door opened and a chubby, fresh-faced man entered. He was greeted with a roar of welcome, and those nearest him slapped his back and pushed him forward.

"What'll you have, Ronnie?" men shouted, and from all sides came the offers to buy him a drink. The chubby one smiled with almost boyish pleasure at his welcome.

"Good to see you, lads," he called out.

Heron poured some water into his Scotch. It was all so jolly and convivial, like a rugger-club social, all hearty jokes and pals together. But Heron knew there was another side. When the heavily buckled belts came off and the nail-studded boots began stomping. They made good weapons.

"What brings you here, Harry?"

Heron turned around. Pearce, the eternal survivor, the man whom closures and management upheavals and half a dozen Press Council censures hadn't put out of business, stood at his elbow. He was smiling, but Pearce's smiles had an unfortunate quality of being similar to his sneers.

"Hello, Tom," said Heron.

"Well, are you buying or not?"

"What's yours?" sighed Heron.

"Vodka," said Pearce. It was his favorite drink because it left no smell.

His eyes swept the crowded bar, then he focused on Heron.

"You still haven't told me. What on earth are you here for? A free punch-up?"

"I came for a drink," said Heron quietly.

Pearce gulped his vodka. "Oh, sure."

"How are things at Château Despair?" asked Heron a little maliciously.

"Christ, what d'you expect? The new bloke is going crackers. He wants pubic hair on page three *and* page five. 'Triple orgasm and the modern woman.' Watch this space next week."

"Well, that'll make you happy."

Pearce's eyes glittered. "You haven't changed, Harry. Still a vintage bastard."

But it was said without heat. They'd been through too much together.

"You sorry now?" asked Pearce.

Heron stiffened. "Sorry?"

"Getting in too deep with your bent copper friend? Wasn't worth it, was it?"

"Oh, fuck off," said Heron.

Pearce burped. "Never put all your eggs in one basket, old son, that's my motto. You should have made sure he wasn't the only one at the Yard feeding you hot tips. That way you would have been safe. Stands to reason they thought you were tied in with him."

And you, thought Heron, looking at him, don't you have your little pet sources? Don't you scratch backs to get the titbits?

"You're a bloody fool, Harry." Pearce took another swig of his vodka. "You should have given evidence against Shayler. It would have made you smell sweet with the law, and Fleet Street wouldn't now be embarrassed to have you around. Just look at yourself. Blacklisted down the line. The crime reporter who played footsies with a corrupt police chief."

Heron wondered if he should do something he'd been keen on for a long time. Smash Pearce right in the middle of that sneering face. But at that moment Pearce turned. He waved to somebody at the back of the bar.

"Hey, here!" he yelled. "Over here, Charley."

She pushed her way through, and there was only a

moment's hesitation when she saw Heron. Then she came forward.

"Hi, Tom," she said. She turned to Heron. "Didn't expect to see you, Harry."

"Small world," said Heron.

"Harry's buying," announced Pearce. "What are you having, lovely?"

"Harry knows," said Charlotte.

Heron ordered her Bloody Mary, and Pearce leered, "Ah, I see you two know each other quite well."

They ignored him.

"You on this demo?" Heron asked her. She nodded. "Shouldn't think it'll make much," she said. "It's pictures they're really after."

"That reminds me," interrupted Pearce. "Has anybody seen my idiot photographer? The stupid git always disappears when you want him."

"Well, why don't you see if you can find him?" suggested Heron, smiling coldly.

Pearce shrugged. "I know when I'm not wanted. Ta-ta."

He shoved his way through the people around them and over to the door. He was grateful for Heron's cue; it got him out of paying for the next round.

"You're looking good," said Heron. She had on her black raincoat, and her dark hair framed her face with those great brown eyes beautifully.

"I called you at the paper," he said.

"They sent me out early." She lit a cigarette. Through the smoke she looked at him. "How is the world treating you?"

"Same as always."

"You know what I mean."

"Listen, Lotte."

"Yes?"

"Doing anything tonight?"

"Working."

"No, I mean afterward."

"I'll be dead. Dead to the world."

"Can't I see you?" he pleaded. Inwardly he cursed himself for sounding so eager.

"I'm worn out," she said gently. "A working girl needs her sleep."

"Okay." His face was blank. "Have another one?"

She hesitated. "I don't know." She glanced at the crowd.

He signaled to the barmaid.

"Harry," said Charlotte.

"Hmm?"

"There's a job going on the paper. They need somebody in Manchester."

"Manchester! Who wants that?"

"It's a job, Harry. It wouldn't interfere with your great masterpiece," she added sarcastically.

"No, thanks."

"Harry . . ."

He swung on her. "Forget it. Face facts. I got my best inside stories from a Yard big shot who's doing time for being corrupt. Of course they think he got kickbacks from me. So you know what that makes me." He saw her hurt expression. "Look, I appreciate it. But you know as well as I do they'd never touch me."

"You could at least try, couldn't you?"

The barmaid put the drinks in front of them. Another Scotch, another Bloody Mary.

"They never tied you in with it . . ." added Lotte. "Not you."

"Ever heard of guilt by association?" Heron gave a wry grin. "I hitched myself to the wrong star." The grin vanished. "So drop it."

"I . . ." she began, but he cut her short. "Cheers," said Heron, and raised his glass. It was like slamming a door.

"Sorry I mentioned it," she said stiffly, and took her drink.

The Scotch warmed him inside. "Don't be stupid. I said I appreciated it. But don't waste your time. It isn't worth the effort. Heron no longer has the Good Housekeeping Seal of Approval."

For a moment she was going to argue. But then she said, "I think I'd better get going." She started to buckle the belt of her raincoat.

"Don't. Not yet. Nothing's happening, Lotte."

As if to prove him wrong, somebody banged the counter of the bar, and a loud voice called out: "All right, lads. Drink up."

The leaders were calling their followers to order.

"Let's be moving!" shouted a man in denims. "Mustn't keep the Pakis waiting."

"It isn't polite," yelled somebody else, and there was a roar of laughter.

They formed a circle around the fresh-faced one, who raised his hands for silence.

"Remember, no trouble with the law. We don't want any aggro with the police. We're strictly law-abiding."

"Hear, hear," chorused several men, and then there was another gust of laughter.

"Follow me," ordered fresh face. "We're forming up in the square. Keep it orderly."

"I'll see you, Harry," said Charlotte, and made for the door. He saw her leave in the stream of people making their way outside.

Suddenly the pub was silent. The barmaid began clearing the glasses from the bar. She glanced at Heron.

"Aren't you joining your friends?" she asked.

"They're not my friends," growled Heron. "Give me another Scotch."

A man entered, stood in the door, and looked around the bare pub. His face was anonymous, his clothes unmemorable, but Heron could smell it: Special Branch. His eyes rested on Heron momentarily, then he nodded to the barmaid and walked out again.

"Copper," said the barmaid. "Tell 'em a mile away."

She gave Heron a second look, as if a thought had struck her. "You're not one, are you?"

"Hardly," said Heron. He gulped down his Scotch and went outside.

They were walking up the street, about a hundred of them, led by a man carrying the Union Jack and fresh face. Two police vans kept pace with them, and a file of police walked alongside.

"The blacks, the blacks, we gotta get rid of the blacks," somebody sang out, and soon most of them took up the chant, clapping their hands in time. The policemen looked stolidly ahead, expressionless, unsmiling. In a doorway an old woman in hair curlers applauded.

Ahead, in the distance, around the square, there were already crowds, held back by cordons of police. Heron could hear the yells: "Nazis out, out, out!"

Everything followed ritual. It was like the traditional choreography of classical ballet, thought Heron. The curtain was about to go up.

He had seen the same show often, with the same performers. But this time nobody was paying him to duck flying bottles, get crushed in the mob, or dodge mounted police charges.

Then he saw Madek.

3

He stood at a corner opposite, half hidden, like a man who wanted to have a good look and yet was anxious not to be spotted by others. He had a tiny Minox camera, and as the demonstrators passed, he took several pictures, quickly, furtively. Then he disappeared around the corner.

A man emerged from a doorway and began to follow him. The man, in a brown check coat, wasn't interested in the crowd, the police, the chants. He had eyes only for Madek, and then he too was gone around the corner.

In a reflex action, Heron crossed the road, went to the corner, and looked down the street. Yes, there in the distance was Madek, and check coat was following him.

Heron enjoyed shadowing people who were being shadowed. He started walking after the two men.

He wondered if Madek realized he was being followed. He wasn't hurrying, just walking at a brisk pace. It was a long road, grubby, with derelict houses and seedy basement flats.

Madek intrigued him. Hanging around a demo. Taking pictures. Being trailed.

Farther up, both men turned right, and Heron kept after them. If they split, he would follow Madek, he decided. There was a lot more he wanted to know about the little man.

A green car slid alongside him and pulled up at the curb. The door opened and the anonymous-faced man got out.

"Just a moment, sir," he said politely.

Heron stopped, annoyed. The two men ahead of him were still in sight, but he might lose them.

"Sorry, I'm in a hurry."

The other three occupants of the car stared at him.

"Police," said the man, and produced the warrant card that was so familiar to Heron.

"Well?"

"I'd like to know what you are doing here." The eyes were unblinking.

"What's that to do with you?" demanded Heron.

"We've been keeping you under observation, and we think you've been acting suspiciously."

"Balls," said Heron.

"You mind?" asked the man.

Heron shrugged. He knew the score. He opened out his arms. It was a very perfunctory pavement search. The man felt his jacket, patted his pockets, slid his hands along Heron's trouser legs. He didn't expect to find anything. Heron knew that as soon as he didn't even check the contents of his pockets.

"Satisfied?" said Heron.

"Just out walking?" inquired the man.

"What's it look like?"

The man took out a slim buff notebook.

"Your name?"

"Heron. Harry Heron."

"Address?"

"Eighty-one Ashfield Gardens."

"Thank you, Mr. Heron."

"Why?" asked Heron.

"Why what, sir?"

"Why all this?"

The Special Branch eyes seemed amused.

"Just routine."

"In broad daylight?"

"We can't be too careful, sir, can we?"

The man turned to get back in the car. Its engine was still running, and the other three occupants were staring at Heron blankly.

"Anything else?" asked Heron.

"No, that's all," said the man. He slammed the door, but the window was down.

"I can push off, then?"

The man rolled up the window and the car slid away.

Madek had vanished. So had the man in the brown check suit.

Heron smiled grimly. They hadn't even done a computer check on him. They hadn't even bothered to see what sort of cigarette he carried. They had stopped him for another reason. Somebody didn't think shadowing people was a very funny game. Especially, perhaps, shadowing Madek and his tail.

An ambulance raced past, its two-tone horn screeching, going in the direction of the demonstration. He could hear other sirens in the distance. The ritual was being played by the book. The punch-up had begun.

Just like Hackney, Red Lion Square, Lewisham, Notting Hill, he thought. The same hate-contorted faces screaming their slogans, shoving, pushing to get at the others, the same screaming women being dragged by the hair, the roar of the mob as it broke through the police cordon, the banners being ripped, the poles broken, the people trampled, the policemen with blood running down their faces.

Heron paused and lit a cigarette.

While the demonstration was on, cabs avoided the area as if it were a plague spot. Buses had been diverted two hours ago. And the nearest tube stations were shut because the transport people were sensitive about rival demonstrators knocking each other off the platforms onto the live rails.

There was nothing for it. He would have to walk.

4

The Nazi salutes didn't matter. The hate slogans. The racial taunts. The provocation. They wouldn't make good copy.

Thirty-one arrests. Two policemen hurt. Bottles thrown. Rival mobs. Banners torn up. Shop windows smashed. That's what people wanted to read about. That's what the desk wanted.

His third paragraph had started "Women screamed as . . ." It was a kind of superstition with Pearce. He firmly believed that if he could insert "women

screamed" into a story, it would make the front page.
Subs couldn't resist it.

"Is that the lot?" asked the copytaker.

"Yeah," said Pearce. "Give me the desk." No harm,
after all, in promoting the story.

"I think Fred got some good pictures of the punch-
up," he told the desk eagerly. "Listen, it was murder.
They bashed the hell out of each other. Then the
mounted police moved in . . ."

"Yes, the usual thing." The desk was bored. "Is
it all over now?"

Pearce knew if he said it had broken up, that they
had all scattered and were making their way home in
little groups, it meant recall to the office.

"Well, I don't know," he said craftily. "It's still
pretty ugly. Something might flare up again."

That ought to give him a couple of hours' drinking
time.

"No," said the desk. "I think you'd better come
back. I'm short of people."

"You sure?" Damn the son of a bitch.

"I'll take a chance on it," said the desk. "You make
your way in."

Pearce slammed down the phone. His feet hurt. He
had done a lot of walking. He wished he could see
a taxi.

He glanced through the glass pane of the phone
booth and saw Charlotte Gordon. He had lost her in
the scrimmage when the demo had become a brawl.
She must have put over her story by now. If they
were both going back to the Street, he could chat her
up. And Heron could lump it.

He opened the door of the kiosk to cross the street
to her just as a car passed her. It was dark green and
there were four men inside. A cop car, no doubt about
it. Two windshield mirrors, the thin black-tipped radio
aerial. Plain clothes.

One of the men gave Charlotte a nod. He could
swear it. Her back was to him, so Pearce couldn't
see her face. But they seemed to know her, all right.

Pearce forgot about his aching feet. He crossed the street to her just as she started to walk away.

"Charley," he called out.

She stopped.

"Who's your friend?" he asked mischievously.

She wasn't amused. "Stop calling me Charley," she said curtly. "I don't like it."

"I say, Miss Gordon, we *are* in a bad mood. Just wondered who your police friends were. Special Branch?" He studied her keenly. "Some inside tip I should know about?"

"Oh, go away, Tom."

Once Pearce was curious about something, he kept at it.

"Buy you a drink?"

"They're not open yet," said Charlotte. "Anyway, I've got to get back."

"So have I." He paused. "You don't have transport, do you?"

"'Fraid not," she said, her tone uninviting.

"Pity."

"I'll see you, Tom." She gave him a noncommittal nod.

"Okay." His inbred malice came to the fore. "Harry's already pushed off. You won't find him around here." He couldn't resist it.

"Really?"

She didn't give him a second look.

He stood, his eyes pursuing her as she strode off. No doubt about it, she had very nice legs.

She had lied about not having transport. He had recognized her Volkswagen. It was parked in a cul-de-sac near the pub.

No question, she was a cool lady. Damn good-looking, but definitely a liar. Not just about the car, but maybe a couple of other things, too.

It was the other things that especially interested Pearce.

5

Heron crossed Lancaster Road. In the first-floor window of a house opposite, he had a momentary glimpse of a woman zipping up her dress.

Pity about Lotte. He would have liked to see her tonight. Well, he'd try her tomorrow. Yes, that was it. He'd phone her flat. Maybe they could get together then. It was something to look forward to.

The way things were, he was grateful for that. He did not face the prospect of a weekend at the typewriter with eager anticipation. He wished he'd never thought of writing the great exposé.

He stopped. In the basement of a derelict house three men were having a fight. Then he saw it wasn't a fight at all. Two of them were beating up a third one, hitting out at him, kicking him. They were brawny characters, one had his sleeves rolled up, and both were enjoying themselves. Their victim was cowering, trying to dodge their blows, vainly putting up his hands to shield his face. He was a West Indian, and he cried out for help. His assailants, silently, savagely, efficiently, kept slamming into him.

Heron winced as the blows thudded home. He looked around quickly. The street was empty. Christ, he thought, hundreds of police crawling around the district a short while ago, and not even one bobby when you need him.

In the basement the West Indian slowly slid to the floor, and now the two men were using their feet to pound him. They were laughing.

"Hey," yelled Heron. They didn't even hear him. "Hey, you!" He started down the steps.

Even as he did, a voice inside him was saying, You're crazy, Harry, what's it got to do with you, stay out of it, there're two of them, you'll only get your face kicked in, stop being Mr. Public-Spirited Citizen, walk on, get out of it. . . .

"You!" shouted Heron. For the first time the two heard him. They looked up, surprised. The West Indian, sprawled by the wall, was spitting blood and vomit.

"Fuck off," said one of the men, and they resumed kicking the black man. They wore open-necked shirts and belts with big buckles. Each had the little badge Heron had seen in the pub.

Heron, his rage mixed with apprehension, grabbed one of the men by the arm.

"You're under arrest," he said.

He hoped it would work. Maybe they'd fall for it. Maybe they'd think he was a plainclothes cop.

"I'm taking you both in," he announced. He tried to make his voice authoritative, official.

The two men exchanged looks.

"You the law?" asked one doubtfully, and Heron knew he had lost.

"You're no bloody policeman," said the other man. But they were still eyeing him warily. If he could have pulled out a warrant card or a walkie-talkie radio, it would have been all right.

He made a final try.

"Let's not have any trouble now. Come along."

At his feet, the West Indian groaned. He spat out a mouthful of teeth.

"What the hell are you? A fucking nigger lover?"

The man was grinning now, and his companion smiled, too.

"You leave that man alone," ordered Heron, and they burst into laughter. One of them launched a kick at the West Indian's head.

Heron knew it was for his benefit.

"I'm making a citizen's arrest," he said. "I'm going to hand you over for causing grievous bodily harm . . ."

"You and who else, mate?" inquired one of the men.

"I don't like wog wankers," said the other one, and suddenly Heron felt a blow, a hard, vicious blow in his stomach, then a kick in the groin, and despite the agony, his mind, like an outside observer, signaled: You won't get out of this, you've had it.

He fell under a rain of blows; he could taste the blood in his mouth and hear grunts. They had no time to say anything; they used all their breath to do a proper job.

A fist struck him in the mouth and nearly drove his teeth through his lower lip. The other man was booting him in the back, and he felt an awful pain around his kidney.

Suddenly one of the men yelled, "Scarper!"

Vaguely, Heron heard them fleeing up the steps, and then something that sounded like car doors being slammed, and confused voices, and then he was out.

6

The policeman was a young constable, shiny-faced, neatly scrubbed. Heron reckoned he'd probably only just finished his two years' probationary stint. He had put his helmet carefully at the end of the trolley, and sat gingerly on the chair in the cubicle.

Nobody else took any notice of them in the

casualty department. An impassive Malay doctor had given Heron a quick examination, not the slightest bit interested in how he came to have his cuts and bruises. A nurse had done some slick first aid with disinfectant and plaster, and now Heron leaned back, aching.

"They gave you a nasty going-over, sir," said the bobby respectfully.

"That's right." It was painful to speak through his swollen lips.

"Did they take anything?" asked the constable. He had his notebook ready.

"Christ, I wasn't mugged," groaned Heron. "I was beaten up."

"Oh," said the young one. He gazed down at the blank page of his notebook, which so far had only Heron's name and address. A thought struck him. "Do you know them?"

"Not personally. Except I know what they were."

The bobby poised his pencil eagerly. "Go on, sir."

"They were fascists," said Heron.

"Fascists?" Almost imperceptibly, the constable was less respectful.

"Fascists. Nazis. Black Shirts. Thugs."

"How do you know?"

"God Almighty, they didn't have to show me their membership cards. They were kicking a black man because he was black. They called me 'nigger lover.' They . . ."

"Maybe they were football hooligans."

"Oh, sure."

The young bobby studied Heron thoughtfully.

"Were you involved in the demonstration at all, Mr. . . ." He looked down at his notebook. "Mr. Heron?"

"No."

"I mean, it wasn't a political argument, was it?"

"I told you. I've never seen them before."

The policeman started writing in his notebook.

"Would it make any difference?" asked Heron.

"If what?"

"If it had been a political argument? I mean, is it less serious if one gets beaten up in a political argument?"

"There are a lot of extremists around, and they go looking for trouble," said the policeman enigmatically. He saw Heron's expression. "On both sides," he added hastily.

"Look," Heron said wearily, "I don't care a shit about any of them. Red bastards, Marxist apes, workers' revolution, Nazi sons of bitches. But I'll be fucked if I let any of them beat me up, or watch them do it to other people. Got that straight?"

The constable winced. "Yes, sir." He closed his notebook, reached for his helmet, and stood up.

"I'll be making a report about this assault," he announced formally. He put on his helmet. "But I don't hold out much hope we can find them. These little brawls happen every day."

Heron felt his face. "Some little brawl."

"If we need any more, we'll be in touch with you," said the policeman.

"What's happened to the other fellow?"

"You mean the colored gentleman?" said the policeman carefully. He wasn't taking any chances. "He'll be all right. He's had X-ray examination. He'll be okay."

After he had gone, Heron stood up cautiously. He put on his jacket, and where they had kicked him still hurt.

He came out into Praed Street, and the cool evening air helped to clear his head. He was annoyed with himself. That little fracas had marked his card. That young copper would soon be typing his memo, informing Special Branch of the name and address of this radical who had been involved in a street fight with political opponents.

That was a laugh. They wouldn't even need to open a new file on him. They could just slip it into the dossier Scotland Yard already had on him.

7

The two calls came in quick succession. When the phone rang the first time, Heron was surprised. Nobody had called him for days, and the phone bill was three weeks overdue. The red final notice lay on the mantelpiece of the bed-sitter, and he had got used to the idea that any moment he'd be cut off.

For the first few mornings after the notice expired, he had tentatively picked up the receiver to listen if there was still a dial tone. Then he'd given that up.

And here it was, ringing stridently.

Heron drowsily looked at his watch. 8:20 A.M. Sunday morning. A hell of a time to call somebody. As he reached for the phone, he groaned. He still ached from the beating up the previous day. His lip was puffy. Moving his limbs was painful. Why the hell did anyone have to wake him? He could have slept on for hours, happily oblivious of reality.

"Yeah," said Heron.

"Harry, are you all right?" Her voice was anxious, urgent.

Suddenly he was very much awake.

"Shouldn't I be?"

"Harry, please. I want to know." Lotte sounded concerned.

"Don't worry. No bones broken. Anyway, what's a bruise between friends?"

"Have you seen a doctor?"

"Relax. I got the full Florence Nightingale bit at St. Mary's. They even gave me a plaster."

"You're not trying to fool me?"

"Come and see for yourself."

"I only wanted to make sure that you're okay," she said evasively.

"That's very kind." Something was bothering him. "How did you know?"

"Know what?"

"About me?"

"I . . . I heard that you'd been hurt. In a fight or something. Must have been at the demo."

"It wasn't at the demo," he said. "Who told you, Lotte?"

She had a habit of getting impatient when something annoyed her.

"Oh, I can't remember," she snapped. "Who cares? You're okay and that's all I wanted to know. See you sometime."

She rang off, and Heron slowly put the receiver back. It was nice she cared.

And yet . . .

How the hell did she know? It wouldn't be on the wire. A back-street brawl would hardly make a Press Bureau release.

He lay back in bed, and there was something he couldn't understand. The pieces didn't fit.

Then the second call came.

For one hopeful moment he thought it might be Lotte again. But it was another woman.

Fennerman's wife sounded muffled, almost far away. She said something indistinct he couldn't quite catch.

"It's a bad line, Ursula," said Heron. "Can you speak up?"

Then he heard her clearly:

"Come over, quickly."

"What is it?"

"I can't talk now."

"What's the matter?" asked Heron.

"Colin's dead."

He froze.

"I'm on my way," said Heron.

Suddenly he didn't ache any more.

8

A mortuary van with blacked-out windows was standing outside the house in Hampstead, and there was a policewoman at the door.

Heron got out of the cab and walked up the garden path, past the two rose bushes, to the porch.

The policewoman barred his way.

"Sorry, sir," she said. "You can't go in there."

"Friend of the family," said Heron briskly, and rang the doorbell. It was the style that had got him past a host of minions in the past, and it still worked.

A man in a cheap suit opened the door almost immediately and looked at Heron without warmth.

"Yes?" he said.

"Mrs. Fennerman sent for me," said Heron. Behind his shoulder, the policewoman was frowning. She resented the way he had ignored her.

"Who are you?"

"My name is Heron."

"All right," said the man curtly. He opened the door wider to let Heron in. "I'll see."

He is armed, thought Heron. The man's jacket was unbuttoned, and he could see the strap of the shoulder holster.

"Wait here," instructed the man, and left Heron standing in the hall. By the telephone table stood the familiar equipment case. The forensic boys were here, too, then. Fennerman hadn't just had a heart attack.

From the living room he heard the murmur of voices, and then she came out, followed by a stout man whose fair hair was thinning on top. Heron's heart sank when he saw him.

Ursula Fennerman had been crying, and she was clutching a handkerchief. Her blonde hair, usually so immaculate, was slightly awry, and her eye makeup was smudged. She wore a green trouser suit, beautifully pressed. It fitted her slim figure well, and for some reason he was surprised. Maybe he didn't expect newly bereaved widows to wear trouser suits.

"Thank you for coming," she said quietly. He had a feeling the presence of the stout man restrained her.

"What's happened?" asked Heron.

"Colin's . . . Colin's been . . ." she started to say, but the stout man interrupted.

"Mr. Fennerman's been murdered."

Heron nodded.

"You don't seem surprised."

"With half of Scotland Yard here? Plus the funny squad?"

"I'd like to talk to you, Mr. Heron," the stout man said, and opened the door of the dining room.

"I want to see Mrs. Fennerman," said Heron.

"Later."

She looked at Heron pleadingly, but the stout man merely repeated: "Later."

Yes, thought Heron. Just my bloody luck. It would be him.

The woman stood undecided.

"Perhaps you'd like to go up to your bedroom," suggested the stout man.

Momentarily, she was nonplused. "The bedroom?"

"We're about to take him away," said the stout

man, a little gentler. "I don't suppose you really want to see any of that."

She nodded. She gave Heron a look and made toward the staircase.

"In here," said the stout man, and indicated the open door of the dining room.

Inside, he closed it.

"Sit down."

Through the dining-room windows there was a good view of the lawn at the back of the house. Things were happening there. An outline was marked with white tape on the grass. A detective with a clipboard was taking measurements.

"You don't remember me, do you?" said the stout man. He didn't wait for Heron's answer. "I remember you, though. I was Shayler's sergeant."

How could I forget? thought Heron.

"And what are you now, Mr. Hood?" He tried to keep his voice neutral. "Chief Inspector? Superintendent?"

"Detective Chief Inspector," said Hood, and he relished it.

"Congratulations. Rapid promotion—well deserved, no doubt."

Hood flashed a sharp glance at him, but Heron could keep his face very bland.

Two other plainclothesmen were prowling about the lawn, carefully avoiding the white-taped area.

Hood followed Heron's glance but said nothing.

"What happened?" asked Heron again.

"Somebody killed your friend."

"Out there?"

"That's where his wife found him."

"How did he die?"

Hood shrugged. "Somebody shot him. That's all I know at the moment."

He was playing with a little silver mechanical pencil.

"I'd like a few answers, Heron."

"I didn't know I was involved."

Hood smiled coldly. "Where have you been all night?"

"Sleeping. At my place."

"Alone?"

"No. With Miss World."

The stout man's lip curled.

"Don't try the smart stuff with me." He peered at Heron's face. "Been in a fight, have you? Bit of a scrap, was it?"

"I tried to make a citizen's arrest," said Heron. "Two yobs were bashing a bloke and I tried to stop them. They stopped me instead."

"Very public-spirited of you." He sniffed. "Makes a change from the old days, eh?"

Heron ignored him. He was watching the detectives on the lawn.

"Speaking of the old days, seen anything of Shayler lately?" asked Hood.

"He doesn't have many visitors where he is," said Heron curtly.

"These things can be fixed. Just wondering if you've kept up with the old connection."

"Just for the record," said Heron, "Shayler was a damn better cop than a few I could name now."

A police cameraman was now taking photographs on the lawn.

"Well," said Hood, "that's not really what we're here about, is it?"

"I wouldn't know."

Sitting at the polished dining table, bare except for a lace mat and a white Allach porcelain bowl in the middle, Heron studied the man opposite.

You haven't changed, friend, he thought. You're better dressed, better paid, better fed, but the same bastard. A cop who actually enjoyed arresting people, especially when they were awakened in the middle of the night. He relished watching people being sentenced, his eyes never leaving their face. He savored their fear.

Shayler's fall was the best thing that ever happened

to him. It meant promotions right down the line. People getting to fill dead men's shoes before they were dead. Hood was wearing a pair of them now.

"You worked for Fennerman, didn't you?" Hood asked suddenly. He had pulled out the usual little buff issue notebook.

"I didn't work for him. I helped out now and then at his shop."

"Like yesterday?"

"Like yesterday."

"Pretty broke, aren't you?"

"I manage."

Hood leaned back in the chair, and it creaked.

"Not easy for you, is it?"

"You care?"

"Hardly being helpful, are you?" said Hood.

"I'm answering your questions."

"I don't know about that." He frowned. "Not exactly in your line, is it, helping out in a junk shop flogging phony souvenirs?" Then he smiled condescendingly. "But I suppose you can hardly pick your jobs now, can you? Lucky to pick up anything, eh? How the mighty art fallen."

"Can't resist it, can you, Hood?" sighed Heron.

"I know you for what you are, Harry," said Hood pleasantly. "You're bent. It would make me very happy to see you put away. You lorded it over us poor peons when you were in with the big boys, you shoved your way in, you were the cat's whiskers, weren't you? Well, me old mate, it's different now, I promise you."

Heron's hands were clenched. He sat white-faced.

Hood leaned forward. "Maybe you'd like to try it with me? How about it? How about a little bribe, eh? See if you still got the touch?"

Heron's chair crashed back, and he stood up and tried to grab Hood across the table.

"Easy, now," said Hood. He was on his feet, the eyes in his beefy face mocking. "I really wouldn't, Heron. You might find that's all I need. You'd make me a very happy man, and that's the last thing you want, isn't it?"

He reached out and patted the white bowl with the eagle design in the center.

"There, you nearly broke that, and I'm sure Mrs. Fennerman wouldn't appreciate it."

Heron put his chair straight and sat down again. His mouth was dry.

"Is there anything else, or can I go?" he asked very quietly.

Hood looked at his notebook again.

"Tell me, do you know a Hungarian called Madek?"

Suddenly Heron was very calm, relaxed. So. Hungarian, was he? Crocodile-leather shoes, perfume, and goulash?

There was a knock at the door, and a man put his head around it.

"You want him taken straight to the mortuary, sir?"

"Where else?" said Hood, and the man shut the door.

Hood beamed at Heron. "He's hardly in a state to have lunch at the Ritz."

"Madek came to the shop yesterday," said Heron.

"And you know him, of course."

Heron shook his head. "That's the first time I ever saw him."

"Really?" Hood chewed his lip. "What makes me think you"re lying?"

"Because you're so damn smart." Heron said it poker-faced, and Hood did a momentary double take. Then he flushed.

"What did Madek want?" he asked curtly.

"He wanted to see Fennerman. I told him to come back some other time."

"And you say you've never had any dealings with Tibor Madek?"

"I didn't even know his name was Tibor. Why should I know him?"

Hood smiled. "I don't think you would say if you did. Not Madek."

Through the door, Heron heard the phone ring in the hall. Again there was a knock on the door.

"Yes," said Hood irritably. It was the man in the cheap suit.

"For you, sir. Urgent."

"Stay with him," grunted Hood, and went out.

The man stood at the door impassively.

"You Special Branch?" asked Heron. The man stared at him without a flicker of expression.

"What are you doing on a murder job?"

The man looked blankly in front of him.

"You often work with Hood?"

There was no reaction.

Heron sighed.

"How's your sex life?" he asked.

For a moment he thought there was a sign of movement. But he was wrong. The man didn't seem to have heard.

The door was flung open without ceremony, and Hood came in again. He looked angry.

"You can go," he said to Heron curtly.

"Just like that?" Heron feigned astonishment. "No signed statement? No interrogation at the nick? I just walk out?"

Hood nodded to the cheap suit, who slipped out. He moved silently.

"On your way, Heron," said Hood.

He clipped his silver pencil into an inside pocket.

"Orders from above?" said Heron softly. "That phone call? Instructions to lay off? Somebody at the top? Telling you?"

Hood held the door open for him.

"I can't wait," he said. "I can't wait for you to be dead, Heron."

9

He knocked softly on the door of the bedroom up-stairs. There was a rustle, and then her low voice called out, "Yes? Who is it?"

"Harry."

She opened the door, and he caught a faint whiff of perfume.

"Come in." She looked much calmer. Her hair was neater, and she had put on some lipstick.

The bed was made, and she sat down on it. She indicated a chair by the dressing table for Heron.

"Did they ask you a lot of questions?"

"It's all right, Ursula. They're not arresting me yet."

She gave a wan little smile, which vanished instantly. The paleness of her face enhanced her high cheekbones. She was a very attractive woman, decided Heron.

"The house is crawling with them." She shivered slightly. "They're everywhere. I feel a prisoner in my own home."

"They'll be gone soon." He wanted to ask her many things, but this was not the time. She was taut, like a wire stretched to its limit.

"Is there anything I can do?" he said simply.

She shook her head.

"I'll be all right."

"Maybe there's somebody . . ."

She shook her head.

"I'll be all right," she insisted again.

"Look, why don't you at least let me . . ."

"You mean the funeral? Make the arrangements? Oh, no, Harry, thank you very much. That's very kind of you, but it's my job."

She said it almost proudly.

"And then?" he asked, and kicked himself for being tactless.

But she took it very quietly.

"I don't know. Perhaps I will go home for a bit. To Freiburg. To my people."

That was where Fennerman had met her. In Germany. Only three years ago. She was his second wife, and not more than half his age. It had happened very quickly, while Fennerman was over on a business trip. He came back with a truckful of stuff for the shop, and a new blonde, blue-eyed wife.

"I don't want to talk about it," she said, and he nodded. "But don't worry. I'll cope."

She had practically no accent, and her English was almost perfect. Fennerman's German had been fluent, and Heron had sometimes wondered which they spoke to each other alone, intimately, when no one else was around . . .

"I don't really know you at all, do I, Harry?" she said unexpectedly.

He stared at her. She was looking at him with those vivid, clear violet eyes.

"I . . . I suppose not." It was true enough. They'd had him over a few times, he'd been out with them, but it hadn't been very frequent.

But then he didn't know much about her, either.

"I know one thing, though. Colin would have trusted you with his life." She reached for a cigarette and lit it.

"Was he in any danger?" she asked. "Did you know if there was anyone . . ."

"Threatening him? No." He shook his head. "And you know Colin. He isn't a man—" He stopped, swallowed. "He wasn't a man you could threaten easily."

She nodded.

"No," she said firmly. "He was not a man who was afraid." She blew out some smoke.

"Did he say anything to you yesterday? He wasn't worried, was he? I mean, you didn't notice anything wrong?"

"I didn't see him yesterday," said Heron. "He wasn't at the shop. A man called Madek asked for him."

"Oh?" She frowned. "I don't understand. I thought . . ."

She fell silent. Nervously, one hand played with a tiny gold pendant around her neck.

"Maybe you could look after the shop until I decide what to do about it," she said. "Is that all right with you? *That* would help me."

"Well," said Heron doubtfully. "I don't know."

"I'm sure Colin would like you to . . ."

"All right, but I'm not a permanent sort of guy." He was trying to word it carefully. "I . . . I don't like being tied down."

"No, I suppose not," she said. "It's not much of a business anyway, is it?"

She stubbed out the cigarette.

"There's plenty of time to decide all that, I guess." She stood up and walked over to the window.

"Well, you make sure you call me if there's anything I can do," said Heron. "It isn't going to be easy for you for a bit. The police will have all sorts of questions, there's the inquest and all the legal formalities, and it can get on top of one. You know where I am . . ."

But she wasn't listening to him. She was standing by the window, transfixed, staring out of it.

Heron went over. He stood beside her, and then he saw what she was looking at. Below, along the front garden path, two men were carrying a plain wooden coffin to the gate.

They were walking slowly, not for any ceremonial reason, but just to step carefully, making sure that they didn't trip. The lid of the coffin, guessed Heron, probably wasn't fastened down. There were still things that were going to be done to that body inside the box.

Ursula stood perfectly still. Heron looked for tears, but she was dry-eyed, erect, never removing her glance from the coffin.

The mortuary van in the front of the house had its doors open, and the two men carefully slid the coffin inside the wagon and then slammed the doors shut. They got into the front, and the dark blue van with its black windows drove off.

Still she stood, watching until it turned the corner.

"You'd better sit down," said Heron.

She turned her head and looked at him, as if she had suddenly become conscious of his presence.

"No, I'm all right." She was very composed.

She went over to the dressing table and glanced at herself in the mirror.

"I think I'd like to be alone now." She was still staring at her reflection.

"Of course." Heron went to the door. "Don't forget, if there's anything you need."

She nodded.

"I mean it," said Heron.

To his surprise, she came over.

"I'm very grateful," she murmured.

"I'll keep in touch." Heron opened the door.

The violet eyes were fixed fully on him.

"Maybe I will see a lot of you, Harry," said Ursula.

And she shut the door gently behind him.

10

They weren't following him after all. He turned around a couple of times and did some nifty dodges, but there was nobody on his tail. It was the kind of idiot thing Hood might have decided to do, and he had fully expected it. Heron felt relieved. He didn't particularly feel like doing a hide-and-seek routine to shake off an unwanted shadow.

In Haverstock Hill, he looked for a phone box. He might as well cash in on it all and tip off somebody about the murder. Fennerman wouldn't mind, that was for sure. He'd buy him a drink on the proceeds, thought Heron.

He dialed his old paper and asked for the news desk.

"It's Heron," he said.

"Yes?" The voice was noncommittal, even slightly bored. He wasn't sure, but he thought it might be Calder.

"There's been a murder in Hampstead. A man called Fennerman. I'll put over a piece, shall I?"

"Just a moment."

Heron was certain now it was Calder. He had a knack of sounding superior.

Heron waited impatiently. He'd soon have to put in a new coin. He studied the graffiti on the phone-box wall. KEEP BRITAIN WHITE, said a scrawl.

"You there, Heron? 'Scotland Yard is investigating the death of Colin Fennerman, fifty-seven, who was found dead in the garden of his Hampstead home earlier today. It is being treated as a case of murder, said a spokesman.' You're too late, old boy. They beat you to it. It's on PA."

Calder couldn't keep the glee out of his voice. Heron, the great crime reporter, being scooped by PA.

"Oh," said Heron. They had been damn quick to get it on the wire. Didn't look as if he'd make much out of it now. Still, he'd have a try.

"Listen," said Heron. The phone started pipping, and he put in another coin. "It could get quite interesting. I'll give some background if you like."

"Don't think so, old son," said Calder languidly. "I mean, it doesn't look much of a story, does it? Who was the chap anyway?"

"He did various things. Ran an antique business in North Kensington. You know, war stuff. He was quite an expert."

"Never heard of him," said Calder. "I don't think it'll make much, thanks all the same."

"All right," said Heron. Pity. He could have used the money.

"Better luck next time," said Calder, and rang off.

That was the worst part. The patronizing. From blokes who wouldn't have been good enough to be his copy boy.

"Yeah," said Heron to himself through gritted teeth. "Better luck next time."

Then he wondered if he had been wrong after all about being followed. It wasn't the kind of fellow he would have expected Hood to set on him, though.

It was a motorcyclist. His head was a huge space helmet, and he was completely clad in leather. He had pulled up on the other side when Heron went into the phone box. And when he came out, the motorcyclist had started up.

And now, three streets away, he was still there, cruising behind Heron.

He was astride a powerful Japanese motorcycle, and it had a little blue pennant.

You're getting jumpy, mate, thought Heron to himself. You'll be imagining next that carthorses are shadowing you.

But he had to jump on a bus and ride as far as Oxford Street before the motorcyclist was no longer in sight.

11

To his surprise, the shop was open when Heron arrived at Monday lunchtime. The light was on, too, and he put the keys back in his pocket as he opened the door.

Already things had been changed. Many of the shelves were bare. Showcases had been cleared. Much of the muddled display had gone. And on the floor, in the middle of the shop, stood several wooden tea chests, packed with things that had gathered dust for so long.

A man in shirtsleeves came out of the back room and gave Heron a friendly nod.

"Good morning," he said. His shirt was an expensive one, and he wore silver cuff links. He was in his thirties, with blond wavy hair. He didn't seem the type who'd run around a junk shop in his shirtsleeves, decided Heron.

"Who are you?" he asked the man.

"Ah," said the man with sudden realization. "You must be Harry."

He smiled pleasantly.

"You must forgive me if I don't shake hands,"

he apologized, "but they are filthy. This place is, well, a bit dusty, isn't it?"

As if to prove his point, he held up his hands. They were grimy.

"I'm sorry," said Heron, "but I don't quite understand what you are doing here."

"Of course not." The man had a definite German accent. "My fault. I'm Dieter Langschmidt."

He made a shallow bow.

Heron looked around.

"What exactly is going on?" he asked.

Langschmidt frowned slightly, like a man who finds it tiresome to restate an obvious fact.

"I'm packing up. Closing the shop. For Mrs. Fennerman."

"She never told me."

"Oh? But surely that is not correct." The man spoke very precisely. "I understood that she asked you to carry on here, but you were not interested. So . . ."

He shrugged his shoulders.

"Is she selling the place?" asked Heron.

"I believe so."

"And when was all this decided?"

"Yesterday."

"What about all the stuff here?" asked Heron.

"I have no idea. Maybe she will sell them. Maybe she will put them in storage. Or ship them home. Perhaps," and Langschmidt smiled thinly—"they have sentimental value."

"I think I'd better talk to her," said Heron slowly.

"But of course, Harry."

Heron glanced across the shelf where the three steel helmets had been. It was empty now.

"There was some mail there," he said. "Bills and things. For Mrs. Fennerman to deal with."

"They have all been attended to," said Langschmidt. "Everything is in order."

Heron nodded, a deceptively mild expression on his face.

"Seems a pity," he sighed, "to see the end of it all."

"I do not think so." Langschmidt was very authoritative. "Mrs. Fennerman has no more use for it."

"I see." He faced the man. "Who precisely are you?"

"But I have told you. Dieter Langschmidt."

"No, Mr. Langschmidt. Not your name. What are you?"

"Ach, so." The man smiled again. "Of course. I understand. That is quite simple. I am a friend of Mrs. Fennerman's. A good friend."

"From Freiburg?"

"From Germany. It is a big country."

"I know," said Heron.

"By the way," said Langschmidt, "is there anything here you like?"

"What do you mean?"

"A little memento, perhaps? To remind you of the shop? Please. Pick it. Whatever you want. Take it as a gift."

"I think you've already packed most of the stuff, haven't you?" said Heron.

"Then I can unpack it if there is something you, how shall I say, fancy."

Langschmidt was hanging on his answer almost eagerly. "Please," he said encouragingly.

"Well." Heron paused. "I wouldn't mind that porcelain figure, if it's still around." That at least was worth something, he thought. A kind of golden handshake.

"The Allach piece?" The man frowned. "I was thinking of something perhaps not so rare. Just a little souvenir."

"I'll let you know."

At the door, Langschmidt clicked his fingers.

"Oh, I nearly forgot. I am so glad you came. There must be some money for you here. You were always paid out of petty cash, were you not?"

You are well informed, thought Heron.

"That's all right, Dieter," he said. "I've already taken it. You don't owe me a thing."

"That is good."

"*Auf Wiedersehen*," said Heron.

"Oh, but Harry, now *you* have forgotten something," said Langschmidt, as if the thought had only just struck him.

"Such as?"

Langschmidt held out his hand. "The keys, Harry. The keys to the shop. You will hardly need them any more."

"I tell you what," said Heron pleasantly. "Why don't I hand them back to Mrs. Fennerman in person?"

"Oh, that's not necessary," said Langschmidt lightly. He was still holding out his hand. "I'm glad to have met you," he said, smiling. Only his eyes were wary.

"I bet," said Heron.

12

He phoned the house in Hampstead, and a man answered.

"Mrs. Fennerman there?" asked Heron.

"Who is that?"

Heron blinked. Another German accent.

"It's a friend."

"But who?" The voice was officious.

"Tell her it's Harry."

"I am sorry," said the man, "but Mrs. Fennerman is not here. Can I take a message?"

"Will she be long?"

"I have no idea."

Something began to nag Heron. "Where is she?" he asked.

"She is out," said the man.

"Well, tell her Harry called."

"Yes," said the man curtly, and rang off.

Heron knew the bastard didn't even make a note of his name. He hadn't even bothered to ask for his number. Nice friends, Ursula has . . .

Friends? He paused. Just who were these characters?

Reason told him they were just that. Friends. Good friends, probably, who'd come over when they heard about Colin. Friends from Germany. Like Dieter, helping her to sort out the shop. That's what reason told him.

But instinct said something else, and what it said made him feel uneasy.

Ten minutes later he was walking up the path to the front of the house. This time there was no police-woman guarding the porch. But a couple of the rooms had the curtains drawn shut. Their windows stared faceless at the street.

Heron rang the bell and waited. He could hear nothing from inside the house. Then a chain was drawn and a bolt pushed back.

The man who stared at Heron had rimless glasses and short hair. He wore a brown suit and a conservative striped tie.

For a moment Heron thought it was Dieter's brother, not because they looked that alike, but because they were identical in style, appearance, haircut, manner.

The man stared at him.

"Mrs. Fennerman, please," said Heron.

"She is not in," said the man. Behind the glasses, his eyes narrowed. "Are you not the man . . ."

"Yes," said Heron. "I phoned."

"She is still not in," said the man, and started to shut the door.

Heron already had his foot in.

"Sorry, pal," he said, and barged through.

The man staggered back and the door slammed shut.

As he swung around, Heron faced him. His arms hung lightly at his side, and he was loose on his feet.

"You have no right," said the man angrily. "I will call the police."

"Do that." Heron was watching his every move.

"There is no one here," said the man.

"You are," said Heron pleasantly.

The man straightened his tie. "What do you want?"

"I told you. I want to see Mrs. Fennerman."

"You understand English, don't you?" said the man, and Heron thought that was rather funny, because the man's German accent had become more pronounced in his anger. "She is not here. You do not believe me? Please." He waved a hand expansively. "Look for yourself."

"Just what is your role in life?" asked Heron.

"Please?"

"What are you doing here?"

"I am a family friend," said the man.

"And a colleague of Dieter's?"

For the first time the man looked friendly. "Dieter Langschmidt? Of course. He is a good friend, too. You know Dieter?"

"We've met."

"Ach, so you are Harry Heron."

"Correct." They've got good communications, he thought.

"I am Jurgen Kiefer." He grabbed Heron's hand and pumped it cordially. Heron was taken aback. "You are very impulsive, Harry. You should have explained who you are."

His grip was firm, confident.

"Ursula has such a lot to do, you can imagine," he

went on. "She is all over the place. Solicitors, insurance, bank. When such a terrible thing happens, it makes much work for everybody."

"You and Dieter have come over specially?" asked Heron.

"But what do you expect? We could not leave little Ursula all on her own over here with such a tragedy. What are friends for?"

The idea of calling her little Ursula tickled Heron.

"Did you know Colin well?"

"You see," said Kiefer, "we are like the three musketeers. All for one and one for all. That is friendship?"

Heron winced.

"Tell me, Harry," said Kiefer, and he was suddenly serious. "Have you any idea who killed him?"

Heron shook his head.

"Or why?"

"If I knew that, we'd probably all know who did it."

"Well," said Kiefer stoutly, "I have every confidence in your police. Scotland Yard, what could be better? They will find out, positively."

"Can you ask Ursula to phone me?" Heron had written his number on a piece of paper and handed it to Kiefer.

"Of course. When she comes in."

"Thank you."

"She will be at the inquest tomorrow. The police, they have asked her."

"Yes," said Heron.

Kiefer looked at his watch. It was an impressive one, with half a dozen dials.

"I must not keep you, Harry. But it has been good to meet you. Another musketeer, eh?"

"Sure," said Heron.

Kiefer opened the door, and watched him walk down the path to the garden gate.

Heron did not turn around. He had found the common denominator, the thing that made the two men so similar. They were military men. They stood erect. Authoritative. They were used to giving orders—and taking them. They were tough, disciplined.

And no more friends of the family than he was a flying Dutchman.

13

The inquest was a brief affair. The coroner announced that at this stage he proposed only to call some preliminary evidence and then adjourn the proceedings.

Heron arrived just as the hearing started, and slid quietly into one of the benches in the dingy courtroom. By the wall sat Ursula, with Langschmidt and Kiefer beside her. She gave Heron an almost imperceptible little nod.

There were few people. The only reporter, a seedy type, shabbily dressed, kept his head bent over his notebook and never looked up. He wouldn't have noticed if an ostrich had stepped into the witness box, reckoned Heron. He felt contempt for the type: not a journalist at all, but a shorthand clerk. The sort who'd phone through and say there wasn't any story in the Prime Minister's speech because the Prime Minister had dropped dead and never made it.

Only two witnesses were called. The first was a policeman, who agreed that he had answered a 999 call to the house in Hampstead. There he saw the body of the deceased lying on the lawn at the back of the house. Mrs. Fennerman told him that she had awakened, found that her husband wasn't in the room, went downstairs to look for him, and discovered him dead in the garden.

Heron glanced at Ursula. She was looking at the policeman impassively.

"Mr. Hood," said the coroner.

Hood self-importantly carried a folder into the witness box.

"You are pursuing inquiries into this matter, Chief Inspector?"

"Yes, sir."

"Is there anything you can tell me at this stage?"

"Not really. This is likely to be a lengthy investigation, and I have many lines to follow up."

"Hmm," said the coroner. He studied a thin file in front of him. "A somewhat unusual weapon was used, wasn't it?"

Heron looked up. Hood had told him Fennerman was shot. He'd never thought much about the gun.

Hood nodded. "Yes, sir, a crossbow." He opened his folder and took out a small cellophane-wrapped object with a label tied to it. "This is the bolt that killed him."

Heron stared at it, incredulous. People got killed by bullets, knives, bombs. Not crossbows. He couldn't believe it.

"It is steel-headed, sir, about ten inches long, and weighs about an ounce. Quite deadly."

He put the object back in his folder.

"This crossbow," said the coroner, frowning. "An antique weapon, you think?"

"No, sir. We believe a modern crossbow was used. A very accurate weapon. At a hundred yards it would have a velocity of about four hundred feet a second."

"It's the first time I've come across such a murder weapon," said the coroner.

"It's just as lethal as a gun. From a criminal point of view, it has some advantages. It is silent. And its possession does not require a firearms certificate."

"Tell me, Mr. Hood, is it difficult to use?"

From the witness box, Hood looked fleetingly at Heron. It was the first time he appeared to have noticed his presence.

"Not really, sir. Anyone can handle one. There is no recoil. As a matter of fact, it is a popular sporting weapon. Even women are expert with it."

Ursula dabbed her mouth with a lace-edged handkerchief, while her two companions kept their eyes on the coroner.

"You haven't found the weapon, I take it?" asked the coroner.

"No, sir."

The coroner looked at a sheet in his file. "I have here the pathologist's report, which says that the dead man was killed by this bolt entering his right eye. Death was apparently instantaneous." He closed the file.

"That will be all, Mr. Hood, for the moment. Thank you."

Hood stepped down from the witness box.

"May I be excused, sir?" he asked. "I have a rather busy schedule today."

"Certainly, Chief Inspector."

He walked past Heron like an actor doing a key exit, knowing the eyes of the entire audience are on him.

Don't you love it, thought Heron, playing the big Scotland Yard ace. The man whose time is so vital that he has to rush off. The detective with a thousand secrets.

"That is as far as I propose to take things at this stage," said the coroner. "I will now adjourn this inquest so that the police can continue their inquiries." He gathered up his papers.

"The body can be released for burial." He peered into the courtroom. "I would like to express the court's sympathy with the bereaved."

Ursula Fennerman and the two men had already

risen. She stopped for a moment now, inclined her head gently, and then the three of them walked out.

Heron rose to follow. She had never called him, and he had some unfinished business.

Then he paused.

Sitting on the last bench, tucked in a corner watching people leave, was Madek.

14

"My friend," said Madek, and got to his feet with a winning smile. "How beautiful to bump into you."

He had a different-colored bow tie, and he wore a big ring Heron hadn't noticed last time.

"Excuse me," said Heron. "I'll be right with you, but I just want to catch somebody before they leave."

"The lovely Mrs. Fennerman, no?" said Madek. "Of course. Hurry. I too would like to talk to her."

They hurried out of the courtroom, Madek eagerly padding alongside Heron.

"I was late," chattered Madek. "It had already started when I got here. Madek has one very bad fault, believe me, he oversleeps too much. Like you, eh?"

In the street outside stood a black Mercedes-Benz, shining and polished. The three were just getting into it.

"Ursula," called out Heron.

"Call me, Harry." She waved and got inside with a flash of slim legs. Langschmidt smiled at Heron and slammed the door. The two men were sitting on either side of her in the luxurious confines of the Mercedes.

There was a chauffeur in front, in a gray suit but

without a cap. He evidently had his instructions, for he started the car immediately, and it slid off, purring. Fleetingly, Ursula's pale face glanced back at Heron from the rear window. Then she turned her head, and the car was lost in traffic.

The last thing Heron saw of it was the registration number: DO 11. The computer in his mind filed it and fed it into the system. Heron was good with numbers.

"Well," said Madek, "maybe the lady is not anxious to talk to us."

"Could be," said Heron.

Madek took his arm. "But nobody can stop us talking. I have a marvelous idea. Are you hungry?"

Heron hadn't even had breakfast.

"Good," said Madek. "We will have a magnificent lunch. If there is one thing Madek knows, it is where to have good food."

"Who's paying?" asked Heron.

Madek was pained. "Please. You are being taken to lunch by Madek." He waved an arm. "Taxi!"

"Look here . . ." Heron began, but Madek was already instructing the driver:

"Greek Street."

"Where are we going, the Gay Hussar?" asked Heron.

"It is so embarrassing, that name," said Madek. "Also, today I feel like frogs' legs and snails."

"I only thought, you being Hungarian, Tibor . . ."

"So. You have been checking up on Madek." The man wasn't displeased. "But the name is not Tibor. I'm Terry Madek."

"I was told that Tibor . . ."

"Tibor sounds foreign," said Madek with dignity. "I am Terry."

He leaned forward.

"And you are Harry Heron. The reporter. The famous reporter. You see, I too do my homework. I didn't know you when I came to the shop, but now I know all about you."

"Who from?" asked Heron coldly.

"I hear things," said Madek. "I hope you can eat a horse." He clearly wanted to change the subject.

The cab turned into Soho Square, and Madek said, "My first home." He indicated the little open space in the center. "You see, there. That's where I slept for three nights when I first came to London."

"When was that?"

"The revolution, of course. I escaped from Budapest right under the nose of the Russians."

"That's a long time ago."

"I will never forget." He lapsed into silence until he stopped the cab outside L'Escargot.

"Ah," said Madek. "Could you pay the cab, dear friend? I have no change. Only ten-pound notes. Would you mind?"

"Try him," said Heron. "Maybe *he* has change."

"You cannot ask a cabdriver to take a ten-pound note for such a small fare," said Madek loftily. "It is like giving a bus conductor a check."

Heron paid. "But the lunch is on you," he said, more to reassure himself.

"But of course."

Inside, the white-haired maitre d' came forward.

"Your best table. For us," said Madek.

"You have a reservation?"

"I am Mr. Lawrence," announced the dapper little man, and his tone implied, Does President Carter need a reservation? Do they ask Prince Philip to book ahead? Heron just kept quiet.

At the table, Madek said, "Do you mind if I sit with my back to the wall?"

"Not in the least."

"I do not like people shooting me in the back," apologized Madek, but his smile was false.

Heron looked at his watch. "Will you excuse me? I have a call to make," he said.

"Please."

Heron went to the phone booth in the corridor of

the restaurant and took out his little black book. He was looking for the number of a man who had access to certain information.

"Why do you want to know?" demanded the man after Heron told him what he wanted.

"I'm playing a numbers game."

"If you're not going to tell me—"

"Reggie, I wouldn't ask if it wasn't important."

"You know this should go through the normal channels. There is a procedure for these things . . ."

"It's urgent. Believe me."

There was a pause. Then Reggie said, "All right. Call me back this afternoon. But it's the last time."

"Of course," said Heron.

When he got back to the table, the wine was already in the ice bucket.

"I have ordered," said Madek. "You will like it, I know. It will be delicious."

"You're the host," said Heron. The point, he felt, couldn't be made too often.

The waiter put before him a dozen snails.

"The garlic butter is . . ." and Madek blew a kiss. He attacked his own snails.

The last time Heron had eaten snails was in Brussels, at an Interpol conference. That must have been. . . . He tried to think. Three years ago? Six?

It was a good meal. Venison, done beautifully. Montrachet '73. A raspberry *sorbet* that delighted. And then the coffee.

"A cigar, my friend?"

"That's very civilized," said Heron, and he picked the biggest from the case the waiter brought. He looked across at Madek through the Havana smoke.

"What is this all about, Terry?"

"You are very direct," said Madek. "Have some more coffee."

"Well? Are you going to tell me?"

"Of course, Harry. Cards on the table. My first principle, always."

Heron blew out some cigar smoke. "What exactly do you do?" he asked.

"I am a businessman," said Madek. "I buy things. I sell things. I sell them for more than I paid for them. Sometimes . . ." He smiled. "Sometimes I even sell without buying. You see how truthful I am. I am very honest. I even admit I used to steal. Before I became a businessman. When I first got to England, I had no money, no job. But I had to eat, so I stole women's handbags. I took the money and threw away the bags. I took nothing else." He hesitated. "Well, except once. There were some beautiful love letters in one handbag. So poetic, so lovely. I kept those. I had no woman, and I read them to myself. Then I burned them."

He searched Heron's face.

"There, have you ever known anyone to be more honest than me? I have told you everything."

"Not everything," said Heron. "The other day, for instance, I saw you taking photographs."

"Oh, you mean this?" Out of his pocket he brought the tiny Minox. "You are quite right. I always have this. So if I see a big fire or a bank robbery, I can go 'click' and I have a fantastic picture I can sell to the newspapers for lots of dough."

"You don't get a lot of money for pictures of fascist demonstrations," remarked Heron. "That's what you were photographing."

"You are wrong," said Madek. "Not here, maybe. But they pay well on the Continent. German magazines, Italian ones. They like pictures of fascist demonstrations in England. Maybe it makes them feel comfortable."

"You were being shadowed. Did you know that?"

"Of course, my dear friend. The authorities, they are so suspicious."

"Why should they be?"

"They do not like free enterprise. I am an entrepreneur. They are afraid of entrepreneurs in this country."

Over the rim of his coffee cup, Heron looked at the little Hungarian. He was quite disarming, almost likeable. Even the perfume smelled less obnoxious. Heron wondered how dangerous he could be.

"And what do you want from me?" he asked.

Madek nodded, like a man who had got where he wanted.

"I think you and I should be partners," he said.

"Doing what?"

"We split fifty-fifty. We get rich together."

"I said, doing what?"

"Please, Harry. No games. You know very well what I am talking about."

"Bear with me. Tell me."

Madek sighed. "The deal with Fennerman."

"What deal?"

"He promised to let me have the Goering Testament."

"The *what?*"

"Why are you so boring, Harry? I made him a good offer."

"The Goering Testament?" repeated Heron, baffled.

"Yes," said Madek impatiently. "The third letter. The secret testament he wrote in his cell before he committed suicide. We had made an agreement."

"I don't know what you are talking about."

"Fennerman told me to come to the shop on Saturday. He would have it there. I had offered very good money. Very good money indeed. But he wasn't there, as you know. He let me down. I am sorry he is dead, but that is not my problem."

"You know he was killed that night . . ." said Heron. "Is that why he was murdered?"

Madek shrugged. "Maybe. All I know is it is very sad. And very inconvenient for me. I am not interested who killed him, or why. All I want is that little piece of paper. I am sure you know how to get hold of it."

"I've never even heard of it."

"Of course you haven't." Madek smiled tolerantly,

like an adult humoring a child who's playacting. "So now I suggest we do it together. We share the proceeds."

"I tell you—"

Madek cut him short. "You can't fool me, Harry. If you haven't got it, you know where it is."

"Maybe you should ask Mrs. Fennerman."

"I don't think she can help me," said Madek. He frowned. "Not any more . . ."

"What's this thing worth anyway?" asked Heron casually.

Madek spread his hands. "You name the price."

"Five thousand pounds? Ten thousand? Fifty thousand?"

"Why not more?" said Madek quietly, and Heron could see he meant it.

"But why?"

"I am not interested, Harry. I play the market. To me, the *Mona Lisa* is just an old piece of canvas, but if some Texas oil millionaire wanted to pay a million to hang it in his air-conditioned cellar, what has it to do with me? I would help him get it. Do you know, somebody once wanted to buy Napoleon's penis? I was in the market for that, too."

"Who's your client?"

Madek laughed aloud. "My dear friend, I love you. I will share everything with you. I will give you my best pair of Gucci shoes. But I am not that stupid. Where would I be if you knew that?"

Heron drank his coffee. It tasted bitter. He had forgotten the sugar.

"Well?" Madek waited expectantly. "Is it a deal? You and I?"

"I'll have to think about it," said Heron slowly.

A look of triumph spread across Madek's face, and he smiled broadly.

"I knew it!" he cried. "I knew it all along."

"Now wait a moment," said Heron. "Why do you think Fennerman confided in me?"

"I see. You like to pretend still you know nothing." Madek pouted. "Come, my friend, you know he had all sorts of connections. In the right places." He winked. "Ah, that is pun, wouldn't you say? The *right* places?"

"You're trying to say that he somehow got hold of this document? In Germany?"

"Right. He did not just trade in silly guns and daggers and Iron Crosses, your friend. You know that as well as I do. That lovely china, for instance."

"Allach porcelain?"

"Of course. Only the top SS had that. Specially made for them. And your friend had lots of it. Very special indeed. Special connections . . ." Madek smiled. "Very special."

"Really?" Heron was noncommittal. "And just exactly what is this Goering thing?"

"A few pages of paper, that is all, a few handwritten pages. But, my friend"—Madek pushed his face closer —"very important pages."

"Why should they be?"

"You are not that stupid, my friend." He shook his head. "You know what they mean to some people, but the important thing is that they can make us both rich. Fennerman had it, you're his colleague. I think you know more than you say, so I think we must make business together."

"You might have the wrong man," said Heron.

"Nonsense." He raised his glass of wine. "Welcome, partner."

"I said I want to think about it," said Heron cautiously.

"Of course, of course."

He wrote something in a tiny gold-edged leather memo pad, tore out the page, and gave it to Heron.

"You can always get me there, or leave a message."

He signaled imperiously, and the waiter brought the bill. Madek pulled out his wallet, crocodile leather like his shoes, and then looked dismayed.

"How stupid of me. I forgot to get any money."

"I thought you had nothing but ten-pound notes," said Heron dryly.

"Never mind," said Madek airily.

From inside his jacket he produced a big, company-size checkbook. As Heron watched, he wrote out a check in huge spidery writing. The name printed on the check, Heron noticed, was Frederick J. Lawrence. And that's how Madek signed it.

He saw Heron's look. "I have several bank accounts, my friend. It is sometimes useful to have them in different names. But that is quite legal, I assure you. This is a free country."

Outside, in Greek Street, he offered Heron a lift in a cab.

"I think I'll walk a bit."

"When you have thought, you call me," said Madek jovially. "I shall be waiting, partner. You know something?"

Heron shook his head.

"You and I, Harry, are going to be very rich. Isn't that nice?"

He strode off jauntily, and Heron, watching him go toward Shaftesbury Avenue, wondered if Madek ever stopped lying.

15

In the Broadwick Street post office, Heron called his friend.

"Well," said Reggie, "if they smashed your headlights, forget about suing them for compensation. They've got diplomatic immunity."

"There's no CD plate," said Heron.

"There doesn't have to be. Some diplomatic missions like to have a few unmarked cars. Can't blame them, with all the terrorists around the place."

"Go on."

"That's it, chum. That Mercedes you're so interested in, DQ eleven, is on the diplomatic list."

"You sure?"

"I checked twice. It belongs to the West German embassy. The ambassador's own car pool."

16

At eleven o'clock in the morning the cemetery was empty. Heron hadn't expected a large crowd, but the lack of people at Fennerman's funeral was something else again.

There was no Ursula. At first Heron thought she was late, but the brief ceremony ended and she still had not come.

Instead, there was a wreath of carnations and roses with a plain white card that said:

"I will love you always. U."

Very touching, thought Heron. She couldn't even be bothered to show. A quick phone call to the neighborhood florist, and that was all. He remembered how unmoved her face had been as they carried the body out of the house. Yes, she was quite a hard lady.

There was one other man present. He stood erect, an elderly gentleman in a dark suit, with white hair and a regimental tie. His shoes were beautifully polished, and he carried a bowler hat and a tightly rolled umbrella.

His bearing was upright and, despite his age, straight as a ramrod.

They both stood, when it was all over, looking down at the fresh grave with its small marker: "Colin Arthur Fennerman, 1920–1978."

Curious, thought Heron. Here we are, the only two mourners. Colin must surely have had some friends. Somebody must have cared that he was dead. His first wife, perhaps. As for Ursula . . .

"Excuse me, sir," said the old gentleman. He had put on his bowler hat after standing bareheaded and silent at the grave. "Did you by any chance know my son?"

Heron nodded.

"I am Colonel Fennerman. His father." The old man held out his hand. "I am pleased to meet you."

His grip was firm and strong. The old boy was certainly well preserved, Heron thought.

"I don't imagine Colin told you about me . . ."

Under their bushy white eyebrows, the eyes, sharp and clear, focused on him. "You are Harry," said the colonel. "Oh, yes, I know all about you. So why are you here, and not his wife?"

"Perhaps the shock . . ." muttered Heron awkwardly.

"Don't believe it. She is no shrinking flower. Even if she's got deplorable manners."

"I'm sure there's a good reason. She was very fond of Colin."

The colonel snorted. "Was she, now?" He looked around. "Not much of a send-off for him, was it? Not even the police. You'd have thought the police . . ."

"I imagine they're too busy on the case," said Heron guardedly.

"Hmm." The colonel started to walk along the path between the plots of graves. "Never thought I'd see this day. Colin, last of the line. I always reckoned he'd bury me." He stopped and faced Heron. "He deserved better. He was a brave man."

A chord struck in Heron's memory. That's what Ursula had said: "He was not a man who was afraid."

"Didn't know much about my son's business," said the colonel. "He had that shop, didn't he? Military stuff?"

"That's right. He let me help out." Heron took the plunge. "Did he ever mention something called the Goering Testament?"

"Should he?" He glanced at Heron. "What is it?"

"Something Colin had, maybe."

"First I heard of it. Goering's, did you say?"

Heron nodded.

"Must be worth something if it is," said the colonel. "Come along, don't dawdle."

He marched on firmly, swinging his umbrella. There was no frailty about this old man.

"So it means nothing to you?" pressed Heron.

But the colonel suddenly appeared to be hard of hearing, striding on without reply.

"How did you two meet?" he asked.

"One of those things," said Heron. "Got to know each other, kept up the acquaintance, you know how these things go."

"No. I don't."

He seemed preoccupied with what was on his mind. Then he came out with it.

"Look here, Colin once said you knew people. In the police. At the Yard. When you were in Fleet Street. I want to know what's happened. What's going on. Why someone killed him. Why his wife isn't here. You follow?"

"Yes," said Heron.

"I live up in Gloucester, but I'll be in town a couple of days. See what you can find out."

"I will," promised Heron.

"I'm staying at Brown's. Come and report to me. Before I go back to the country. That's not too much to ask, is it?"

"I'll try to find out," said Heron quietly.

At the gate of the cemetery stood Lotte. She came forward, nodded to Heron, but was interested only in the old man.

"Excuse me," she said. "Colonel Fennerman?"

"What do you want?" snapped the old man curtly.

"A couple of words, if you don't mind," she said. "I'm Charlotte Gordon of the *Chronicle*."

"Journalist, are you?" rumbled the colonel. "Don't hold with it. Not at funerals. Not any time. And let me tell you, it's no job for a woman, scavenging."

"I'm sure it won't take long, sir," said Heron, and Lotte flashed him an angry look. The message was clear: Don't bloody well try to smooth things for me, I can handle this myself.

"Well, what is it?" growled the colonel.

"About your son," said Lotte. "I'd like to get just a little background. His service career, for instance."

"My son did his duty. He always did his duty," said the colonel. "Right to the end."

"He served in Normandy, didn't he, sir? And later in Germany?"

What's your angle? Heron wanted to ask her. War service? Who cared now?

"Of course he did."

"Was this him, sir?" She had produced, from her shoulder bag, a photograph. It was Fennerman, all right. A youthful Fennerman. In his twenties. In the uniform of an army captain. He had a neat-trimmed moustache. Something he never had while Heron knew him.

"Where did you get that?" asked the colonel. "He was much younger then. This was taken in the war."

"If you like, Colonel Fennerman, I'll get the paper to send you a copy," said Lotte.

"How did you get hold of it?" he repeated.

"I think the paper had it in its files." She sounded vague.

The colonel was still studying the photograph.

"Yes, I'd like a copy of that." Almost reluctantly, he gave it back to her.

"I'll give you my address in the country," he said.

"That's all right, Colonel, I'm sure the paper has it."

Heron blinked. Check and double-check, that was the rule. And that's usually exactly what Lotte did. This time it didn't seem to matter.

She glanced around the empty cemetery. "Who else was at the funeral? Any relatives? Friends?"

"No," said the colonel stiffly. "Just myself. And this gentleman."

She ignored Heron. "No family at all? No old army comrades?"

"Colin had no close family left. Apart from me," said the colonel. The question about comrades he left unanswered.

"I hope you don't mind the—the intrusion," said Lotte. "I know it's not the time. I do apologize."

"I suppose you have your job."

"But his wife? Was she here? He *was* married, wasn't he? Didn't she come?"

"Maybe you'd better ask her," snapped the colonel. "Good day."

She was about to say something, then nodded. "Thank you again."

At last she acknowledged Heron's presence.

"Let's meet sometime, Harry," she said as she walked off.

"You know that girl?" asked the colonel.

"Yes," Heron answered. But he wondered whether he really did.

As they came out of the cemetery gates, Lotte was getting into her Volkswagen. She had parked it on a double yellow line.

"She's nosy," muttered the colonel. "Well, I suppose that's what they pay her for."

"Yes," said Heron again. As she drove off, Lotte waved a gloved hand at them.

In the distance, a taxi approached. It had its FOR HIRE sign lit up.

"Can I take you back to your hotel, sir?" offered Heron.

"In London I go by tube," snapped the colonel. He saw Heron's expression. "Blast you, man, I'm not that decrepit yet, and if I were I'd thank you not to remind me of it."

"Yes, sir." Heron felt like a subaltern dressed down on parade.

"Well, you coming?"

"No, thank you. I've got a few things to find out."

"So you have. Damn it, she does owe me an explanation, that wife of his."

"And I'll contact you at the hotel."

"Good." The colonel drew himself up stiffly. "Thank you for coming to the funeral, Heron. I appreciate it. At least my son hasn't been forgotten by everybody."

He turned abruptly, but not quickly enough to hide the tears in his eyes.

17

Messrs. Rowntree, Middleton and Chandler, auctioneers, valuers, and estate agents, were polite and correct but hardly helpful.

Yes, they confirmed, the late Mr. Fennerman's house had been placed on the market. They did not think they would have any difficulty in disposing of it; it was a good property and Hampstead was a desirable district.

"Isn't this a bit rushed?" Heron asked the suave

man opposite him. He didn't know whether it was Rowntree, Middleton, or Chandler, but he was sure they all spoke with one voice. "I mean, Mr. Fennerman only, er, died on Sunday, the inquest has been adjourned, the funeral was only this morning, and already you're selling the house."

"Those are our instructions," said the voice of them all.

"I went over there Monday, and the house was still occupied. Today it's empty and your FOR SALE board is up. Who gave you your instructions?"

"Mrs. Fennerman." The man looked at Heron with some distaste. "Excuse me, sir, but are you interested in the property? Are you inquiring as an intending purchaser?"

"Maybe," said Heron.

"Well, in that case I can assure you that everything is perfectly in order. Would you care for a cup of tea?"

"No, thank you. Do you know where I can get hold of Mrs. Fennerman?"

The man looked pained. "Believe me, Mr. Heron, there's absolutely no need for that. We have been granted full powers of attorney in this matter, subject to Mrs. Fennerman's approval of the price finally offered."

"What about the shop?"

The man sucked in his breath. "The shop in North Kensington?" He looked slightly disturbed.

"That's the one. Near Ladbroke Grove."

"Yes, that's a great pity." The man sighed.

Heron's eyes narrowed. "What's a pity?"

"Well, you see, we were also asked to put the shop on the market. Although," he stressed hastily, like a lady whose virtue might be impugned, "our main line of business is, of course, in high-class residential property."

"So?"

"I'm afraid the shop won't really fetch a viable

price at the moment," said the man sorrowfully. "As of today."

Heron sat up. "Why not?"

"I'm sorry to say it was burned down during the night. Arson, I'm told."

"What exactly happened?" asked Heron.

"The police tell me that it appears to have been a petrol bomb. Somebody threw it into the premises during the night, and I'm afraid there was nothing anybody could do."

The estate agent's second chin quivered. "Isn't it shocking, all this vandalism these days?"

He brightened. "However, luckily it was empty. With great foresight, Mrs. Fennerman had closed down the business and removed all the contents. That was very fortunate, wasn't it?"

"Oh, indeed," said Heron.

"But I take it your real interest is in the house?"

"Could be."

"Would you care to look over the property, Mr. Heron?"

"I'd like Mrs. Fennerman's present address," said Heron.

"I'm sorry," said the man. Heron was sure he was Middleton. He didn't seem a Rowntree or a Chandler. "Her instructions are quite specific."

"Is she in this country?"

Middleton-that-might-be cleared his throat. If this was a purchaser—and he wasn't convinced of that—he didn't want to antagonize him too much at this delicate stage.

"Well, Mr. Heron, I suppose I can go so far as to say that the lady has moved abroad. That is why she wishes to dispose of her late husband's property over here."

"Germany? Is that where she is? Freiburg, perhaps?"

"I'm sorry, Mr. Heron, I'd like to be more helpful, but you understand, a client's instructions are sacred."

He liked the way he put it. "I really can't go beyond confirming that she is no longer in England."

"Thank you," said Heron, and stood up.

The estate agent was slightly dismayed.

"But wouldn't you like to view the house? I can arrange . . ."

"Sometime," said Heron.

The man looked at him like a grief-stricken spaniel.

"If I were you," said Heron kindly, "I'd make sure nobody chucks a petrol bomb into the house, too."

"Oh, surely not . . . ! Anyway, Mr. Heron, if you're really interested in the property, I wouldn't leave it too long. I've already had one inquiry for it."

"Really?"

"Yes, indeed. A lady came in and asked about it. Just after lunch. I hope she wasn't too annoyed—when she left, she found a parking ticket on her Volkswagen." He allowed himself a chauvinistic smile. "Amazing how some women drivers simply ignore the yellow lines, isn't it? Must cost them a pretty penny."

"I wouldn't worry," said Heron, at the door. "I've got a feeling the people she works for pay her fines."

18

Geist, who was down as a commercial attaché on the Foreign Office diplomatic list but fulfilled a completely different function at the embassy in Belgravia, came out of the communications room.

He had just sent a signal to Bonn, in his special code, about the suspected presence of an ex-Bader-Meinhoff adherent in Southampton. It was information the liaison man at Special Branch had passed on to him to relay to the federal authorities.

A mild-mannered man, considering his career, Geist was wearing his new Savile Row suite. He had ordered it as soon as he was transferred to London from his attachment to NATO headquarters, but it had taken six months to be ready.

It fitted him well, almost as well as the major's uniform he wouldn't wear while at the embassy.

"There's a man downstairs asking some funny questions," his assistant, Ludwig, told him when he returned to his office.

"Well, give him some funny answers," said Geist, wondering what the *Geheimt Sache* file on his desk contained.

"I think maybe you should see him yourself, sir." Usually, Ludwig did as he was told, but this was different. "He is asking about Langschmidt and Kiefer."

Geist forgot about the file.

"Are you sure?"

"That's what downstairs says."

"Very well," said Geist. "Send him to the interview room."

Heron was examining a print of Heidelberg Castle when Geist came in.

"How can I help you, Mr. Heron?" he asked, looking at the slip of paper reception had filled in.

"I'm trying to find somebody, and maybe you can help me," said Heron.

"A German national?"

"Well, her name is Fennerman. She married an Englishman, and—"

Geist cut him short. "Then I cannot assist you. She must now be a British citizen."

"But Langschmidt and Kiefer aren't," said Heron.

"Who?" He had learned long ago how to play dumb in a most convincing way.

"Dieter Langschmidt and Jurgen Kiefer," said

Heron. "They're very German. I'd like to know something about them."

"But what is the connection, Mr. Heron?"

"If I find them, I think I'll find her."

"My dear sir," said Geist—he could have been educated at Eton—"do you realize how many of our tourists visit London? Thousands and thousands. The embassy has no way of knowing who is over here."

"Who said they're tourists?" Heron looked at him coldly. "Maybe they're here on business."

"That has nothing to do with us." Mentally, he photographed Heron. He wanted to remember that face.

"Then why are they using one of your cars?"

"I don't understand."

"They've been chauffeured around in a Mercedes that belongs to your embassy. The number is DQ eleven. It is an unmarked car, but it is on the diplomatic list. Now, can you tell me why two people you've apparently never heard of should have the use of one of your cars?"

"I'm sure you've made a mistake," said Geist lightly. "You misread the number." He shook his head. "Unauthorized people do not use our embassy cars."

"Perhaps they've sent me to the wrong man." Heron nodded as if he had found the answer. "What is your department?"

"I'm a commercial attaché," said Geist stiffly.

"There you are. The wrong man. I need to see somebody else. As you say, this has nothing to do with the commercial attaché, has it?"

"Mr. Heron." His face was bland. "I do not believe anyone else can help you, either."

"How strange," said Heron. "Don't you even want to know why I'm anxious to find Mrs. Fennerman?"

"Perhaps this is a matter for the British authorities. Have you tried the police?"

"Isn't that a good idea!" Heron smiled, and Geist

began to look a little relieved. "Now, why didn't I think of that?"

"Well, in that case, I'm glad to have been able to be of some assistance. I hope you find what you're looking for."

"So do I," said Heron.

"Please." The man held open the door.

"Oh, by the way," said Heron, "what do you know about the Goering Testament?"

Geist's gray eyes stared straight into his. "I've never heard of it. What is it?"

"Never mind," said Heron. *"Auf Wiedersehen."*

19

When Geist sat down at his desk, Ludwig said, "The military attaché would like to arrange a meeting tomorrow and—"

"Later," said Geist. He looked thoughtful.

"What did he want, this man?" asked Ludwig.

Geist did not reply. He pulled a ruled yellow pad toward him and started writing. He covered only six lines. Then he tore the page off and handed it to Ludwig.

"I want this encoded as well," he ordered, "and marked 'Priority.' "

Ludwig, who in order to work with Geist had his country's highest security clearance, looked at the sheet and whistled.

"Yes," said Geist. "You're quite right. I told you London isn't a dull post."

After Ludwig had gone, Geist picked up one of his two phones.

"Get me the Ministry of Defence," he requested. "Mr. Ross."

His call came in thirty-five seconds.

"As if we haven't got enough on our plate, I have a little goody for you," said Geist. "It's a man called Heron."

20

"Drop me here," ordered Hood, and the police driver stopped in Wardour Street.

He walked up the cul-de-sac to the shabby entrance of the second house. Paint was peeling off the door, and all kinds of posters were stuck on the wall: IRANIAN STUDENTS RALLY, WORKERS SOLIDARITY DEMONSTRATION, FREE ABORTION MEETING, ANTI-ZIONIST MARCH. Most of them were weeks out of date.

Over each of the three doorbells was a notice. One, tacked to the wood by two drawing pins, simply read "Yvonne, top floor." "Manhood Film Productions" was on the ground floor. They had once made porn films in an empty warehouse in Bermondsey but had gone out of business seven months ago. The ground floor was now empty, but nobody had bothered to remove the notice. Over the middle bellpush was a tiny brass plate: "Heron Associates. Public Relations."

There were no associates, and they had no public-relations account. Heron rented the tiny second-floor office, containing a desk, two chairs, a telephone, and a toilet. He got it cheap because it wasn't used for prostitution. Yvonne, upstairs, had to pay eight pounds a week for her hovel.

Hood didn't bother to ring the bell. He mounted the creaking stairs and tried to breathe in as little as he could. The place smelled rancid. On the landing somebody had torn off much of the wallpaper, and the only light came from a single unshaded light bulb.

Heron was sitting behind the desk when Hood walked in. The door hadn't been fastened. Heron had become fatalistic about creditors.

He didn't stand up. Hood looked around the cramped, bare excuse for an office with distaste. Stuck on one wall was a London Transport map of the underground system. The telephone perched on a stack of old magazines. It still worked, to Heron's surprise. The final demand had expired six weeks ago.

"Official business?" asked Heron. He indicated the other chair.

Hood eased himself down. "What the hell do you do here, anyway?" he asked.

"Didn't you know? I'm J. Walter Thompson's biggest competitor. PR the big way."

"You aren't even a registered company," said Hood contemptuously. "You've never done a stroke of PR work in your life. You hire this dump to have a place to park your arse. You haven't even got any stationery. Look at it."

"My company doesn't believe in unnecessary trimmings," said Heron. "And the secretaries are on holiday, at the moment, in Bermuda. What do you want?"

"To give you some advice," said Hood.

"That's very friendly of you."

"It isn't meant to be, believe me. I'm simply warning you to stop bothering people."

"People?"

"You've been making a nuisance of yourself, Heron. You know what I mean."

"You must have a case of mistaken identity," said Heron, wide-eyed. "I haven't been drunk and disorderly. I haven't caused an obstruction in Piccadilly or shouted rude things at the Archbishop of Canterbury, have I? You've got the wrong man."

Hood did not smile. "Please yourself. You don't have to listen. But I'm telling you to watch your step. You've been annoying people."

"Such as?"

Hood took a deep breath. "All kinds of people. Estate agents. The German embassy. Asking them questions."

Heron reached over to a dusty shelf and took down a blue book. It was a book policemen knew well: *Moriarty's Law*. Heron's edition was four years out of date, but he looked through the index, then glanced up, smiling.

"Can't see that's a crime, asking questions." He smiled.

"No," said Hood heavily. "But obstructing police in the course of an inquiry is. And so is interfering with the course of justice."

Heron shut the book with a loud snap.

"I don't think you know much about justice," he said. "Not that it matters. Now, you tell *me* something, What's happened to Mrs. Fennerman?"

"I don't see it's any of your business, but I understand she's gone away."

"Aren't you bothered?"

Hood scraped back the chair. The floor was uncarpeted, and as he stood up the wooden boards creaked.

"No, Heron, I'm not," he said. "But I hope you take this seriously. I could have pulled you in, officially. But I thought I'd talk to you man to man, for old times' sake. It's the last warning you'll get. Keep your nose out of things that don't concern you."

"I'm quite touched that you care," said Heron mockingly. "Secretly, you must be very fond of me."

"Oh, one other thing. That fight you got into. Have you gone political, Heron?"

"What's that supposed to mean?"

"There's a report about it. You scrapping with some right-wing gentlemen. Not like you, Harry, is it? I wondered if you've suddenly got some new allegiance."

"If I have, I'll let you know. Right now I'm an undercover infiltrator of the Flat Earth Society, but that isn't on your list, is it?"

Hood scowled.

"Or maybe it is?" added Heron. He contemplated Hood. "You've turned into an odd sort of copper, you know that? No straight stuff for you any more, eh?"

"What the hell's that supposed to mean?"

"You're Special Branch now, aren't you?" said Heron. "New rank, new job. The moment I saw you and your armed chum at Fennerman's place, I knew. No more safe blaggings and break-ins for you. It's the cloak-and-dagger stuff now. Right?"

Hood shrugged. "Please yourself. The point is, it all spells trouble for you, believe me."

"I do," murmured Heron. "I always believe you, Hood."

He heard Hood thumping down the stairs and then cautiously picked up the phone. The dial tone came through loud and clear. They still hadn't cut him off.

It worried Heron.

21

The leather-clad motorcyclist in the big space helmet cursed. Brown's Hotel had two entrances, one in Albermarle Street and the other in Dover Street. No way could he watch both at the same time.

He sat astride the big Japanese motorbike, the little blue pennant drooping. There was no means of knowing which side Heron would emerge from. He'd have to whistle up reinforcements.

Heron had only just arrived, so he'd be in there for a little while. It gave the motorcyclist a chance to request a backup.

He found a call box and dialed.

"He's inside now," he said, "but I need somebody here. I can't cover two exits by myself."

"Okay," said the voice. "I'll see what I can do."

"I'll be in Albermarle Street," said the motorcyclist. "Who'll be coming?"

"Sean, I think."

"Well, tell him to find me, and then he can take over the other side."

"Okay," said the voice again. "Just make sure you don't lose *him* in the meantime."

"Oh, sure. But he'll be there for a bit. He's only just come."

"Better hurry back. It might not be a very long meeting."

The voice chuckled.

22

Colonel Fennerman was sitting in a deep leather armchair in a corner of the hotel lounge. In the armchair next to him sat a sharp-featured man in a navy blue blazer. The brass buttons had little crowns on them.

"There you are," said the colonel. He was slightly

flushed, as if something had been annoying him. "You're late, Heron."

"The traffic . . ." apologized Heron.

"This is Mr. Ross," said the colonel without further ceremony. "An old friend. Ministry of Defence and all that."

He sounded grudging, as if he were introducing him only reluctantly.

"How do you do?" said Heron.

He sat down, and Ross said, "Shall we have some coffee?"

Without waiting for a reply, he signaled the waiter. He appeared to be in charge; the colonel might be the man who was staying at the hotel, but Ross had taken over as host.

"Well?" said the colonel. He was clenching and unclenching his hands.

Heron hesitated.

"You can talk all you want in front of Ross," growled the colonel. "Told you, he's an old friend."

"Actually, I haven't got much to report," said Heron. "As far as I can make out, your daughter-in-law has gone abroad. I think she's probably back in Germany."

"Ah," said Ross. "That's that, then."

He sat back in the armchair like a man who's pleased that the business at hand has been so efficiently resolved.

"I don't know," said Heron.

"What do you mean?" asked the colonel. He seemed nervous.

"It doesn't smell kosher to me." The other two had the look people have who never use the word "kosher." "She's put the house on the market already."

"She has, has she?" said the colonel, but Ross put a restraining hand on his arm. The waiter poured them coffee.

Something has happened to the old boy, thought Heron. His shoulders drooped. His eyes avoided him;

he looked drawn. Maybe the death of his son had finally caught up with him . . .

The colonel was staring at Heron. "Did you see her?" he asked.

"No. It's almost as if she's been spirited away by her friends."

"What friends?" demanded the colonel, frowning.

"Two Germans. Langschmidt and Kiefer. Have you ever heard of them, sir?"

Before the colonel could reply, Ross said breezily, "Spirited away is hardly the way to put it, is it? I imagine they're old friends who came to help her tidy up things. I mean, here was the poor lady all on her own, husband murdered, nobody to turn to, so naturally they rushed to her side. What are friends for, Mr. Heron?"

"That's exactly what Kiefer said, and he sounded phony, too."

Ross sipped his coffee without batting an eyelid.

"I also find it curious," Heron went on, "that these gentlemen have the use of a German embassy chauffeur and a diplomatic car."

"Oh, I'm quite sure you're wrong about that, Mr. Heron," said Ross.

"And do you think I'm wrong in thinking something peculiar's happened with the shop? If you call being burned down by a petrol bomb peculiar."

"Well, I dare say it was insured," said Ross.

Old Fennerman's mouth twitched. He really does look distinctly unhappy, thought Heron. A far cry from the firm, authoritative, commanding old man at the funeral.

"Did you know Colin, Mr. Ross?" inquired Heron mildly.

"No."

"But you're a friend of the colonel's. Did you serve together?"

"I know I haven't worn well, but I'm not quite that

old, Mr. Heron. He was a little before my time." Ross
was quite amiable.

"May I ask what you do at the Ministry of Defence?" Heron inquired.

The old man's hand shook slightly as he stirred
his coffee, but Ross didn't appear perturbed.

"You've been a journalist, Mr. Heron," he said. "So
you know that asking certain questions is an offense
under the Official Secrets Act, and answering them
is even more heinous."

"That's what I thought," said Heron.

Ross shot back an immaculate cuff and looked at
a wafer-thin watch.

"Well, Colonel," he said. "Don't forget your train.
I think it's about time to depart, don't you?"

Fennerman nodded.

"I've checked you out, the luggage is in the hall,
and the bill is paid," said Ross, and suddenly Heron
felt a shiver go down his spine.

A porter came over and said to Ross, "Your car is
here, sir."

"Excellent. If you're ready, Colonel, I'll drive you to
the station."

"Thank you," mumbled the colonel. "Very good
of you."

The old man stood up. Ross dropped two pounds
by the coffee pot.

"Come along, then, Colonel," he said.

"Colonel Fennerman." Heron's tone brought the old
man to a halt. "I'll find out. Don't worry, I'll find out
what's happened to her. What's going on. Why Colin
was murdered. I'll keep you posted. You can depend
on it."

"Personally, I'd leave it to the authorities," murmured Ross. "After all, they get paid for it." His look
jeered at Heron.

"Yes, very grateful to you," rumbled the colonel.
"Appreciate everything you've done, Harry, but I can't
really expect you to . . ."

"It's not for you, sir," said Heron. "It's for me."
He ignored Ross. "There's a lot I want to know. You
can probably help me." The colonel started to shake
his head. "Anyway, when I know exactly what I'm
after, maybe I can come to see you. With a long list
of questions . . ."

"Come along, Colonel," said Ross.

They all walked to the Dover Street exit. A two-
tone Rover was parked in front, and the driver was
already loading the suitcases. Ross held open the door
for the colonel.

"Au revoir, Colonel," said Heron, and for one
moment the old man gave him a searching look. Then
he climbed into the car.

"Don't bother to check this one for license numbers, Mr. Heron," said Ross. "You'll find it's a mini-
cab." He got in beside the colonel and slammed the
door.

A motorcyclist followed Heron as he walked up
Dover Street and into Piccadilly, where he turned left.
The motorcyclist had no problem trailing him. But
outside Burlington House, Heron crossed the road and
strolled into Fortnum and Mason's just as the ornamental clock was striking.

He didn't buy anything, but walked right through
the store and emerged from the back entrance into
Jermyn Street.

It was very annoying for the motorcyclist, because
the lights into Duke Street were against him, and
by the time he roared down into Jermyn Street, Heron
had disappeared.

That was at 11:10 A.M.

23

When the 11:45 A.M. train from Paddington arrived in Gloucester at 1:56 P.M., a porter noticed that the door of a first-class compartment was swinging open.

At first, he merely slammed the door shut. But when, ten minutes later, a suitcase was found in the empty compartment, he remembered that there had been no one inside when the train pulled in.

Half an hour later a body was found on the track, about four miles from Gloucester. It was that of an elderly white-haired man, and papers in his wallet gave his name as Fennerman.

At 5:30 P.M., Heron bought the final city edition of the *Evening Standard* from the newspaper seller outside the London Casino in Old Compton Street.

It was not until he got home that he saw the stop-press item that said Colonel Charles Arthur Fennerman, eighty-three, had died in a fall from a London–Gloucester train that afternoon. Foul play was not suspected.

At 8:41 that evening, Lotte phoned.

24

"You sound surprised," she said.

"I always am when the phone rings," said Heron. "I haven't paid the bill. I thought they'd cut me off weeks ago."

There was a long pause. Then she said, "Harry, you must really get yourself a job. You can't go on like this."

"Is that what you've called to tell me?" he asked wearily.

"Not really. I wondered . . ." She paused "I wondered if you're busy."

"I'd like to see you," he said.

"Well, I'll drop by, if you like."

"I'll be here."

She was about to hang up when she said, "Have you eaten?"

"I thought we'd go to the Ritz," fantasized Heron. "Or the Savoy, if you're bored."

"I'll bring something with me," she said, and rang off.

He was pleased that she was coming. The prospect of seeing her suddenly made everything else seem much less important.

He sized up the room and swung into action. He gathered up the newspapers that littered the floor, put the two dirty shirts in the carrier bag he used as a laundry basket, made the bed, emptied the ashtray, removed the unwashed cups and plates and put them to soak in the basin. Quickly he hung up his other trousers, which he had flung across a chair, in the wardrobe.

He found himself humming tunelessly, feeling glad that she'd be here soon, that they'd be by themselves, just she and he. He gave everything a last-minute once-over, kicked his slippers under the bed, and put his old pajamas, which he hadn't changed for ten days, in the carrier bag, too.

Then, in front of the house, he heard her Volkswagen, and soon afterward she was ringing the bell of what the ads had described as a furnished bachelor flat, he called a bed-sitter, and most people a dump.

He kissed her lightly as she came in. She was wearing an open-necked shirt, slacks, and a leather jacket. But she managed to look extremely feminine, and Heron felt the excitement rise in him. He kissed her again, but she pushed him away gently with one hand. In the other she was holding a bag.

"Careful with that," she said. "Don't spill anything."

She had brought a Greek take-away meal—taramasolata, kebabs, Greek bread, salad, and two bottles of wine.

"Get out the plates," she commanded, and then he stood by and watched her turn the table into an appetizing spread that made him realize how hungry he was.

Afterward she sat in the armchair and he on the bed, drinking coffee. They had turned off the light for the meal and stuck two candles in a couple of bottles. Now the candles were flickering.

"I've missed you," he said.

"That's nice," she said, but not smugly or arrogantly.

"I had started wondering . . . if you were trying to avoid me."

"Don't be silly. You know how things are."

"Sometimes I don't," said Heron.

"I've got a job. It isn't always easy."

"Oh, sure," said Heron a little bitterly.

She reached for the shoulder bag that lay on the floor beside the armchair.

"I've got something for you," she said. She took out a piece of paper and passed it over to him.

It was marked, in one corner: "Private and Confidential."

Heron hadn't seen a D-notice for a long time, but they hadn't changed much, evidently. This one was quite firm in its instructions:

> It is requested that no reference be made in any publication to the movements or activities of the following:
>
> 1. Mrs. Ursula Fennerman
> 2. Dieter Langschmidt
> 3. Jurgen Kiefer
>
> Editors are also reminded that police inquiries into the murder of Colin Arthur Fennerman may involve questions of security, and that it is, of course, against the public interest to publicize such matters.

"Where did you get this?" asked Heron.

She lit a cigarette. "I nicked it from the editor's desk. I thought you'd want to see it." She blew out a cloud of smoke. "Oh, don't worry, I'll slip it back tomorrow and nobody will ever know."

"What else have you heard?" He passed the D-notice back to her.

"Not much," she said. "That's what I wanted to ask you. You knew him, didn't you? What's it all about?"

He looked across at her and he wanted to ask, Is that why you are here tonight? To find out things? To pump me?

"Something's going on," she went on. "Haven't you noticed how little coverage the murder's had? Crossbow and all? They've hardly mentioned it. And you know, I heard a really silly thing."

She had curled her legs under her.

"I heard a rumor there's another D-notice on the way."

"Oh?"

"Yes. About you, Harry."

"You're crazy."

"Story I heard was they want everybody to lay off you. On grounds of security. What have you been up to?"

"Where did you hear this?" asked Heron tersely.

"Oh, God, you know what the Street is. Probably a lot of rubbish, but it set me wondering."

He poured himself another cup of coffee out of the percolator.

"Tell me," he said. "What were you chasing the old man for?"

"Background. The paper's all intrigued. They're gathering up background stuff. Might be useful one day."

"And the photo?"

"We had it in the library, but there was some mixup about the identity. They wanted me to make sure."

"You know the old boy is dead, do you?" he asked casually.

Lotte froze. "No!"

"Today. Here." He threw the evening paper across. "Stop-press."

She read it quickly, then looked at him, wide-eyed. "Do you believe it?" She was pale. "Do you really believe it was an accident?"

He shrugged. "He was getting on, wasn't he? A very old man. Old people do funny things, like opening compartment doors by mistake while the train is traveling."

But he kept seeing, in his mind's eye, the man in the blazer with the silver cuff links who appeared so solicitous that the old colonel shouldn't miss his train.

"It's terrible," said Lotte, and she seemed to shiver. "Well, it's the end of the Fennermans, that's for sure," said Heron. "The old boy was a widower, and with Colin gone, there's nobody else left. The end of a long line. Colin once told me there'd been a Fennerman in the army since seventeen eighty-three."

She uncurled herself. "Oh, let's talk about something else," she said. She walked over to the switch and turned on the electric light. "I'll do the washing up."

"No," said Heron. "Leave it. I'll do it after you've gone."

She faced him, arms akimbo. "But I'm not going anywhere," she said.

He got to his feet slowly.

"I thought I'd stay. Unless, of course, you don't want me to."

He took her in his arms, and his mouth eagerly sought hers. It was a long, passionate, sensual kiss, and when it was over he knew that she was as eager as he was for what was to come.

"To hell with the washing up," said Heron, and switched off the light.

25

Heron bought all the daily papers at Paddington Station after breakfast and then settled back in a corner seat on the train to Gloucester. None of them carried a single line about the old man's death. No one bothered to follow up the previous evening's stop-press item.

It was a gray, nasty day, raindrops spitting at the window and then running down it in rivulets. Heron watched the countryside flash past, and a ridiculous

little limerick from the forgotten past kept going
through his mind:

> Dr. Foster went to Gloucester
> In a shower of rain;
> He stepped in a puddle
> Right up to his middle
> And never went there again.

He hadn't told Lotte he was going. The questions
that nagged him he had kept to himself.

At Gloucester, he asked a taxi driver at the station
to take him to police headquarters. The cabdriver
gave him a funny look. In a cathedral town like
Gloucester, people didn't talk about police headquarters. Official buildings had their old-fashioned
names. Like Shire Hall. Like police station.

"I'd like to see somebody about Colonel Fennerman," Heron told the sergeant behind the counter.

"Colonel who?"

"He was killed yesterday. Fell from a train here."

"Relation, are you, sir?" asked the sergeant.

"Press," said Heron. "From London."

It used to impress local coppers in the provinces.
It made them feel they were on the map. But no
longer, apparently.

"Oh," said the sergeant. "What do you want?"

On a desk at the back was a cup of tea with a half-
eaten sausage roll in the saucer. Heron guessed the
sergeant wanted to get back to it.

"Who's the officer in charge of the case?" demanded
Heron.

"I'll see," said the sergeant, and went through a
door. He reappeared after a moment with a tall man
smoking a pipe.

"Come all the way from London, have you?" asked
the tall man.

"Yes," said Heron. "The Fennerman story."

"What story?" said the man, sucking his pipe.

"There is no story. The old gentleman fell from the train."

"You're on the case, Mr. . . .?"

"Detective Inspector Robson. And there is no case. What paper are you from?"

"The *Chronicle*," lied Heron.

"You have any identification?"

Heron pulled out his NUJ card with the cheap passport photo taken in a do-it-yourself booth in a penny arcade.

"Well, Mr. Heron," said Robson, handing it back, "you'd better tell your editor he's sent you on a fool's errand."

Heron looked around the charge office. "Can we talk somewhere more privately?" he suggested.

"Nothing to talk about," said Robson. "The colonel fell out of his compartment."

"Just like that?"

"Just like that."

"A sheer accident?"

Robson took his pipe out of his mouth. "I didn't say that."

"Oh?"

"I think you can assume he took his own life. That's for the coroner to decide, of course, but you can take it from me." He took out a box of matches and began to relight his pipe, making sucking noises.

"How do you know?" asked Heron.

"Well, off the record, he left a note. It was on his seat."

"What did it say?" asked Heron.

Robson drew himself up. "You know better than that. But I'll tell you, off the record, the note satisfies us it was suicide. The old gentleman had just lost his son, you know. Very tragic. First the burglary, and then his son . . ."

"Burglary?"

"Not very important, really. Nothing was taken. But the house was ransacked. Must have upset the colonel. That, and his son. Well, he *was* pretty old."

"I see," said Heron. "Who was the note addressed to?"

"To somebody at the Ministry of Defence."

"A Mr. Ross?"

"You have been busy," said Robson. "Yes, rather sad. Explaining that life had become a bit too much for him. They were an old army family, you know."

"I know," said Heron.

"Now, you tell me something," said Robson. The sergeant at the desk was finishing his sausage roll. Somewhere a phone rang.

"Yes?"

"Why all this interest? None of the other papers have bothered."

Heron smiled. "Maybe that's why we've got a bigger circulation."

"Up to you." Robson shrugged. He went over to the desk, knocked his pipe on an ashtray. He looked across at Heron. "Still, you could have asked the Yard and saved yourself a trip." The sergeant was listening.

"The Yard?" said Heron. "Why them? It's out of their jurisdiction. What's it got to do with them?"

"I suppose it's because of the son. They made a routine query for background. We told them the same thing. That there's nothing sinister to it. You can check with Detective Chief Inspector Hood. You know him?"

"Yes," said Heron. "I know him."

"Well, that's all there is to it." He peered at Heron through the smoke from his refilled pipe. "Are you staying here for a while?"

"No," said Heron. "I have something to do in London."

26

Heron went straight to the Ministry of Defence the next morning. As he ascended the broad steps of the massive building, he knew he'd come to the wrong address. But Heron was a fisherman.

The reception-desk woman in the overalls with the MOD badge on each lapel was as impersonal as a supermarket cashier.

"I want to see Mr. Ross," said Heron.

She pushed the admission-slip pad toward him. "Is he expecting you?"

"I think so."

"Fill in one of those," she instructed. "And do you have any identification?"

"My face," said Heron.

On either side of him people streamed past, flashing their staff passes. He felt strangely illegitimate without one.

Heron wrote his name and address on the slip, and where it said *name of person to see* he put: "Mr. Ross." But he left both *department* and *purpose of visit* blank.

The woman looked at his piece of paper and frowned.

"Did you say you have an appointment?"

"I think he'll see me," said Heron.

She pulled a big blackbound, looseleaf volume from a shelf in front of her. It reminded Heron of the undesirable-foreigners book immigration officers thumb through at airports.

"What department is he in?" she demanded.

"I don't imagine it's listed," said Heron.

"But you've got him under something. Somewhere."

Her disapproval was unconcealed. The way he had filled in his slip was untidy. Everything about him was untidy.

"You sure he's in this building? We have many establishments . . ."

"Try again," said Heron.

She didn't answer. Instead, she picked up a phone and dialed. All the time her critical eyes surveyed Heron.

The extension answered.

"Horseguards Reception here," she said. "There is a Mr. Heron here wishing to see Mr. Ross . . . That's right, Heron." She waited. Then the extension came on again. "I see," she said, and put the receiver down.

"You are to wait," she ordered.

Heron stood by the reception counter, watching the traffic of people, some in uniform, some in civilian clothes that were just as uniform. No wonder, he thought, that sentries at St. James's Palace can spot officers in civvies so accurately they give them a correct present arms each time.

Across the big entrance hall, a woman walked toward Heron. She was slim, gray-haired, in her fifties. I bet you play golf and go hiking on weekends, he reflected. Well preserved and hard as leather.

"Mr. Heron?" she asked. She seemed to have no problem spotting him right away.

"That's right."

"I'm Miss Foley," she said primly. "You want to see Mr. Ross, I believe?"

"Yes."

"Well, I'm afraid you've come to the wrong place. We have no Mr. Ross."

Heron sighed. "Miss Foley, you're doing a marvelous job, but I need to see Ross. In a hurry."

"Unfortunately—"

"Unfortunately, I haven't got much time. Also, my feet are too tired to keep looking for the latest hidey-hole. So if Ross isn't in this marble palace, just tell me where he is, that's a good Miss Foley."

She was one of the senior sweater-set-and-pearls bunch, no doubt about that, he had already decided. She had stayed on in the service instead of making a desirable match with a show-jumping sprig straight out of the Guards. Probably been a fixture for twenty years.

"What is it, actually, you want to see Mr. Ross about?" she asked. He had to admire the smoothness with which she switched channels.

"The Goering Testament," said Heron quietly.

There was no reaction from her.

"Do you ever feed the pigeons in Trafalgar Square?" she asked instead, as if she hadn't heard him.

"I don't like pigeons, and I don't feed 'em."

Miss Foley allowed herself a frosty smile. "Well, Mr. Heron, you should try it sometime," she said. "For instance, at four o'clock this afternoon."

Heron nodded. "Four o'clock."

"Good," she said. "I don't think there's anything else, is there?"

"Any idea what I feed them wtih?" asked Heron.

"Anything that tempts them, Mr. Heron," said Miss Foley, and already she was walking back to the corridor from which she had emerged.

He wondered, when he saw the face of the reception lady, why she had taken such an intense dislike to him.

"Nice day," said Heron pleasantly.

Her look made him conscious of what it must be like to be caught in a mosque wearing street shoes.

27

Kelly, whose professional name was Yvonne, came down the stairs from the top floor, feeling sorry for herself. She wasn't having a good week. Not only was business slack, but an Arab client, whom she had hopefully picked up in a Park Lane coffee bar, had given her a black eye, which didn't exactly help attract new customers.

She had screamed blue murder, hoping he'd at least make it worth her while, but he had earlier lost eight thousand pounds in a casino, and she had to be content with ten. And when she swore at him, his English was so bad that the full, rich potency of her venom simply didn't have any effect.

She stopped on the second-floor landing, where a small, dapper man was knocking on the door of Heron's pied-à-terre.

Kelly took in his sharp suit, the little bow tie, the Gucci shoes. Clients were rare in the afternoon. Also, he was slightly built, hardly likely to knock her about. She was feeling sensitive about that at the moment.

"I don't think he's in," said Kelly.

Madek looked up at her. "You know where he is?"

Kelly shook her head. "He comes and goes all the time. Maybe he'll be back soon."

"I must see him. Quickly." She thought he sounded a little desperate. He banged on the door again.

"Would you like to wait?" suggested Kelly invitingly. "In my flat? Upstairs?"

She was really quite a pretty girl, but she had no idea how to make up her face, and the black eye, compounded with the garish lipstick, the smudged mascara, the false eyelashes, created a blotched caricature, which Kelly firmly believed to be alluring and teasingly demimonde.

"No," said Madek. "It is very urgent I see Harry. I must find him."

"I'll make you a cup of tea, if you like," offered Kelly. She had other services in mind, but at least if she could get him upstairs . . .

"You have no idea where I can find him?" repeated Madek. "Now?"

His spaniel-like eyes appealed to her almost frantically.

"Now, you come upstairs with me," she said firmly. "He'll be back any minute, I'm sure, and you'll be right here. There's no point in standing about on a landing, is there?"

"Well, maybe . . ." said Madek doubtfully.

She was sure he had plenty of money on him. Those shoes alone must have cost seventy quid or more.

"Of course," she said soothingly. She wondered what was making him so nervous. "Come along, now."

She actually took his hand and led him up the stairs.

"What is your name?" asked Madek.

"Yvonne," said Kelly.

28

"You can look him up on the diplomatic list yourself," said Reggie reproachfully.

"He's listed as a commercial attaché," cut in Heron. "I've checked."

"So what do you need me for?"

"I want to know what you've got Herr Geist listed as," said Heron. It was a comfortable leather-upholstered phone booth, making a change from the smelly, fetid call boxes the post office provided in the neighborhood. Like everything else in the luxury hotel, it was spotless.

"You know what you're asking," said Reggie.

"I think I know the answer already, but I'd like it confirmed."

There was a pause.

"Where are you calling from?" asked Reggie finally.

"Don't worry, it's safe."

Reggie grunted. "You're starting to ask too many favors, Harry."

"Reggie, please."

"All right, hold on."

Heron didn't have to wait long.

"You there?" said Reggie after a couple of minutes.

"Yes."

"Well, your friend is one of the lads."

"A big boy?"

"You could say that."

"I thought so. Goodie or baddie?"

"Depends which side you're on, doesn't it?" said Reggie dryly.

"Thanks for the help."

"Listen, Harry, what are you up to?"

Heron smiled to himself. He was going to tell Reggie the truth, and the man wouldn't believe it.

"I'm off to feed the pigeons in Trafalgar Square," he said.

29

"Shut the door," said Kelly.

"But I want to know when he comes back," objected Madek.

"You'll know," she said impatiently. She went over and closed the door.

It wasn't a flat at all, and Kelly didn't live there. It was a strictly functional room, with a big bed, two chairs, a mirror on the wall, and a cupboard.

"The office is in there," said Kelly, nodding at a door.

"The office?" Madek looked puzzled.

"The loo. In case you want to use it."

He shook his head.

"This is very kind, but I think I should wait downstairs," he said, smiling weakly.

"Cup of tea?" asked Kelly, but didn't wait for his answer. She went into the bathroom, came out with an electric kettle she had filled with water, and plugged it into a socket. It stood on the floor, hissing.

"Sit down, for God's sake," she told Madek. The way he stood there, awkward and nervous, you'd think he'd never been with a woman.

Madek eased himself down on a chair. From the cupboard Kelly produced two cups without saucers, a carton of lump sugar, and a spoon. She put a tea bag into each of the cups.

"Milk?"

Madek nodded. She disappeared into the bathroom again, emerged with a half-full milk bottle. She poured the hot water into the cups, passed one over to him.

"There you are," said Kelly.

He leaned forward.

"Listen, I think that's him," he said.

They were silent. There was no sound from the stairs. He looked disappointed.

"Don't worry, you'll hear him," said Kelly. She sat on the bed and saw to it that her skirt showed plenty of thigh. Her sweater was too tight, and she wore a padded bra. By the time her clients found out, she had usually made up for it in other ways.

"Well?" said Kelly, and smiled invitingly.

Madek took a sip of tea with no great enthusiasm.

"Very nice," he said politely. It was clearly the tea he was talking about.

She wanted to shake him.

"What would you like?" she asked instead. Mustn't rile the customers.

Madek blinked.

"Nothing, thank you," he said.

"For you, only a tenner," she offered. "Whatever you want. All yours for half an hour. French kiss, anything."

To encourage him, she suddenly stripped off her sweater. She kept on her stuffed bra, not in modesty, but as a selling point.

Madek eyed her. "Very nice," he said again.

"Worth ten quid."

"I don't have time," he declared sadly.

"Don't be silly. You'll have a quickie until he's here."

"You don't understand. People are after me."

"It'll relax you," she said, and stood up, unzipping her skirt. Then what he had said sank in.

"What people?" she asked sharply as the skirt fell around her ankles. "Who's after you?"

"Please, I cannot tell you. But I must find Heron."

"Oh, come on, you're safe here," she said, stepping out of her skirt. She had on black briefs and a black garter belt with stockings. Kelly was a firm believer that in her line of work, tights were not sexy enough.

"I have to go," said Madek. He put down the teacup he had been clutching and got up.

"That's great," she snapped. She faced him, arms akimbo. "You come in here, leading a girl on, have a private strip show for free, and then walk out."

"No, no!" cried Madek. "There has been a misunderstanding."

"You bet there has," spat Kelly. She thought of the Arab and her black eye. Now this jerk. What a week she was having. "It's bloody false pretenses." She looked him up and down contemptuously. "I don't suppose you could make it with a real woman anyway."

"Please," said Madek. "You do not understand . . ."

"Too chintzy to pay a girl her bloody ten quid, that's what you are."

Madek sighed.

"You take a check?" he asked hopefully, reaching inside his jacket.

"Fuck off!" screamed Kelly.

He fled to the door.

"Whoever they are, I hope they get you!" she yelled after him. "I hope they chop you into little pieces!"

She slammed the door behind him, and he ran down the creaking stairs. On the first floor he stopped outside Heron's door. He banged hard. There was still no reply. He knocked again, but he knew no one was there.

He stood silent on the landing and licked his dry lips.

Madek was afraid.

30

Heron reached for the paper towel next to the washbasin and dried his hands. The men's room of the hotel was one of the best on his list, and he was no mean judge; Heron had long experience grading the free facilities of central London's luxury hotels. He utilized them with critical discernment, giving points for ready availability of telephones, comfortable armchairs, spaciousness and appointment of the washrooms, the necessity to hand out tips. This one came pretty near on top of the league.

He looked at himself in the mirror. He hadn't shaved too well, and his eyes were slightly bloodshot. But at least, apart from one tiny scab, the marks of the beating he had gotten were no longer visible.

In just over an hour he was due in Trafalgar Square. Trust Ross to pick a place like that for a meet; the faceless ones were quite childish in the way they played their games. They really believed in red carnations in buttonholes, or a *Financial Times* stuck under the left arm, or blowing the nose with a polka-dot handkerchief. Above all, they loved Hitchcockian meeting places.

A man came into the washroom. He went straight to the marble washbasin next to Heron's. Hot water was already in all of them. He started to rinse his hands.

Heron, in the mirror, had seen him enter and taken little notice. If there was one thing he avoided, it was catching the eye of strangers in men's rooms. He had covered too many cases, when he was doing police courts, in which some poor devil had glanced at the man next to him and been promptly arrested for importuning; half the Chelsea vice squad seemed, at one time, to have been boosting their arrest records that way.

The man kept rinsing his hands, and suddenly Heron was uneasy. The fellow didn't look particularly fastidious, yet he was making such a big job of washing his hands before he had used any of the facilities.

Heron turned to the door, which was pushed open. Two more men came in, one with a university scarf.

"Excuse me," said Heron, because they stood in his way.

"Just walk straight out of here, Mr. Heron, and stay with us," said a voice behind him. He knew it was the man who had been washing his hands. He also knew that what pressed into his back was a gun.

The character with the university scarf was already holding the door open.

"Come along, we're all good friends, aren't we?" said the man behind him, and the gun pressed just a little harder.

Usually Heron was pleased when there wasn't a cloakroom attendant in sight; it meant he didn't have to give a tip for a perfunctory, useless brush of his coat. But this was one time he wished there were half a dozen of them.

Grouped around him, they marched him through the lobby, the gun making itself felt. The place was crowded: a party of tourists had arrived with all their luggage; a sheik with his entourage came sweeping out of the bank of lifts; a man was being paged; people were greeting each other. And nobody took the slightest notice of Heron and the three men.

For one wild moment Heron wondered whether, in the swinging doors, he could somehow get away, elude the one with the gun, run for it in the street; but if they had planned it, they couldn't have organized it better. To let the tourists in with their bags, the swinging doors had been folded and the way into the street was clear.

A black Daimler was drawn up by the sidewalk, with a chauffeur behind the wheel.

"Get in the back," said the man with the gun. There was nothing furtive about them; the one with the university scarf even tipped the majestic head porter in front of the hotel and received a respectful salute. It was so respectful that, thought Heron wryly, it must have been a hell of a good tip.

Heron sank into the luxury of the cushioned back seat, between two of the men. The one with the gun was on his left, and it pressed into his side. University scarf sat in front beside the chauffeur. Smoothly, the car merged into the traffic.

Heron looked at the three men in turn. They were in their late twenties, he judged, or maybe early thirties. Clean-cut, handsome men, open-air types, maybe. The man with the gun had a very expensive wristwatch.

"All right," said Heron, "what's all this in aid of?"

The man with the university scarf, in front, turned slightly. He had a finely chiseled profile, rather haughty. For some reason, he reminded Heron of a Roman centurion.

But that changed when he heard him speak.

"You know perfectly well, Mr. Heron," he said politely, and his accent was American.

There must be some mistake, Heron was about to say, but he knew there wasn't; they had used his name from the start.

"What do you want?" he asked.

"Shut up," ordered the man on Heron's right. His hair had started to turn gray early, and his tone of authority was unmistakable. University scarf turned away from Heron and stared ahead at the windshield without saying another word. For the first time, Heron realized that the graying man's right eye was glass.

"Who the hell are you?" asked Heron. He was very conscious of the gun in his side.

"We'll tell you when to talk," said glass eye. "You'd better sort your mind out. You've only got two hours."

"What happens then?" asked Heron.

"You'll be dead," said the man with the glass eye.

31

The clock on top of St. Martin in the Fields indicated ten minutes past four, and down below, in Trafalgar Square, Ross stood by one of the Landseer lions and frowned.

He had arrived five minutes early, and now, a quarter of an hour later, there was still no sign of Heron. He decided to walk around Nelson's Column once more, but his feeling of apprehension was growing.

Ross sidestepped a flock of scrawny pigeons scavenging for a handout and glanced across the road to South Africa House. Maybe Heron was being cautious; maybe he was hanging around on the edge of the square, sniffing out the lay of the land. But Ross, deep inside him, knew Heron wasn't coming. Not there or outside the National Gallery or, across the other side, in front of Canada House. Heron wouldn't show.

"Sir, where is George Washington's statue?" a woman in horn-rimmed glasses and sensible shoes asked Ross. She was carrying a flight bag with TWA emblazoned on it.

"Over there," said Ross irritably, pointing vaguely northward.

She looked confused.

"Oh, ask a policeman," snapped Ross, and destroyed one Kansas spinster's illusion that all Englishmen, especially those whose blazer buttons have crowns on them, are gentlemen.

After another half hour, he gave it up. He made his way over to Northumberland Avenue, where a blue car was parked.

Ross got inside and sat brooding.

"Where to, sir?" asked Bowler, the driver. He was more than a chauffeur; as a member of the Special Air Service, he had done deadly undercover work in Armagh. Now he was attached to Ross's department, and it was useful that most people, even in the Ministry of Defence, should think that he was merely a civilian employee in the motor pool.

"He didn't turn up," said Ross.

"Yes, sir."

"I think we're in trouble."

Bowler said nothing.

"Back to the office," ordered Ross.

There were several things he had to do, urgently. One was to put out a security tracer on Heron.

He only hoped it wasn't too late. Heron a corpse was no good to him at all.

32

They had put a hood over Heron's head, and within minutes he had lost his sense of direction. He could breathe and hear, but the blackness gave him an awful taste of claustrophobia. He would have given anything to tear this shroud off, but he knew he didn't have a chance. The last glimpse he had of the gun, it was lying in the lap of the man, his finger on the trigger.

They did not talk, and Heron tried to take advantage of the silence to get a clue, a hint, of where they were driving. The car stopped periodically, evidently at traffic lights, and then moved on after a few moments. He wondered if they were driving a long distance or just going around in circles to confuse him. He had no idea whether they were still in the center of London or somewhere on the outskirts. Ealing? Hampstead? Islington? Farther out—Epping? Richmond?

Once he tensed, when he heard a siren behind them. It came nearer and nearer, and for a glorious moment he thought a police car was gaining on them. Then he realized the men had said nothing, and the car's speed hadn't altered; they were ignoring the siren. He heard the police car shoot past, and then its sound disappeared in the distance. He wondered why the police hadn't noticed that one of the men in the Daimler they passed had a black hood over his face.

They'd been driving about half an hour, maybe twice that, when the car stopped.

"This is where you get out, Mr. Heron," said the voice of the man with the glass eye.

He heard the Daimler's doors open, and firm hands helped him out of the car. Even under the hood, he could sense the sudden fresh air. He heard sea gulls. Then he felt himself being led along until the American said, "We got you, don't worry. Just step carefully. Slowly now. You're okay."

They guided him along what seemed to be some kind of wooden plank or gangway, holding him like the blind man he was, and he moved warily, step by step.

"Take it easy now," said the American.

He had stepped onto something, and it seemed to move under his feet.

"This way."

They were almost solicitous the way they helped him, made sure he didn't trip, guided him, made sure he didn't lose his balance.

"In here."

It was the man with the glass eye. Authoritative. Like an officer in charge of a detail.

Very carefully, he was half hauled, half led, down what seemed to be very narrow steps, and then the fresh air cut out and he no longer heard the sea gulls.

Now he was in some kind of room, he knew that. Yet the floor seemed to move slightly, and if they hadn't held him, he would have staggered and lost his balance.

"Sit," instructed the American, and he was forcibly pushed down onto what seemed to be a chair. Then, much more roughly than they had handled him up to now, somebody grabbed his arms and twisted them behind his back. He heard a click, and he couldn't move his arms any more. They had put handcuffs around his wrists.

"Take that thing off," ordered the man with the glass eye. One of them whipped the hood away, and Heron blinked, trying to regain his sense of equilibrium.

He was in a dark space. The only light came from an electric bulb overhead. Around him were the American and the man with the glass eye. To his surprise, the third man and the chauffeur were missing; Heron had been sure they had all brought him down together.

"Are you all right?" asked the glass-eyed man. There was no concern for Heron's welfare in his tone, just a clinical interest.

"Isn't it time you stopped playing bloody games?" said Heron. The handcuffs hurt his wrists.

"This isn't going to take long, Mr. Heron," said the glass-eyed man. "We're going to kill you unless you tell us where you've got it."

"Got what?" asked Heron. He suddenly realized why everything moved slightly. He was afloat. A barge, maybe. The room had no portholes and there was nothing nautical about it, but he could smell a kind of boat smell. And the movement was caused by the gentle lapping of waves or current, he didn't know which.

The American took off his university scarf and hung it on a hook. "I'll say it only once, Heron. Where have you got the document?"

"Document?"

"The Testament. You either have it or you know where it is. I think you've got it. Either way, you tell us."

The light bulb was swaying slightly, and it began to mesmerize Heron. He screwed up his eyes.

"I know nothing about it," he said. "I've never seen it, I've never had it, I think you're all crazy."

"Fennerman gave it to you, didn't he?" It was the glass-eyed man. "He gave it to you or you took it, right?"

"Why are you so interested in something I haven't got?" asked Heron, wriggling slightly. His arms, clamped in their enforced captivity, ached.

He began to orient himself. He saw the steps that led down from a trapdoor above. Those were the steps he had been brought down. So he was under the deck, in the bowels of the boat. A storeroom, maybe. Once up those steps . . .

"The Goering Testament is very important to us, Mr. Heron," said the glass-eyed man gravely.

"I think you're a bunch of fucking Nazis," spat Heron. "Go to hell."

The American with the centurion's profile hit him.

"That's right . . ." gasped Heron. "Fucking Nazis."

"Stop that," barked the glass-eyed man to the American. Then he turned on Heron. "Don't you ever call us Nazis, you understand? Not ever." His face was white, and only his cheekbones were flushed.

"That's what you are," croaked Heron. He tasted

blood in his mouth. "The new breed. The new generation. You and your pals."

"He's just a stupid bastard," said the American contemptuously. "I think we . . ."

The man with the glass eye held up his hand.

"No," he said sharply. He regarded Heron with distaste.

"It doesn't matter who we are, Mr. Heron," he said. "You don't matter, either. We will find this piece of paper with or without you. If you tell us where it is, we'll let you go . . ."

"Oh, sure. So that I can run to the police and have the lot of you put inside."

The glass-eyed man laughed unpleasantly. "If we were to disappear now, you don't even know who we are, where we come from, where we go to, do you? You haven't even heard a first name, have you? You don't know a thing about us. Run to the police, you idiot."

"Listen," said Heron. "If I knew where your holy relic was, I'd see you damned first. I'd fucking well burn it, if it means so much to you lot. So go and sing *sieg heil*."

"All right," said the American, and this time the glass-eyed man did not interfere. "You've had your chance, Mr. Heron. Now you're through."

33

"Who are you, caller?" demanded the operator at the government switchboard, eighteen feet underground. It was an exchange whose number was a defense secret, whose whereabouts were classified, whose one thousand two hundred lines, all proofed against electronic eavesdropping, were reserved for the use of departments whose existence no one admitted.

The exchange also had a special routine. No one ever asked for their party by name. They merely gave an extension number. And if they called from outside, they had to say a key word.

"Who are you, caller?" repeated the operator. Procedure wasn't being followed. Yet whoever it was knew the clandestine exchange, knew the extension they wanted.

"Never mind that," replied a woman's voice. "Just put me through to four-five-two."

The call, as was routine on this exchange, was already being automatically tape-recorded. But now the operator activated the crash procedure for tracing an incoming call. If only he could keep the conversation going . . .

"Hurry up," ordered the caller.

Miss Foley picked up the green telephone and listened. Her pencil flew across the shorthand pad. The caller said only a few words.

"Who is this?" asked Miss Foley, but the caller had already rung off. She buzzed the switchboard urgently.

"That call on four-five-two, where did it come from?" she asked.

"We've been trying to trace it, but there wasn't enough time," said the exchange supervisor.

"How did they get onto this line?" demanded Miss Foley. She was a very precise woman and made a fetish of observing security procedures. "This is a secret number."

"We have no idea," said the supervisor.

"Did it come through the Ministry of Defence?"

"No," said the supervisor. "Whoever it was knows about our special setup, the exchange, the extension. There was only one thing she didn't seem to have."

"What's that?"

"The key word."

"Ah," said Miss Foley. "Thank you."

She typed the few words of the caller's message on a sheet of paper, then left her office in the restricted corridor and knocked on another door.

"Yes?" said Ross irritably. A file marked "Secret, Not To Be Removed From This Office: HERON, H. J." lay open on his desk.

"I think," said Miss Foley, "that I've got what you've been waiting for."

She handed him the message.

34

The third man came down ten minutes later. He was screwing a silencer onto his pistol.

"Now, look," said Heron. He was feeling sick to his stomach. "This is crazy. Why kill me?"

The man said nothing. The glass-eyed one was standing back a little, almost aloof.

"What good does it do?" gabbled Heron. He was searching for words, arguments, anything that might stall them. His defiance began to ebb at the sight of the gun. Once that silencer had been screwed on . . . "I can't do you any harm. You said yourself I don't even know who you are. What's the point of killing me?"

"Shut up," said the American. "Stop whining. You had your chance."

"Okay," said the man with the gun. "All set."

The other two looked inquiringly at the glass-eyed man. Clearly, it would be his order that fired the shot.

"For the last time, Heron, where can we get hold of it?" asked the man.

Suddenly the trapdoor above them was flung open. The Daimler's chauffeur looked down at them.

"They're coming!" he yelled.

"You sure?" the man with the glass eye called up to him.

"They're on their way now," shouted the chauffeur. "Move it. Come on."

"All right," said glass eye.

The man with the gun raised it. The long, elongated muzzle was a foot from Heron's forehead.

"No," ordered glass eye.

The gun did not waver.

"No," repeated the man, and his authority over the others was clear.

Slowly the gun was lowered.

"You're a lucky man, Mr. Heron," said the man with the glass eye. "Only don't count on luck any more. It may have just run out . . ."

The three scrambled up the steps, and he heard the clatter of their footsteps over his head. Then there was silence.

Heron sat in the chair, his arms still handcuffed behind his back, and shut his eyes. He felt drained.

He tried to raise himself from the chair, but with his wrists manacled, it was impossible. If he pushed too hard, he would overbalance, still chained to the chair. The cramp in his shoulders, his arms, his back, was agony.

The sound of steps overhead came down to him, and, through the open trapdoor, a bulky figure started to descend. The man navigated himself down the awkward steps with caution and then turned to face Heron.

"So," said Detective Chief Inspector Hood. "You're still in one piece. Pity."

All Heron said was, "Get these damn things off me."

Hood walked around the chair, studying Heron like an exhibit.

"The bracelets, you mean? I think you should get used to them, Harry. I really do. They'll become quite familiar to you, God willing. When you finally get nicked, they'll snap 'em on you, of course. You'll wear 'em on the way to court and, if you're naughty, in the dock. You'll wear 'em on that long ride to jail and every time you're out of the lockup. The only place you won't be needing 'em is in the wooden box, six feet underground."

"Get them off, Hood," said Heron quietly.

"No, you get the feel of them. Look on them as a taste of things to come."

Heron lashed out with his right foot, but it was a futile move, and the big man just laughed.

"Are you all right, sir?" came a call from the deck.

"Yes, Sergeant," Hood shouted back. "Everything's under control. He's down here."

A man's face appeared in the opening.

"Is he okay?"

"Fit as a fiddle." Hood smiled. "You just carry on, Sergeant."

The face withdrew.

"I'm sorry we got here so fast," said Hood. "Maybe if we had stopped at traffic lights, it might have been simpler all the way around. Would have given your pals a chance to do what they wanted."

"You care a lot, don't you?"

"Heron, I'm only interested in the law-abiding citizens of this realm," said Hood tightly. "What happens to the rats—you're right, I couldn't care less. And you know which category I put you in."

A man in a navy blazer came down the steps and Hood swung around.

"There you are, Heron," said Ross amiably. He nodded to Hood. "Good work, Chief Inspector."

"Thank you, sir," said Hood stiffly. He glared at Heron.

Ross saw the handcuffs.

"Can't you get those things off?" he asked mildly.

"They're looking for a key," said Hood. "I'd better hurry them up." He began heaving himself up to the trapdoor.

"You would have been much better advised to feed the pigeons," murmured Ross.

Heron tried to ease his cramp. "I never got the chance."

"What went wrong?"

"You could say I was hijacked," said Heron.

"Oh?" Ross raised his eyebrows. "Who by?"

"A bunch of thugs. Latter-day Nazi boys."

"No," said Ross firmly. "You're wrong. They were not Nazis."

Despite his pain, Heron sat up straight suddenly. "So you know who they are? You'd better tell me. Because right now I don't believe you."

Ross shrugged. "Please yourself. I'm working on . . . an educated guess. Never mind."

"And how did you know you'd find me here?"

Ross glanced around, his eyes resting for a minute on the university scarf.

"That yours?" he asked.

"Hardly."

Ross went over, took the scarf off the hook, examined it idly.

"Interesting. London School of Economics, I think."

"I asked how you knew where I'd been taken," insisted Heron.

Ross stroked the scarf. "Oh, *that*. Information received."

"From?"

Ross shook his head. "Fancy! You of all people. You know one doesn't divulge one's sources, ever."

A man in a windbreaker came down the steps.

"Mr. Hood thinks this will fit," he said, and unlocked Heron's handcuffs. They snapped open, and

Heron rubbed his wrists gingerly. The steel rings had bitten into them.

"They'll be a bit sore, but the cuffs never do any damage," said the man. Heron thought that if he were not a detective, a saint could be forgiven for thinking he was a mobster.

"You should know," said Heron, and the man grinned. He went up the steps again.

"Well, come on, Heron, we'd better go," said Ross.

Heron stopped by the steps. "How come Hood is involved? What's he doing here?"

Ross seemed surprised by the question. "Chief Inspector Hood? Why do you ask? My, er, department requested police assistance to get you out of this. In case we met some trouble. The heavy stuff isn't really our scene."

"Of course not," agreed Heron, poker-faced. "But why Hood?"

"Because, I imagine, he and his men happened to be available."

"And his murder inquiry? What's happened to that?"

"Perhaps they're all part of one and the same thing," said Ross, and his sharp features momentarily broke into an arctic smile. "Come along. We have business together."

Heron couldn't help thinking, as he followed him through the trapdoor, that the last man he recollected going off with Ross had been old Colonel Fennerman.

And that a few hours later the colonel was dead.

35

Hood stood glowering as they came off the barge and went over to Ross's car. Heron was surprised at how close his floating prison had been to Kingston Bridge. The barge, old, disused, was moored by the bank of the Thames, a gangway linking it with the towpath.

Nearby, several police vehicles were parked, and a group of Hood's men were standing around. There was even a dog handler with a nasty-looking Alsatian. Hood had brought a small army with him, and they watched silently as Heron got into Ross's car.

Ross sat next to him, and Bowler drove off without being given any instructions; clearly, he knew their destination.

"You weren't really badly treated, were you?" asked Ross solicitously.

"By Hood?" said Heron, still rubbing his wrists. The handcuffs had left red rims.

"No." Ross betrayed a touch of annoyance. "I mean the gentlemen who grabbed you."

"Well, I'm still in one piece."

Ross nodded and pulled out a silver cigarette case. He clicked it open and offered it to Heron.

"Only Turkish, I'm afraid," he apologized.

Heron shook his head.

"I got very fond of Turkish cigarettes," said Ross somewhat enigmatically.

For the rest of the journey they didn't speak much. Only once did Bowler turn his head.

"Straight there, sir?" he inquired.

"Straight there," replied Ross.

"Where's there?" asked Heron.

"Home territory," said Ross.

In twenty minutes they were in the West End, and then the car swung into King's Road.

Unexpectedly, the car suddenly turned into the gates of Chelsea Barracks. It came to a halt at the barrier, just past the railings with DUKE OF YORK'S HEADQUARTERS blazoned on them.

Heron expected to see a sentry, but instead, a black man came out of the guard lodge and walked over to the car. He nodded to Bowler, glanced at the two men in the back. Then the barrier swung up and the car purred through.

"What's all this?" asked Heron.

Ross smiled. "Come along, Harry, you know perfectly well there are other things in King's Road apart from dolly birds, boutiques, and hash."

The car stopped on the other side of the parade ground, near a couple of similarly anonymous-looking civilian automobiles parked behind rows of army vehicles.

"This way," said Ross, letting Heron out of the car. On the square, a couple of soldiers in camouflage smocks walked past.

"We're going to enlist?" asked Heron. Ross held open a door for him, and then they were walking down a corridor. Heron thought he could hear, faintly, the stammer of a teleprinter and the rattle of typewriters.

They turned a corner and came to another door. It was guarded by a soldier who also wore, incongruously, thought Heron, a camouflage smock and combat boots. He had a beret on, and Heron knew what the winged-dagger badge meant. He had a mighty respect for the Special Air Service Regiment; SAS didn't let Queen's Regulations stand in the way of what they had to do.

Ross and Bowler showed the soldier a little pass.

"He's with us," they said, indicating Heron, and for a moment the soldier's cold gray eyes raked him. Then Ross knocked on the door—two raps, followed by a single one.

The door opened, and a man in a turtleneck sweater immediately stood aside to let them in. His well-creased trousers were khaki, but the sweater was yellow. His brown shoes had a mirror polish, and his haircut was army-regulation length.

"Anything come in?" asked Ross.

"No, sir," said the man.

"All right, Simpson. We'll be a little while."

"Very good, sir," said Simpson. "I'll be in Records, if you want me." He left, shooting a curious glance at Heron as he passed.

"Sit down, Harry," said Ross.

The room's windows were barred, but Heron could see part of the parade ground through one of them. Ross sat behind a desk. In the corner was a table with a typewriter and a couple of trays containing papers. Bowler sat down at it, his back to them.

The wall behind Ross was covered with photographs. They looked like news pictures: people coming out of buildings, crowds in the streets, demonstrators with placards, several shots of policemen struggling with rioters. And there were many photos of people's faces, mostly blurred and fuzzy, as if they had been taken out of focus or enlarged many times over. Heron stared at one of them; he recognized the face. It was familiar, but at first he couldn't place it. Then he remembered: it was the fresh-faced man called Ronnie, who had been in the pub before that demo.

There was another man, in a check cap, hard, scowling. His name Heron didn't know, but the face was impressed on his memory.

"You know him?" asked Ross, friendly.

"Yes," said Heron. "He and his chum were beating up a black. Then they turned on me."

"Ah, yes." Ross nodded. 'They gave you quite a going-over, didn't they?"

And Heron suddenly realized that Ross didn't even pretend he didn't know all about it. That young policeman's memo had certainly percolated upward . . .

"What is this place?" asked Heron.

Ross brushed some Turkish tobacco ash off his blazer.

"We're terribly short of space, and they had a spare office here . . ." he said vaguely.

"We?"

"We tried for Hobart House," Ross went on as if he'd never heard Heron's question, "but the Coal Board was really bloody-minded, so when the army very kindly said they could fit us in . . ."

"With the SAS?"

"Oh, they've got all sorts of things at Chelsea Barracks," said Ross dismissively. "I don't even know half of them. Do we, Bowler?"

"No, sir," said Bowler without turning his head. He was staring at the *Times* crossword in front of him.

"Well, what am I doing here?" demanded Heron.

Ross nodded. "Yes, of course, you want to get away." He stood up. "Tom, have you got the stamp collection?"

Bowler reached over and handed Ross a big white album.

"We call this our stamp collection, Harry, because it has pictures of heads in it, just like a nice book of stamps," said Ross, putting the album in front of Heron. "Now, just look at them and see if you can identify any of the people who snatched you. Take your time."

Heron had done the rogues'-gallery routine in his time, but this album was somewhat different. The passport-size photographs, four to a page, had no identification at all, not even a code number. They had been stuck down blankly, anonymous. Heron wondered how they were referred to—"top, on the right"? "the one at the bottom, on the left"?

"Just take your time," repeated Ross. He stood next to Heron, looking down at the album. Heron started to turn the stiff pages. Like some of the larger photographs pinned on the wall, some of these were also grainy, out of focus. Others, though, were sharp, almost studio quality.

There were all kinds of faces: swarthy, bearded, youthful; ferret faces and open, frank ones; smiling faces and scowling. Some heads were blond, some long-haired or bald. There were men with scars and thin moustaches, men whose eyes were fearless or furtive.

"Recognize anybody?" asked Ross gently.

Heron shook his head and turned another page. Then he paused. He peered closer. Curious that this should be the one he recognized.

"Yes," he said. "This one. He was the chauffeur. He drove the car."

"Ah," said Ross. "That's Mr. White."

"Who is he?"

Ross wrote something down on a pad. "I told you, Mr. White."

Heron tightened his lips. Ross liked playing games. Maybe there would be one game soon he didn't like.

A page later he found two more of them, side by side, the top row on the page.

"These two," said Heron. "Definitely."

One was the man with the glass eye. The other, the man with the gun and the expensive wristwatch.

"Indeed," said Ross. "How interesting. Mr. Brown and Mr. Green."

Heron looked up at him. "What does that mean?"

"Keep looking," urged Ross.

The Roman centurion was last.

"Of course." Ross nodded, as if it all fitted. "Mr. Gray." He made a final note. "He had the LSE scarf, didn't he?"

"Yes," said Heron. "Now tell me who they really are."

"I told you. Messrs. White, Brown, Green and Gray." His sharp features allowed themselves to look amused. "A colorful lot." He saw Heron's look. "I'm sorry, Harry, it's a terrible weakness I've got."

"What do you know about them?"

"The same as you, Harry. They're after the Goering Testament."

"And so are you," said Heron.

Ross walked back to his chair and sat down facing Heron.

"Yes, Harry," he said very quietly. "So are we."

"You know I haven't got it."

Ross leaned back. "Well, if you haven't got it, you know where it is."

"I've been told that, too," said Heron.

Bowler seemed to have had a sudden inspiration. He picked up a ballpoint pen and began to fill in one of the crossword clues. A big one, with about ten letters.

"I'm curious about something," said Ross conversationally. "How well did you really know Colin Fennerman? Or should I say, what did you know about him?"

Heron shrugged. "He was a friend."

"That doesn't mean anything," said Ross sharply, and his eyes were ruthless. "I asked you what you know about him."

"Well, he . . . he was in the army. His father was a distinguished officer." He gave Ross a sharp look. "As you well know. After the war, Colin drifted around a bit. Did this and that. He had a bit of money. He started his little business. The shop. We got to know each other. He gave me a part-time job. And somebody murdered him."

"You don't know much at all, do you?" said Ross coldly.

He opened his desk and took out a file. Inside,

resting on some papers, was a photograph. He pushed it across to Heron.

It was the young Captain Fennerman, with the neat moustache and the clear, honest eyes. And it was the photo Lotte had had at the cemetery.

"Your friend Fennerman," said Ross. "In nineteen forty-five."

Heron handed the picture back to him.

"Fennerman spoke German fluently, did you know that?" asked Ross.

The chair Heron sat on was uncomfortable. He shifted his weight. "Ursula . . . his wife is German. I knew he could speak it quite well."

"Not quite well. Fluently. Perfectly. Maybe that was the reason they put him in intelligence. First he interrogated Class A prisoners. The big Nazis. He was in Germany from the start, with a special outfit." Ross didn't glance at the file once. He seemed to know all the details by heart. "He did some things with Twenty-one Army Group, too. He was all over the shop, nineteen forty-four, forty-five. And he wasn't always in uniform . . ."

"You mean he was a spy."

Ross looked pained. "I hate the word 'spy.' And I loathe 'agent.' No, he did what I said, intelligence work. Some of it covert. Some of it in tandem with Americans."

"Go on."

"He was doing it in forty-six, too, with the occupation forces. They had a lot to do with the intelligence boys—ferreting out big-shot Nazis, hunting down war criminals, investigating, you name it. Fennerman, it so happened, did work at Nuremberg. For the trials. A couple of times he interrogated Goering."

Ross momentarily gazed out of the window, as if a thought had struck him. Then he went on.

"Anyway, Fennerman attended the execution of the war criminals. Ribbentrop, Streicher, the lot. There was a lot of confusion in the prison that night.

Goering poisoned himself just before he was due to be hanged."

Heron nodded.

"Well, just before he killed himself, Goering wrote three letters. One to Colonel Andrus, the prison commandant. One to Emmy, his wife. And the third letter. That's the one, Harry. His Testament. Goering's political testament. It disappeared."

"Are you saying Fennerman had it?"

"He was offering it for sale," said Ross triumphantly. "Didn't you know that?"

Heron stared at him, gaping.

"After thirty-two years, he suddenly started putting out feelers."

Heron blinked. "No. I don't believe it."

"And it fits, it all fits. Your friend was a bad 'un. That's why the army finally court-martialed him." For the first time he looked at his file. "In March nineteen forty-seven, Fennerman faced a general court-martial at Hanover and was cashiered. He pleaded guilty. I think the army made a deal to avoid his shooting his mouth off. That's why he didn't go inside, or didn't you know that, either?"

Heron frowned. "What was he tried for?"

"Black-marketeering. Stealing army drugs, supplies, and flogging them on the black market. But he was suspected of a lot more they could never prove."

"Would you like some tea, sir?" asked Bowler.

"Yes, please." Ross glanced at Heron. "You, too, Harry? Good. Both without sugar, Tom."

So, thought Heron, he even knows that. He even knows that I take no sugar in tea, only in coffee. Without ever asking.

"The old colonel . . ." he began.

"What about him?" asked Ross sharply.

"He didn't talk as if his son had turned a black sheep. He said he had always done his duty. He was very proud of him . . ."

"The old boy was past it," said Ross brutally. "He

probably didn't even know the time of day any more."

You liar, thought Heron. The colonel was all there. The colonel was no fool. Maybe that was why he had to commit suicide . . .

"Now the only question is what has happened to the Goering Testament. The third letter. That's why you are here, Harry." Ross was playing with his pencil. "I think Fennerman was killed because he was trying to be too clever by half. I think he still had the document, waiting for the best price. Now that he's dead, what's happened to it? What do you say?"

The door opened and Bowler came in, skillfully balancing three cups of tea.

"Here you are, sir," he said. "Two without sugar."

Ross took a sip and looked at Heron across the cup. "Well?"

"Maybe the wife knows where it is. She seems to have had stome strange friends. And now she's scarpered. I think to Germany."

"You think so?" muttered Ross. He put the cup down. "Hmmm," he grunted.

"Excuse me, sir, but your conference with the admiral . . ." Bowler coughed apologetically. "I think, sir . . ."

Ross looked at his watch.

"Damn right," he said. He stood up. "Well, you've been very helpful, Harry, thank you."

"I have?"

"Well, you've identified those four characters, thank you very much." He edged Heron to the door.

"Don't call us, we'll call you?" said Heron.

"Something like that." Ross smiled, but it was not a warming smile. "Turn right in the corridor, then straight out, across the parade ground, and you're in trendy King's Road. Sure you'll find your way?"

"Don't worry," said Heron. "I'll find my way. I always do."

36

While Heron waited for the cuttings, he soaked in the atmosphere once so familiar to him. The smell of paper and glue and printing ink, the people at their desks cutting up newspaper, the shelves of folders and files. It was a long time since he had been in a newspaper morgue, but right away he felt at home.

He had no right to be there, officially, but he knew the layout of the building, and he had walked straight past the commissionaires and taken the lift up to the fourth floor. Reid, the librarian, knew him of old, and hadn't made any trouble when he had asked for the clippings he wanted.

But when Reid finally appeared from behind the steel cabinets, he looked despondent. Reid hated being caught out.

"Can't find anything on your man," he said. "The only thing on any Fennerman I have is this."

He had a thin envelope with one cutting: the stop-press paragraph reporting the death of Colonel Fennerman.

"No," said Heron, "it's the son I want."

"Nothing on him," said Reid sorrowfully. He put the cutting back in the envelope. "Sorry."

"But there must have been something on a British officer in Germany being court-martialed," insisted Heron. "It didn't happen every day, did it?"

"I checked all over the place," said Reid. "Under Fennerman, under British Army of the Rhine, under Courts-Martial. Nineteen forty-seven, wasn't it?"

"About March. He got cashiered."

"Well, there's nothing."

Reid was eager to help. He took it personally if a news item had slipped through his net.

"Only one thing I can suggest, Harry," he said. "Why don't you look through the papers for March of that year? We've got the bound copies."

He made room for Heron at a desk, and a stack of big, heavy volumes was put down.

"Shouldn't think you'll find anything; otherwise we'd have cut it. But you never know."

"I'll try anyway," said Heron. "Thanks."

Quickly he skimmed the newspapers, glancing through the headlines, making a special point of checking smaller paragraphs. It was like looking into ancient history. Britain had been icebound. Big Ben had stopped. Princess Elizabeth had become engaged to a naval lieutenant named Mountbatten. In a wadi in the Middle East, the Dead Sea Scrolls had been found. Eros, the god of love, had returned to Piccadilly Circus from his wartime evacuation. A raft called *Kon-Tiki* had sailed the South Pacific.

Heron hadn't even been a reporter then. He turned the pages, and a forgotten world passed before his eyes. There were pictures of women wearing long skirts called the New Look. The sentries at Buckingham Palace were still in khaki. Britain was poor, and so was Europe. There were headlines about something called the Marshall Plan. The British left India, Pakistan was born, and a singer named Maria Callas made a sensational debut.

But about the court-martial of a British officer called Fennerman there was not a line.

"Well?" asked Reid.

"You were right. I can't see anything."

He shut the last volume. It was the old, defunct *Daily Herald*.

"Maybe nobody covered it," suggested Reid. "Not unless it was rape or hanky-panky with a colonel's wife. You know the boys. What did he do, anyway?"

"I don't know," said Heron slowly. "I really don't know."

"He must have done something to get cashiered."

"Black-marketeering, somebody said."

"There," said Reid triumphantly.

"At least that's what they say." Heron got up. "Thanks again, anyway."

"Anytime," said Reid. "You back in the Street?"

"Not really," said Heron.

On the second floor, three people came into the elevator that was taking Heron down.

One of them was Lotte. She looked startled when she saw him.

"You! Here?"

"I sneaked in to check on something," said Heron. "Nice to see you."

She had on a new lipstick, a color he had not seen her use before, but it suited her. She looked very desirable.

"You got time for a cup of coffee?" he suggested.

"I wish I did," said Lotte. "But idiot-man is sending me to London Airport. Just in case aging Rod Stewart comes in with a new blonde."

In the lobby she said, "Can I give you a lift? On my way there?"

"Well," said Heron, "if you could drop me near Wardour Street . . ."

He loved the perfume she wore. Now he got a good whiff of it.

In the Volkswagen he enjoyed her closeness as she sat beside him.

"Well," said Lotte while they waited for the traffic light to change at the Aldwych, "what's been happening to you lately?"

"You'd be surprised."

"Not with you, I wouldn't, Harry. You attract trouble. Nothing would surprise me."

As the light turned green, the thing that had been worrying him began to nag again.

"You still haven't told me," she said lightly.

"What?"

"How things are."

"Untidy," he said.

She gave him a sidelong glance, but he didn't elaborate.

It wasn't until they were past Charing Cross Station that he asked the question.

"Lotte, wasn't your brother at the London School of Economics?"

"Ricky?" There was surprise in her tone. "No. Why do you ask?"

"Don't know," he said. "Just wondered."

"You must have got him mixed up," said Lotte. "Ricky went to Harvard Business School. In the States."

That could be right, thought Heron. That could be so right. The man with the scarf and the Roman centurion profile had an American accent. People do acquire American accents . . .

"Do you mind if I drop you here?" said Lotte. "You know what the traffic's like. I don't want to go too much out of my way."

"No, of course not," said Heron. "This will do fine."

He gave her a quick kiss, but as he watched the Volkswagen drive off he could not help feeling that suddenly she had seemed curiously eager to get rid of him.

37

As soon as she heard him come up the stairs, Kelly rushed out to the landing. She had kept the door ajar to make sure she wouldn't miss him.

"My, you're a popular man," she said, and giggled.

Heron could see she was drunk. She carried it off well, actually, but he knew the signs. Makeup smudged, eyes a little glazed, and, above all, the giggle.

"How's business, love?" inquired Heron pleasantly. He had an automatic affinity to all free-lancers, whatever their trade, and Kelly was a hard-working lass.

"Rotten," said Kelly. "Won't even pay the electricity bill at this rate." And she giggled again.

"I know what you mean," said Heron, thinking of his telephone. Maybe she'd be lucky, too. Maybe they wouldn't cut her current off. But he knew that wasn't likely, not in her case . . .

"You had some callers," said Kelly. "Everybody in town's after you, you lucky man."

Heron stopped on the landing. "What sort of callers?"

"Funny chap," she said, and giggled again. "Foreigner. Came again this morning."

"Little fellow with a bow tie?"

"That's him. Very excited. Kept saying he had to see you. 'Must see him, must find him.' " She burped. "Said people were after him or something."

"Who's after him?" asked Heron sharply.

"Search me." She lowered her voice. "If you want to know, I don't think he's a gentleman."

"Maybe you're right," said Heron.

"No gentleman at all."

"Well," said Heron, getting out his key, "I'd better get on. Did he say he was coming back?"

She shook her head; the tousled hair fell all over the place. "No idea. Couldn't care less. Bloody foreigner." The gin was well into her bloodstream.

"See you later," said Heron.

She took his arm.

"There was somebody else," she said. She reached inside her bra and brought out a visiting card. "Him."

Heron took it. "Francis Shobbington, M. A.," said the card, and in the bottom left-hand corner, one word: "Solicitor."

"He said would you call him. The number's on the back."

Heron turned the card over. In ink, somebody had written a phone number. The number code was 629, the Mayfair exchange.

"Sorry about that," giggled Kelly.

He didn't have to ask what she was sorry for. In her world, solicitors meant trouble. Writs, summonses, bills, fines.

"I must hire you as my secretary," said Heron.

Kelly came closer. "You wouldn't like to come upstairs and have a drink?" She was both inviting him and pleading.

"I got work to do, love."

"Just a quick drink," said Kelly.

"I'll tell you what," said Heron. "We'll have one tomorrow."

She giggled. "Promise?"

"Absolutely."

She blew him a kiss and turned to go upstairs. She was quite steady on her feet, but she held on to the rickety banister just in case.

He unlocked his door. Somebody had pushed a note under it. He picked it up.

"Harry," said a scrawl of a handwriting. "Must see

you quickly." The "Must" and the "quickly" had been underlined twice. "No time to lose. Swiss House, 8:00 P.M. Do not tell anyone. Your friend, Madek. P.S. Please hurry." The "Please" had been underlined, too.

Heron, managing director and sole employee of Heron Associates, public-relations experts, sat down behind his secondhand desk thoughtfully. Something was wrong, he knew it, but he couldn't put his finger on it. He looked at the visiting card again.

A curious solicitor, Mr. Shobbington. He had his name and his profession on his card, but no firm, no office address, not even a phone number. That he had to write specially.

Heron reached out for the S to Z phone directory, on which a tin of tomato soup rested. He searched the pages, but in the great sprawling city of London, with its millions of telephone subscribers, there was not one Shobbington listed.

He picked up the phone. Yes, it was still connected. Still no bill paid, but service remained normal. Heron dialed the number on the back of the card. It rang, but there was no reply. Not only was Mr. Shobbington unlisted, but he appeared elusive. Still, it was after office hours . . .

Strange, thought Heron, Mr. Shobbington hadn't even indicated what he wanted. He left his phone number and nothing else, as if his name were enough.

38

Madek was sitting in a corner, anxiously scrutinizing the people who came in. When he saw Heron threading his way among the tables, he gave a little wave and then looked around hastily, as if afraid he had made himself too conspicuous.

"Thank God you're here," said Madek dramatically when Heron sat down. "I have been waiting hours."

"Come on, I'm not even late," protested Heron.

The little Hungarian seemed fretful, uneasy. Even his bow tie drooped.

"I feel sick with coffee," he complained. "I think I've drunk a dozen cups. They keep coming, these schmucks, asking if I want anything else, and I have to keep ordering their coffee."

"Well, why did you pick this place?" asked Heron. He loathed the Alpine Centre. He loathed the officious little men who ordered one around, the assembly-line service, the organized turmoil, the constant hubbub. And he didn't like the Swiss.

Madek leaned forward. "It's safe," he whispered. "Too many people for anything to happen. It is best to hide in crowds."

"And just who are you hiding from?"

Madek stared at him reproachfully, but a blond youth appeared. He stuck a menu in front of Heron.

"Yes?" he demanded.

"Coffee," said Heron.

"And?"

"Nothing," said Heron.

"You must eat," declared the waiter.

"Just coffee," insisted Heron ominously.

"And you?" the waiter challenged Madek.

"Another coffee, please," requested Madek, cringing.

The blonde youth gave him a look of contempt and wrote something on a bill before disappearing into the maelstrom.

"You are very difficult to find, Harry," said Madek resentfully. "I phone your flat. Nothing. I call your office. No one there. I come around. No Harry. Where have you been? Yesterday? Today?"

"Busy," said Heron. "Quite busy."

"That woman—what is her name, Yvonne? She is a prostitute, no?" He said it very disapprovingly.

"She is a business girl," Heron corrected him. For some reason, Madek's smug statement of fact annoyed him. "Just as you are a businessman."

Madek did not even blink. "That is what we must talk about. Our business. We have no time."

Heron sat back in the chair as the waiter put down two coffees, none too gently.

"Tell me," he asked, "what are you afraid of?"

Madek fingered his gold bangle nervously.

"We have competition," he said in a low voice. "Bad people. I am no hero. You also must be careful, my friend. So far you have been lucky. No one has touched you."

"I wouldn't exactly say that." He decided that, for what they cost, the cups of coffee were rather small.

Madek gave him a hard look, but Heron didn't elaborate. Instead, he asked, "What is suddenly so urgent?"

Madek lowered his voice even more.

"I think I know where it is," he whispered hoarsely.

"The Goering thing?"

"Ssh. Not so loud. But maybe we have found it." He leaned back and looked at Heron expectantly.

"Go on."

"Now you must get it," Madek added triumphantly.

Long ago Heron had learned to look unexcited when somebody finally told him something he wanted to know. It helped to keep low the gratuities he had to pay.

"Who's got the thing?" he asked, almost languidly.

Madek hesitated. Then he leaned close to Heron. "You were right. I think she has it. The wife."

"Ursula?"

He nodded. "And I know where she is. In the Black Forest. You have heard of Freudenstadt?"

Heron shook his head.

"She is there. In a house called Adlerhof. You must get it from her."

"Just like that?" said Heron.

"You can do it, Harry," said Madek earnestly. "She has some bodyguards, but you will manage it. And then we are rich."

Two *au pair* girls sat down at the table on Heron's left. He knew they were *au pair* girls. They had shiny noses, they spoke German, it was their day off, they were both about ninteen or twenty . . . and he just knew they were *au pairs*. They chattered busily, and he picked up the words "kino" and "Clint Eastwood."

"You will do it quickly, yes?" pressed Madek.

"Why don't you go yourself?" asked Heron softly. "You wouldn't even have to split with me. Why not go it alone?"

Madek shifted awkwardly.

"It is not so simple for me," he said a little uncomfortably. "You see, I have a small problem. With the German *polizei*. You know how stupid the Germans are."

"What is the problem?"

"Oh, it's all a mistake, Harry. Two or three checks . . . I could get it all cleared up, but in Germany you are guilty till proved innocent. It could take a long time. Meanwhile, we lose the"—he shot a glance at the girls—"we lose the goods."

Heron grunted. "You mean you're scared to go to Germany?"

Madek smiled nervously. "Not exactly scared, my dear Harry. There is nothing to be afraid of there. It is just that—that they might not like me to visit the country." His soulful eyes looked innocent. "So you go for me. Okay?"

"I've also got a technical problem, I'm afraid," sighed Heron.

"What?" asked Madek anxiously.

"Bread." He saw the Hungarian was confused. "Money. It costs money to go junketing. Air ticket, hotel, car hire, maybe. I haven't got any."

Madek lapsed into gloomy silence. Then: "You could borrow it, maybe?"

"Sure. From you."

"Not at the moment," said Madek hastily.

"That's it, then."

"No, no," Madek almost cried. He controlled his voice. "You must get the money. Somehow. If we do not have the testament quickly, we . . . we . . ."

He looked quite desperate.

The blond waiter appeared.

"You ready to order?" he asked heavily.

"Another two coffees," said Heron.

The waiter scowled. My, thought Heron, you'd make a perfect little Hitler Youth.

"You cannot just drink coffee," said the waiter curtly. "This table is for dinner. You must have a meal."

He again thrust the menu at Heron.

"I'm not hungry," said Heron.

"It is a regulation," said the waiter proudly.

"Why don't you send for the Swiss navy?" suggested Heron pleasantly.

"I get the manager." The youth marched off, and Heron half expected him, idiotically, to goose-step.

"We'd better leave," said Madek nervously.

"Suits me."

At the cash desk, Madek somehow managed to disappear into the cloakroom, leaving Heron with the bill. The amount confirmed Heron's dislike of the Swiss.

"Expensive, just for a few cups of coffee," he said pointedly when Madek emerged.

"Oh, is it?" said Madek. "Thank you so much."

Upstairs, in Coventry Street, there were crowds from the cinemas in Leicester Square. Heron and Madek weaved their way among them. A police car, its blue light flashing, klaxoned its way urgently from Piccadilly Circus and swept around the corner into Wardour Street.

"You will go, Harry?" said Madek. He gave a piece of paper to Heron. "Here is the address. Just outside Freudenstadt. That's where she is."

Heron took it.

"Please?" repeated Madek.

Another police car shot past them, siren going, and also turned into Wardour Street, its tires screeching.

"Why do you trust me?" asked Heron. "Supposing I did find the bloody thing and flogged it to the highest bidder myself?"

"You wouldn't," said Madek. He grinned crookedly. "Besides, you're not a Hungarian bandit. You're an English gentleman."

Heron raised his eyebrows.

"You could fool me," he said.

"Also, if you did that, I would be very sad."

Heron nearly burst out laughing. But he kept his expression serious.

"And I am a coward and do not like killing people," added Madek quite sweetly.

"Well," said Heron, "I'm not promising anything. I'll see."

"One thing, Harry." Madek was very grave. "Watch yourself. Everywhere. You are a target. Like me."

"You know something?" said Heron. "Statistics prove that the most dangerous place in the world is bed. That's where most people die."

"Very funny," said Madek, unamused. "Just be careful. At least until I've had my share."

Heron grinned.

"I'll see you," said Madek.

A third police car raced past, going all-out, its klaxon scattering people trying to cross Coventry Street. It too careened into Wardour Street.

"There must be some big trouble," said Madek.

"There must be," agreed Heron.

"*Ciao*," said Madek hastily, and the next moment he had disappeared into the crowds.

Heron turned into Wardour Street.

39

He didn't have to look far. The traffic was already snarled up, and harassed cops were trying to untangle the jam. Halfway down ahead of him, he saw clusters of blue lights flashing. They were stationary.

It was his cul-de-sac, all right. There was a lot of activity. At the entrance stood a few sightseers, their passage barred by three policemen. The radio cars parked around had the stamp of police cars who have arrived at an emergency—drawn up at all angles, some half on the sidewalk, their doors open; the crews didn't even bother to slam them as they piled out.

Heron pushed his way through the gawkers.

"Hold it, chum," said one of the bobbies. His lapel radio was muttering, but he turned it low.

Over his shoulder Heron could see men in plain clothes and uniformed officers milling around at the second house. The house where Heron Associates rested its weary feet.

"That's my place," said Heron.

"You live there?"

Heron nodded. He didn't want to explain things to this helmet. Office, flat, tenant, resident, what the hell did it matter? The important thing was why the police were crawling all over the place.

"You'd better go through," said the policeman, letting Heron pass.

In the blind alley nobody took much notice of him, but at the entrance of the house, a man consulting with a uniformed inspector looked up when Heron approached.

"What do you want?" he asked.

"My office is on the second floor," said Heron. "What's happened?"

"What's your name?" asked the man.

"Heron."

He and the inspector exchanged looks.

"I think you can help us, Mr. Heron," said the man. "Come upstairs."

Heron followed him up the creaky stairs. There were a lot of people inside, and some of them squeezed past on the narrow staircase on their way down. Voices drifted down from the upper floors.

"Careful," said the man, "you don't want to step on anything."

On the second-floor landing, Heron understood what he meant. The door of his office was standing wide open. Some of the wood was splintered, and the lock had been smashed.

But that wasn't what Heron was looking at. Instead, he stared at the woman who was lying halfway across the threshold. Her head was lying in a pool of blood, which soaked her tousled hair. The blood came from a raw, gaping slash across her throat.

Kelly's throat had been cut, and death did not make her look beautiful.

"You know her, of course?" asked the man. He wore a smartly cut suit and suede shoes.

"Yes," said Heron, white-faced. He felt the nausea rising in him. Her blood, so it seemed to him, was still flowing from that yawning red trench in her neck. "Yes. She—she's the girl upstairs."

"That's right," agreed the man unemotionally. "Linda Doreen Jenkins. Alias Kelly, alias Yvonne. Your neighborhood tom. But I expect you know all that . . ."

A detective was crouched beside her, drawing the outline of her body on the floor with chalk. He looked up.

"You want me to . . . ?" he offered, getting to his feet.

"No," said the man in the nice suit. "Just carry on."

"Okay, sir," said his underling, and began drawing more chalk lines on the floor.

Heron leaned against the wall, staring at her body, almost mesmerized. Poor Kelly. And that wasn't even her name, after all. Not Kelly. Not Yvonne. Linda Doreen . . .

She had a dressing gown on, and it covered much of her demurely. One of the nylon stockings had a long run in it terminating in a hole.

"What happened?" croaked Heron. He felt surprisingly sad about her.

"Maybe you'll be able to fill in some of the gaps, Mr. Heron."

He saw Heron's look and hastily added, "I don't mean about the murder. But with the motive, maybe."

"How can I possibly—" began Heron, but the man cut him short.

"Why was somebody so anxious to break into your, er, office? That would be interesting to know."

Heron stared at him.

"You see, at first we thought she'd been done in by one of her clients." Heron felt sure he reserved "done in" for street girls and the like. Respectable citizens were "murdered" or "killed," not "done in."

"It happens quite a lot, doesn't it? Sort of occupational hazard. But that isn't the case here."

"No?"

"Indications are that somebody was breaking into your place and she heard them upstairs, came down, tried to stop them or something, and they did this to her."

Heron swallowed.

Another plainclothesman came running up the stairs.

"Excuse me, sir," he said, "but Mr. Hood is on his way. Just came over the blower."

"Thank you, Sergeant," said the man. "You tell him that I've taken this gentleman to the nick."

"Yes, sir," said the sergeant, and started clumping down the stairs.

"You don't mind, do you, Mr. Heron?" asked the man politely. "We can't really talk here. Not with things like this, and the forensic boys having to do all their stuff."

"You mean you want me to assist the police with their inquiries?" said Heron dryly.

"Exactly," said the man. "I knew you wouldn't mind."

40

Something bright exploded in Heron's face as he emerged from the house. Momentarily, he was blinded, then gradually the faces around him came into focus.

"I'll be damned," said Tom Pearce. "So you're the bloody mystery man . . ."

Pearce stood beside the photographer, his tie loosened, a day's growth of beard on his chin, grinning like a Cheshire cat.

He looked at the man beside Heron.

"Have you nicked him, Inspector?" he asked hopefully.

"Come along, now, we don't want the press around here," said the inspector. He seemed annoyed.

"But he's an old buddy-buddy," crowed Pearce. "Aren't you, Harry my boy?"

"Fuck off," said Heron.

"Oh, come on, you know what it's like, they're screaming for a bloody story," said Pearce. "Don't get all snotty with your old mates because you're at the receiving end. What's going on, Harry?"

"Mr. Heron is helping us," announced the inspector impatiently. "Now, please move on."

"Just one moment," said Pearce, self-important. "So they *have* nicked you, Harry."

He dug the photographer in the ribs with a delighted look.

"Mr. Heron is not under arrest," insisted the inspector.

Another flashbulb went off. The photographer had understood the signal.

"That's great," cried Pearce. "If he's not under arrest, he can talk. What's it all about, Harry?"

"Go to hell," said Heron.

Pearce looked up at the house.

"Didn't know you ran a cat house." he sneered. "Must be tough, losing this tart. Can't live off her now, can you?"

Heron hit him. Heron hit very hard, and very suddenly, and Pearce never saw the blow. He staggered and fell, and for a few moments he lay on the cobbles, quite still.

The inspector grabbed Heron's arm.

"That's enough," he said.

"You heard what that bastard said," snapped Heron.

"Well, I'm not doing anything about it," said the

inspector, and for a moment there was a hint of a grin. "But you get into that car, quick."

Pearce groaned and sat up. He felt his jaw gingerly.

"Jesus," he said, dazed.

The inspector slammed the door of the police car, and it reversed up the cul-de-sac, the policemen hastily clearing the way for it. It backed out into Wardour Street.

Slowly Pearce got to his feet.

"Hey," he yelled at the photographer. "Did you get that? Did you get that son of a bitch?"

He was still rubbing his jaw.

"Not exactly, Tom," said the photographer. "But I got a good one of you out cold."

"You're a bloody idiot," announced Pearce.

He picked up the notebook he had dropped.

"Which nick covers this patch? Vine Street? Savile Row? Bow Street?"

"Don't know, Tom," said the photographer. "Might be Goodge Street. It all gets sort of mixed up in this part of Soho."

"That's not the only fucking thing that's mixed up, mate," declared Pearce savagely. "Where the hell's a phone box?"

In his mind, he already had the opening paragraph of his story for the first edition:

"Murder Squad detectives were last night questioning an unemployed man in the brutal sex murder of a Soho good-time gal. . . ."

He liked that. He liked it a lot.

He was so busy looking for a telephone that neither he nor anyone else noticed the taxi that drew up a few doorways from the cul-de-sac. A man got out, paid the driver, and then stood quietly, watching everything that was going on.

The man had a glass eye and seemed very interested in the police activity.

41

The nick turned out to be not a police station, but Scotland Yard. A plain interviewing room on the fourth floor, where a rather studious-looking girl in plain clothes took Heron's statement straight down on a typewriter.

Yes, he knew the dead woman. He rented an office on the floor below. No, he did not know much about her. Yes, she had a lot of acquaintances who visited her for short periods. Yes, they were all men. Yes, he had last seen her earlier in the evening. No, he did not know if she was expecting anyone. Yes, he believed her professional name was Yvonne. He knew her as Kelly. No, he did not know that her surname was Jenkins.

Heron signed the statement. The man in the smart suit, who said his name was Detective Inspector Westbrook, thanked him and left the room with the typed sheet.

"Would you like a cup of coffee?" asked the plain-clothes girl.

"Yes, please," said Heron. They were really being rather nice to him.

But it wasn't the girl with a cup of coffee who came back into the room. The door opened, and Hood stood looking at Heron. Slowly he shut it and sat down at the table where Heron had signed his statement.

"Well," he said, "you've been busy, Harry, haven't you?"

"Makes two of us," said Heron. "It's been a busy day."

Hood grunted. "You seem to be in the clear on this one," he growled finally. "You got a good alibi."

"I haven't even put one up," remarked Heron mildly. "Nobody's asked."

"They've fixed the time of death pretty accurately," Hood said almost reluctantly. "It puts you in the clear. You were with your pal Madek just about that time."

Heron stared at him. He hadn't told anyone about seeing Madek. He hadn't even mentioned where he had been.

"Lucky for you," added Hood ungraciously.

"Sorry," sneered Heron. "Hate to spoil your evening."

"Don't get cocky, Heron," snapped the burly man. "I still got some questions."

"I'd like to ask one first. Who found her?"

"A would-be client. He went up the stairs, saw her lying there. He nearly shit himself," said Hood crudely. His grin was unpleasant. "Ran out of the place screaming for the police." The grin disappeared. "Now I want some answers. What the hell is it all about?" he scowled. "Rubbish who break into seedy little back rooms in broken-down dumps don't cut a girl's throat. And what would anybody expect to find in a slum like that? In a stinking little hidey-hole? You stashing away some goodies I should know about?"

Heron sat silent.

"They were looking for something, Heron. Must be the same lot who broke into your place in Ashfield Gardens tonight."

Heron sat up. "What?"

"Didn't you know?" said Hood, all mock surprise. "Somebody's turned over your bed-sitter. Made a bit of a mess. The landlady called us. I don't think they took anything. Didn't find what they were looking for, I imagine. What would they expect to find, Harry? Tell me?"

"Why don't you ask Ross?" muttered Heron.

Hood took a deep breath. "Ross is security service. DI Five. You know that bloody well. They're not talkative. But I've got a couple of murders, an abduction, and two petty break-ins on my books. And you're involved in all of them."

Heron said nothing.

"You'd better help me, Heron," said Hood sulkily, going to the door. "If you don't, you're going to get burned."

He slammed the door.

Heron looked at the wall. There was a recruiting poster on it. A smiling, clean-cut young policeman. CAN YOU DO A MAN'S JOB? asked the poster. "If you're British, aged 18½ or over, and are 5' 8" (172 cms), write today . . ."

The young policeman on the poster, helmet in the left arm, was invitingly declaiming the oath:

". . . I will well and truly serve our Sovereign Lady the Queen without favour or affection, malice or ill will . . ."

They don't give the rates of pay, thought Heron wryly.

Then Westbrook came in with Heron's statement.

"That's fine, Mr. Heron," he said pleasantly. "Thank you very much." He glanced at the bare table. "Oh, dear, didn't she ask you if you wanted any tea?"

"It was coffee," said Heron, "but don't worry about it."

"Oh, all right, then," said Westbrook. "I think you've seen Mr. Hood?"

"Yes," said Heron.

Westbrook held the door open.

"Thanks again. It was good of you to come."

"I didn't realize I had any choice," said Heron.

Outside, in Victoria Street, he was still trying to work out how Hood knew he had been with Madek.

He glanced around. The sidewalk was deserted. Nobody was following him.

That, he felt, was even more curious.

42

Breakfast was spoiled for Aleksei Shilenko when he saw the urgent decode from the Director waiting for him in his cultural attaché's office.

The Director was terse to his London resident:

"Important we make progress CRAYFISH. Other parties also interested. Imperative CRAYFISH does not elude us or fall into wrong hands. Advise."

CRAYFISH was the code name for the Goering Testament.

Shilenko chewed his lower lip, which he often did when he was concerned. He had feelers out for the damn thing, but could one really trust a renegade Hungarian emigré like Tibor Madek?

43

In the same hour that Shilenko's coded reply was being transmitted to the Director in Moscow, and that Heron, managing to get hold of Mr. Shobbington on the phone, arranged to meet him at noon, John D.

Wurtzberg—as he was listed on the United States embassy diplomatic roster—showed his pass to the Marine guard and rushed for the elevator.

Wurtzberg had slept badly, and while his wife was telling him over breakfast about the art show she planned to visit that day, he suddenly realized what was nagging him. Ten minutes later he was on his way to Grosvenor Square.

He nodded briefly to his secretary in the outer office, unlocked the door of his own office, hung up his coat, and then opened his personal safe, of which only he knew the combination.

In the safe lay twenty-five thousand pounds in neatly bundled pound notes, fifteen thousand dollars in greenbacks, and five thousand dollars in blank American Express traveler's checks. There was also some specially marked and easily traceable currency. As chief of covert operations at the London station, Wurtzberg had twenty-four-hours-a-day access to ready cash for which only he was accountable.

But it wasn't money he took out of the safe. It was a file, all the pages of which were stapled together at the top. Wurtzberg sat down at his desk and began to read. He knew it all, but he had started wondering. . . .

Finally he buzzed his girl.

"Send Seltzer in," he ordered. He lit one of his four daily Havana cigars, a vice that he felt, in his position, had a special piquancy.

"Morning, John," said Seltzer. "Looks like the weather will clear up."

Seltzer began every day with a remark about the weather. Being stationed in London, he had plenty of justification.

"Sit down, Glen," said Wurtzberg.

Seltzer saw the file on his desk and the photograph that was attached to one of the pages.

"Not *that*," he said.

"They're all after it," said Wurtzberg, sour. "But

that's not what's bugging me. What's your feeling, Glen?"

"About the Goering Testament?" asked Seltzer, raising his eyebrows in surprise.

"No." Wurtzberg hesitated. "Do you think we're being double-crossed?"

"The little guy?"

Wurtzberg nodded.

"Look, I'll tell you," said Seltzer. "Madek sells to the highest bidder. It's as simple as that. When he knows a lot of people want a thing, he doesn't care who gets it as long as they pay the most. He's a businessman, that's all."

Wurtzberg rolled the Bolivar around in his mouth. "Is he really essential?"

"You mean, do it all ourselves?" Seltzer, who had been stationed in Saigon, shook his head. "It's like the black market, John. You don't go looking for the stuff yourself. You leave it to the operator who can come up with the goods. It's cleaner that way."

"But if he's double-dealing . . ."

"I guess at one time I'd have said he gets terminated."

"Not these days," remarked Wurtzberg dourly.

"No, boss." Seltzer smiled. "But we couldn't very well stop anybody else doing it, could we, now?"

44

The address Mr. Shobbington had given Heron was in a mansion block just off Berkeley Square and within a pistol shot of Claridges.

"You'll find my chambers on the fourth floor," he had said.

Heron rode up in an antiquated elevator of ornate ironwork. It ascended very slowly, like an old man who doesn't want to strain his heart. The gates were heavy and shut with a loud clang.

"Ah," said Mr. Shobbington when he opened the door to let Heron in. "Punctual. Very nice."

It wasn't an office at all. It was a richly furnished flat, with thick carpets, and oil paintings on the walls. Each frame had its own little overhead light.

"This way, Mr. Heron," said Mr. Shobbington. He was a tall, spare man with a cadaverous face, dressed in a clerical black suit. He wore a stiff collar and a discreet gray silk tie.

He led Heron into what looked like a sitting room, with two armchairs opposite each other in front of a fireplace, above which hung a painting of an air battle. A dog fight, Heron noted, showing a Spitfire, guns blazing, tackling two German bombers.

Heron had the impression that nobody lived in the flat. It was well dusted, perfectly looked after, but it had the slightly stale smell of an unoccupied place. Mr. Shobbington's black overcoat and a briefcase were on a chair, together with his homburg hat. He too seemed to be a guest.

"Nice place," said Heron. Everything was costly here: the slim twenty-four-inch television set in the corner, the crystal ornaments on the sideboard, the heavy damask drapes.

"Please," said Mr. Shobbington, indicating one of the armchairs. Heron sank into it, and Mr. Shobbington eased his long, thin frame into the one opposite.

He cleared his throat. "Thank you for coming, Mr. Heron." He had a prominent Adam's apple, but the stiff collar was a little too large for him. "I hope this hasn't inconvenienced you."

"Don't worry about that," said Heron.

Mr. Shobbington nodded approvingly.

"I represent the Caversham Foundation," he announced, and waited expectantly.

"Oh, yes?" Heron had never heard of it. "I don't think I know it."

Mr. Shobbington's thin lips smiled dryly.

"That's the problem, Mr. Heron. Nobody knows it. Nobody has heard of it. That's why we need you." He paused. "We want you to look after our public relations."

"Me?" Heron looked at him in disbelief.

"You are a professional. You have your own public-relations firm." Heron thought of the ridiculous sign that said Heron Associates, and swallowed. "We think you're the right man for us."

"Why?" asked Heron coldly.

"You've been well recommended. Commander Shayler said you are just the person we want."

Shayler! Doing ten years for accepting bribes while at the Yard. Shayler, his best contact and the cause of his downfall. Shayler, the man who, a judge said, had brought disgrace to the Metropolitan Police.

"But Shayler—" began Heron.

"He is no longer incarcerated. Didn't you know?" Mr. Shobbington, in turn, seemed surprised.

Heron was trying to do some quick calculating. Shayler had been inside now, let's see, eighteen months. If he got full remission, he'd have to do at least seven years. Eighteen months? No way would they parole a ten-year man after only eighteen months.

"You sure?" said Heron. "You sure he's out?"

"I dare say nobody wants to advertise the fact, least of all the authorities," said Mr. Shobbington. "They wouldn't want to give the impression that there's any, shall we say, preferential treatment. Not, of course, that there is," he added hastily. He took out a little silver box from his waistcoat and sniffed a pinch of the brown powder. He held out the box to Heron. "You partake?"

"No," said Heron. "Where is Shayler now?"

"In the bosom of his family, I dare say. Recovering from his dreadful ordeal. A man like him in a place like *that*." Mr. Shobbington gave a slight shudder. "Anyway, he's put your name up to us, and here you are."

He got up and went to a little table on which there was an array of cut-crystal decanters and some glasses on a silver tray.

"Sherry? Sweet? Medium? Dry?" he offered.

"Any Scotch?" asked Heron.

"Of course," said Mr. Shobbington. He filled a measure. "As it is, I hope?"

"Water, please," requested Heron, and Mr. Shobbington, momentarily disapproving, complied. He poured himself a sherry and went back to the armchair.

Heron took a sip. It was good, old whiskey, expensive, like the flat.

"Tell me about the Caversham Foundation," he said. "What is it?"

"It's a very worthwhile body." Mr. Shobbington actually showed some enthusiasm. "It promotes historical research. It helps historians with grants and bursaries. Modern history, you understand."

"You don't need somebody like me," said Heron. "You want an academic type. History, research, that's not my scene, Mr. Shobbington. I've never been to a university. The only exam I passed was in blackjack and roulette."

"My dear sir, you are so wrong," insisted Mr. Shobbington. "You're exactly what we're looking for. We need a hard-hitting professional journalist, a PR expert, a man who knows his stuff. Like you."

He reached over for his briefcase.

"We'd like to offer you a year's contract, Mr. Heron," he said simply, the briefcase on his lap. "We suggest a salary of twelve thousand pounds." Heron sat rock-still. "Plus expenses, say five thousand a year, tax-free."

Heron's hand, holding the whiskey glass, registered his surprise. "That's a lot of money," he said, his voice a little hoarse.

"We are quite a rich institution," murmured Mr. Shobbington.

The telephone rang. He shot up and walked rapidly over to a little inlaid side table on which the ivory-colored phone stood.

"Shobbington," he said. He listened. "Yes, sir." His eyes turned toward Heron. "Yes, he is. Of course. Very good, sir."

Funny, thought Heron. Someone, somewhere, always seems to know where I am.

Shobbington hung up and smiled at Heron. "That was the chairman. Would you be free tomorrow afternoon at five? He'd like to meet you." He picked up his briefcase, which had fallen to the floor in his hurry to answer the phone.

"It might be an idea if you told me who the chairman is," said Heron.

Mr. Shobbington looked positively abashed.

"I *am* so sorry, how remiss of me. It's Wing Commander Defoe. The VC, you know."

"Oh, yes," said Heron, like a man who doesn't want to show his ignorance.

"He won the Victoria Cross in the Battle of

Britain." He smiled slightly bitterly. "You're too young to remember, probably. He shot down five German planes in one day."

Heron was impressed. "In one day!"

"You'll find he's a very modest man. He shot down twenty-two in all, but he doesn't like to talk about it. He's the chairman of the foundation, as I told you. I"—and Mr. Shobbington looked suitably deprecatory —"am the treasurer, and there's a small committee. You'll find it very convivial."

"Aren't we rushing things a bit?" asked Heron. "I'm not so sure I'm taking the job."

"You'd be a fool not to, Mr. Heron," said Mr. Shobbington, but his tone was so mild no one would've taken offense. "I'm sure you'll see the sense of that when you think about it."

He picked up his overcoat and the homburg. "You ready?" he inquired politely.

Heron got to his feet as Mr. Shobbington glanced carefully around the room, like someone who wanted to ensure he had left everything as he found it.

"I'll come downstairs with you," he said finally.

He double-locked the front door of the apartment, and then they descended in the crotchety elevator. During the agonizing, drawn-out ride to the ground floor, Mr. Shobbington said nothing. But between the second and first floors he gave Heron a little smile. An encouraging, friendly, avuncular smile.

Downstairs, in the hall, Mr. Shobbington, homburg on head, stopped.

"Very nice meeting you, Mr. Heron," he said, holding out his hand. "You won't forget, will you? About five tomorrow. Number three Knightsbridge Square. The wing commander is looking forward to it."

Heron took his hand. It was clammy.

"Good-bye," said Heron.

Mr. Shobbington smiled and held the door for him.

Interesting, thought Heron, watching him walk toward Berkeley Square. The Goering Testament hadn't been mentioned once.

45

Heron stepped off the train at Pangbourne and saw Shayler standing by the ticket barrier.

Shayler looked well preserved. A little thinner, perhaps, and some of the hairs on his temples that had been slightly gray were now whitish. But only a few. He looked prosperous, decidedly prosperous.

"Harry," said Shayler, clapping him on the back. For a moment he stood looking straight into Heron's eyes. "Harry, it's good to see you."

"You look great, Bill," said Heron, and immediately thought it was a tactless remark, considering where Shayler had been.

"This way," said Shayler. He led Heron down the slope from the station. "I imagine you could do with a drink."

They went to the White Swan, by the weir, and found two chairs on the pub's veranda, facing the Thames.

"Cheers," said Shayler, raising his glass of beer.

Heron half downed his Scotch.

"What a surprise," said Shayler. "You came down quick. One minute I put the phone down, next minute you're here."

"I had a much bigger surprise," said Heron quietly. "I didn't even know you were out. Why didn't you get in touch?"

"I've got to get used to things again," said Shayler slowly. "Adjusting, I think it's called." Again he looked hard at Heron. "How's it been with you?"

"So-so."

"Back on the beat?"

Heron shook his head.

"I'm sorry," said Shayler.

"Bill," said Heron. "Mind if I ask you something sort of embarrassing?"

Shayler waited.

"How come they've let you out so soon?"

Shayler put the beer down on the table in front of them and lit a cigar. A thick cigar.

"Ask the Home Office."

"I'm asking you."

"No mystery, really," said Shayler. "Only I'm not supposed to talk about it. I made myself useful. Did a bit of detecting. Tipped 'em off about a would-be mutiny. A group of cons were ready to seize two wings of Wormwood Scrubs. Take warders hostages, all that business. They had a smuggled gun, razor blades. It would have been nasty, bloody. But it didn't happen. So the powers that be showed their gratitude." He blew out the cigar smoke. "Also, it wouldn't have been easy to look after me inside. Not once I had shopped the others. They were glad to be rid of me."

"Lucky for you."

"Lucky nothing," rasped Shayler savagely. "Don't talk bloody garbage, Harry. Do you know what it's like for a copper who goes inside? A copper who's put many of them there? On my first day somebody emptied a pot of urine over my head—and that was only for a giggle. They got serious later on."

"You had a rough deal," said Heron. "Sometimes I think if you hadn't pleaded guilty, they couldn't have proved anything. They might have kicked you out, but you'd never have been charged."

"Forget it," said Shayler curtly. "It's over and done with."

"I never believed you'd been taking those kick-backs," said Heron. He paused. "Had you?"

"I told you, forget it," snapped Shayler.

Heron went into the bar and got them another round. When he returned, Shayler was just coming back to the table.

"I phoned Dot," he said. "Told her I'd be bringing you around for lunch."

The last time Heron had seen Dot, she was sobbing in the corridor outside court No. 1 at the Old Bailey after Shayler had been led down the steps to start his sentence.

"How is she?" he asked awkwardly.

"Couldn't be better," said Shayler.

"You . . . still have the house?" inquired Heron.

Shayler nodded, quaffing his beer.

Somehow Heron was surprised. The Shaylers had a splendid four-bedroom house at Tilehurst, a few miles from Pangbourne, with a large garden, a big garage, even a swimming pool. The prosecution had made much of that at the trial. And Heron had been convinced it would be one of the first things Shayler would lose, together with his pensions, his friends, his life-style.

"You remember Hood?" asked Heron.

Shayler smiled grimly. "Who could forget him?"

"He's riding high. Detective chief inspector. Full of glory."

"Of course," said Shayler. He looked at his watch. "I think we'd better take off. Drink up, Harry."

Shayler's car was a brand-new shiny Citroen station wagon, full of automatic gadgets. Not bad for a man just out of jail, whose career lay in ruins, thought Heron.

"I felt very sorry for you when it all happened," said Shayler unexpectedly as they drove along the Thames-side road. "Talk about guilt being tarred by the same brush!"

"Well, I suppose you can't blame them," mused

Heron. "You *were* my best contact inside the Yard. I did get the really big scoops from you, exclusive. Of course, they thought I was greasing your palm." He smiled crookedly. "Maybe I was, in a way. Building you up. Boosting your image. That's how I paid you back for gleaning tips."

"Nobody seemed to mind using your stories," said Shayler.

"Not while you were king. I was the star crime man because I had the in, a direct line to the top man in the squad, and they didn't care how I had it. But once the king was dead . . ."

"Here we are," Shayler broke in, and swung the car into the drive. Its tires crunched on the gravel as it drew up outside the front door.

Dot, an apron over her flowered dress, came out from the kitchen to greet Heron.

"How nice to see you again," she gushed. "Make yourself at home, Harry. Food won't be a minute."

It was bizarre, thought Heron. Throughout the meal she talked as if he had been there only last week. Shayler's suspension, his trial, the last eighteen months inside . . . none of it had ever happened.

Afterward they sat around balancing little cups of coffee and making small talk. In the hall, a grandfather clock struck.

"Oh, dear," said Dot, "will you forgive me? I must wash up. I've got a WI meeting I mustn't miss, and I can't leave dirty dishes." She beamed at Heron. "So nice to see you, Harry."

The two men sat silent for a while. Then Shayler said, "I'll show you the garden."

They strolled around the lawn, and suddenly Shayler came out with it.

"What do you want, Harry?" he asked quietly.

"Want?" repeated Heron.

"You don't suddenly ring me out of the blue and dash down an hour later to discuss the injustice of my case. What is it?"

"What's the Caversham Foundation, Bill?" asked Heron.

Shayler stopped by a rose tree and frowned.

"Don't think I've heard of it," he murmured.

"You know Wing Commander Defoe?"

Shayler's face broke into a smile. "The VC? Of course I do."

"How come?"

"I've known John Defoe since the RAF. Great bloke. Practically won the Battle of Britain single-handed. At least that's what we thought."

"I didn't know you were in the RAF," said Heron.

"You don't know everything, Harry," said Shayler. "Sure I was in the RAF. Special Investigation Branch. That's how I went into the police, straight from the SIB. What about Defoe? Why do you ask?"

"This Caversham Foundation has offered me a job. As public-relations officer. Your old pal is the chairman, and they said you'd recommended me. Why?"

"Oh, I met John in London recently, and he said something about needing some publicity work done or something, so I suggested you." Shayler looked at Heron shrewdly. "I thought you could probably do with the work. Has he got in touch with you?"

"Yes."

"Well, he's a good bloke. I don't know what he wants, but you can rely on him." He paused. "Caversham, did you say?"

"That's right."

Shayler scratched his chin. "Only Caversham I know isn't far from here. That's where the BBC does radio monitoring. For the Foreign Office and the intelligence bods. You know, ears on the world . . . Shouldn't think it's got anything to do with your foundation."

"Shouldn't think so," said Heron.

They walked back to the house.

"Are you going to take the job?" inquired Shayler.

"We'll see." Mentally, he was starting to put a few

pieces in a jigsaw. But many were missing. "I think I'd better get back to town."

Shayler didn't attempt to dissuade him.

"I'll drive you to Reading," he said. "You can get a fast London train there in half an hour."

As Heron got out of the car in front of the Reading station, Shayler asked, "You still at Ashfield Gardens?"

Heron nodded.

"Well, maybe I'll give you a ring sometime when I come to London. Not that I do very often. The place stinks these days. Too . . . khaki." His lip curled.

"You can try," said Heron. "Unless they suddenly wake up."

"What do you mean?"

"I haven't paid my bill for months, but at the moment it still works, cross my fingers."

"Really?" said Shayler. "Ah, well, maybe it's better not to know you."

"I don't follow," said Heron.

"Oh, come on, Harry. You must be under surveillance. They never cut off the phone of anyone who is under security surveillance. They like to know who he chats with."

He slammed the door and accelerated, so that Heron couldn't even say good-bye.

46

Lotte lay naked beside him, and he leaned over and kissed the place between her breasts. Slowly he moved upward, until his lips met her mouth, and they kissed, long, sensually, their tongues meeting. Lotte's arms embraced him and pressed him to her.

They had already made love once, exploring each other's bodies with their hands, their tongues, their mouths, but now, once again, desire surged through both of them, and they let it have its way.

How long they lay there afterward in the dark, Heron never knew or cared. He felt relaxed and at peace. Lotte's warm body snuggled up to him, and they were silent, contented.

In the darkness, Lotte traced an invisible pattern on his chest.

"You're a hairy brute," she whispered. "Has anybody ever told you that?"

"Yes."

"Who was she?"

"I forget."

"Why are you such a liar, Harry?" she asked, but there was amusement in her voice.

He kissed her, hard, and she responded, their bodies entwined. Then, gently, Lotte released herself and lay staring up at the ceiling. After a while she reached for her handbag, which lay on the floor by the side of the bed. She felt for her lighter and a cigarette. The flame vaguely illuminated Heron beside her.

"Don't," he protested sleepily.

"Why not?"

"It gets in the way . . ." His right hand caressed one of her breasts.

"I can always put it out," she said.

"That's very coldblooded," sighed Heron. "Ready, steady, put out cigarette, go . . ."

She laughed, and the tip of her cigarette glowed.

"You know something?" said Heron. "I thought you'd gone off me."

"Why?" she asked softly.

He had his eyes closed. "Oh, the other night, in the car. When I asked about your brother. You clammed up suddenly. Couldn't get rid of me fast enough."

"Don't be silly," she said gently. "I was in a hurry, that's all."

Heron grunted.

She bent over him and kissed the tip of his nose. "I wouldn't be here now, would I?"

He stretched his legs. "I suppose not."

"Sometimes," said Lotte, "you really are an idiot."

"You talk too much," said Heron.

They lay still, both awake, both with their thoughts. They could hear an airliner passing over the house, thousands of feet up but its noise very close. Heron glanced at the phosphorous digits of the alarm clock. It was just after 6:00 A.M.

"I got a funny question, Harry," said Lotte suddenly.

"Hmm?"

"You won't mind, will you?"

"Well, I won't know till you ask me, will I?"

For a while she said nothing.

"Well?" said Heron.

"Maybe I shouldn't . . ." she said, so low it might've been to herself.

"What's the funny question?" insisted Heron.

"Harry," she said, "you're not . . . you're not a . . . spook, are you?"

"A what?"

"A spook. You know, an . . . an agent. You're not in intelligence, are you? Something to do with security?"

He burst out laughing. "Me? You're nuts." Then he was serious. "What on earth makes you ask a damn stupid thing like that?"

"Oh, I don't know . . ." she said vaguely.

He sat up.

"Oh, yes you do," he said a little harshly. "You don't ask people if they're a spy just like that. You must have a reason."

"I didn't say you were a spy," she protested. "I asked if you worked for security."

"Which would you like? CIA? KGB? Come on, take your pick." His tone was not amused. "Or just plain old DI Five?"

"Forget it."

"Lotte, I want to know what brought this about."
She also sat up now. "I said forget it."

He grabbed her naked shoulders and shook her. She tried to twist away, but he held her too firmly.

"Harry," she cried, "you're hurting me!"

"Why?" he yelled.

"Oh, for God's sake, I only asked a question!" She freed herself from his grasp and swung her legs out of the bed. "What's the matter with you?"

She stood on the carpet facing him, naked, quite unashamed, her face flushed.

"I'm sorry," said Heron. "You don't know what a fool question that is with what I've been through. Me in security! It's a bad joke."

"Well, that's all right, then, isn't it?" said Lotte coldly, slipping on a pair of briefs.

"Christ, you know all about me," declared Heron. "You know everything."

"Do I?" she asked. She was putting on her bra, but she stopped. "Do I really, Harry?"

He stood in front of her, arms akimbo.

"What the hell's biting you?" he demanded.

"Would you like a cup of coffee before I go?"

She dressed herself with speed and ran a comb through her hair.

"Well?" she repeated. "Would you?"

"For God's sake, it's only just after six. What's the bloody hurry?" snarled Heron. "We've got lots of time."

"No," said Lotte. "I want to get to the office really early. I've got some unfinished business."

But, at the door, she suddenly kissed him.

"It was nice, Harry," she said quietly, and kissed him again. Then she was gone.

47

Two hours later the deer found the man near a clump
of trees in Richmond Park. They sniffed at him, but
he was of no interest and they moved off.

Shortly afterward, one of the park police spotted him
from a passing Land Rover and got out to have a
closer look.

The man was dead. Sticking out of his neck was a
steel bolt. His right hand was a bloody mess. It looked
as if someone had torn out the fingernails, and judging
by the horrific grimace on the man's face, it had happened while he was still alive.

Death must have come as a great relief.

The police officer ran back to the Land Rover and
radioed for assistance.

Luckily, at that time of morning there were not
many people in Richmond Park, and the police were
able to work without crowds gathering. They closed
off the Robin Hood Gate, and the murder squad took
over.

There was some difficulty at first in establishing the
man's identity. He had, for example, several checkbooks
on him, but they were in different names.

His shoes were Italian, hand-sewn and expensive. A
gold bangle on his right wrist had no initials. He
had a Swedish passport on him in the name of Carl
Jensen, a French identity card made out to a Yugo-
slav national, Boris Zadlev, and an unpaid bill from the
Cumberland Hotel.

No doubt the man had been a dapper dresser,

thought the detectives. His shirt was silk, he had a neat bow tie, and his elegant trousers had razor-sharp creases.

Within an hour, however, Special Branch said the man was definitely Tibor Madek, a Hungarian. He had apparently been shot by a crossbow but had obviously been tortured beforehand.

Clearly somebody had been very anxious to make him talk.

He also had Harry Heron's phone number in his calf-skin address book.

48

"Why me?" asked Heron in the police car on the way to the mortuary. They had fetched him, so they said, to identify the body.

"He hasn't got any relations in this country," replied Hood. "You were his friend, weren't you?"

"Not friend, exactly," said Heron.

Hood had cut himself shaving and a tiny scrap of cotton wool was still stuck near his lip. Heron resisted an insane urge to pull it off.

"You know, you've become very dangerous company, Harry," Hood said amiably. He was in a good mood and quite pleasant to Heron. "I wonder you got any chums left. Look at 'em. One by one, they get knocked off."

"I don't think it's me anybody's interested in."

"Come off it," said Hood.

They pulled Madek out of the refrigerated cabinet, and Heron stood silent, gazing on the little Hungarian's face for the last time.

"I must ask you formally," interrupted Hood, strangely gentle. "Do you identify this body as being that of Tibor Madek?"

"Of course," said Heron a little regretfully. True, Madek had never meant anything to him personally. He knew him only for what he was, a parasite, a grafter, a confidence trickster who'd cheat the Pope. All to earn a quick buck so that he could buy yet another pair of expensive shoes. And yet . . . poor schmuck, he thought, where's it all got him?

"Who did this?" he asked Hood out in the corridor.

"The same people who killed your other pal, Fennerman," said Hood. "You don't need to be a genius to work that out."

"And Kelly?"

Hood shrugged. "Maybe." He pushed open a door. "I'd like you to take a look at these. Just in case they mean something."

They were Madek's things, taken from his pockets and neatly laid out on a table. There were four checkbooks, a membership card of the Playboy Club, two ten-dollar bills, an alien's registration certificate issued by the Home Office, a one-pound chip from the Victoria Sporting Club, a wallet containing twenty-two pound notes, the address book, and about fourteen visiting cards Madek had obviously collected from various people. There was also a photograph of Ursula Fennerman in a bikini. She was smiling at the camera. She had a magnificent body and her pose displayed it proudly.

"Yes," said Hood. "Not bad. Holiday snap, wouldn't you say?"

"Could be."

Hood held up a bunch of keys.

"We've been trying to check these out," he said. "A couple belong to his flat, of course. But the rest are anybody's guess. Two Banhams, two Chubbs, four Yales—he certainly could open a lot of doors. And there's this one . . ."

It was a long, thin key.

"Skeleton?" said Heron.

"Right. Very naughty, very illegal. He could turn quite a few locks with this one. What do you think, Harry?"

"Why ask me? Anyway, some of those keys have numbers. You can trace them all from the firms . . ."

"Of course," said Hood mildly. "I just thought it would save time if you could help."

"Sorry," said Heron. "What are you getting at, anyway? That he was some kind of burglar?"

He thought of Madek lying up the corridor in his frozen chamber, naked, the raw right hand, the bloody wound in his neck, and he felt defensive about him.

"Madek wasn't that sort of man," said Heron.

"Well, he wasn't an angel, Harry. He dropped phony checks like confetti. Must have had the devil's own luck to get away with it."

They left the room, and as they pushed through the swinging doors Hood asked, "Why do you think he got killed?"

Heron looked him straight in the eye.

"I think you know," he said quietly.

49

The three men looked like business executives as they sat lunching at a corner table in the hotel in Queen's Gate, South Kensington, and in a way, they were. No one was the host, and it was an understood thing that they all went Dutch. Two had arrived in taxis because parking was awkward in Queen's Gate, even for cars with diplomatic plates, and their embassies had given strict orders that there were to be no more traffic offenses.

It was an off-the-record meeting, but that fooled none of them; indeed, each would transmit a full précis to his control.

"Well, gentlemen," said Seltzer, "I think it's a mess."

"My people are not, of course, involved," announced Shilenko. "But I agree. It is unfortunate."

Major Geist put down his coffee cup. "Bonn isn't exactly overjoyed," he said.

"Of course, it was very foolish of any of us to become mixed up with an emigré like this man Madek. He was playing us all against each other," complained Shilenko.

"Madek was only one of the irons in the fire," Seltzer began, then stopped. The other two were staring at him. He cleared his throat. "I mean, he's not the end of the road."

"Correct," said Geist. "He is incidental."

The manager came over diffidently and coughed politely.

"Excuse me," he said. "Which of you gentlemen is Mr. Shilenko?"

"Why?" asked Shilenko somewhat coldly.

"I'm awfully sorry, sir," said the manager unhappily, "but is that your car outside? In front of the hotel?"

"Yes," said Shilenko.

"You'll have to move it, I'm afraid, sir." The manager cringed. "It's . . . it's causing an obstruction."

"I'm a diplomat," declared Shilenko. "I have immunity."

"The traffic warden . . ."

Shilenko tightened his lips. "I will speak to this traffic warden. All this bureaucratic red tape. I will not be long."

"Well," said Seltzer, after he had gone, "that's why I always use a cab."

"Between you and me, you don't think Madek had the thing when he was killed, do you?" asked Geist.

Seltzer produced a cigar case, offered one to the German, took one himself. They were King Edwards. Unlike his station chief, Seltzer was patriotic in his smoking.

"No way," he said. "It's still floating around, up for grabs."

"I hope so," murmured Geist.

Shilenko came back.

"There is no problem," he reported triumphantly. "I warned them against causing a provocation, informed them who I was, and that was that."

He poured himself a fresh cup of coffee.

"I have been thinking, my friends," he announced. "It is time, I feel, to put all our cards on the table."

"Sure," said Seltzer.

Geist nodded. "Absolutely."

"Our three countries share the same interest in this matter, and we should therefore cooperate," Shilenko went on. It was a prepared speech, which he had cleared with Moscow. "None of us wishes this so-called Goering Testament to fall into irresponsible hands. The Soviet Union is anxious to have this relic of Nazi mythology destroyed once and for all. The United States is embarrassed."

Seltzer frowned.

"I mean, dear friend, that the document was your responsibility. The fact that it has surfaced after all these years is due to lack of security on your part."

"Wait a moment . . ." Seltzer began, but Shilenko raised a hand.

'No, this is not recrimination. Just a statement of fact. Now, of course, like us, you are anxious to get hold of it. You too do not want it in circulation."

"That's true," said Seltzer.

"As for the Federal Republic, it has enough trouble

with resurgent fascism in its midst not to need the unveiling of such a document," continued Shilenko smoothly.

"There is no point in trying to make propaganda at this table, Aleksei," said Geist.

"So," Shilenko went on, ignoring him, "our countries have a common objective, and we must use the combined resources of our various agencies to achieve it."

He leaned back and beamed.

"Well," said Seltzer, "how do you suggest we work that?"

"We must learn from our mistakes. This man Madek, for example. He was using us. None of us knew what he was saying to the other. He was out to cheat one of us at the expense of the other. We should have dealt with him as one."

"The guy's dead, there's no point in talking about it now," muttered Seltzer.

Major Geist stubbed out his King Edward. It was not to his taste.

"You have some new leads, Aleksei?" he asked invitingly.

"There is a man," said Shilenko. "A very dubious character. He worked in Fennerman's shop. This man interests me. His name is Harry Heron. A funny name. Have you come across him?"

"Never heard of him," said Geist firmly. When he lied, he looked extremely honest.

"You, my friend?" Shilenko asked Seltzer.

"Aleksei, you know my people are always the last to know anything," Seltzer said deprecatingly.

Shilenko smiled. "That is not our impression. Anyway, this man Heron. I think we should cooperate about him."

"What about the British?" said Seltzer.

"The British, as we all know, move in their own peculiar way." Shilenko finished his coffee. "Is it agreed, then?"

"Not a bad idea," said Seltzer. He made a mental note that the Second Directorate in Moscow must be getting uptight about the Goering Testament.

"A very constructive proposal," said Geist. "His name is Heron, did you say?"

Shilenko was pleased when he finally left the hotel. It was a good way of telling them that he wasn't anybody's fool, that he knew about Madek and his double-dealing. And about the man called Heron.

He stopped smiling when he saw his car. That bitch of a traffic warden had stuck a ticket on it after all, diplomatic immunity or not.

It was typical of the British, said Shilenko to himself. You couldn't trust them.

50

Bowler read from his notebook:

"They arrived at the hotel individually between twelve-thirty and twelve-forty-one. They had booked a table in the dining room."

"Go on," said Ross.

"They ordered two soups and one melon as starters, and then—"

"I'm not interested in their menu."

"No, sir." Bowler looked at the book again. "While they were having coffee, the manager told the Russian that his car was illegally parked. Shilenko came out and had an argument with the traffic warden."

"He would," sniffed Ross.

"They broke up eventually about two-thirty. Seltzer returned to Grosvenor Square, Major Geist to the

German embassy, and Shilenko did some shopping at Fortnum and Mason's before going back to Kensington Palace Gardens."

"Hmm." Ross sighed. "I don't suppose you got a clue what they were talking about?"

"I had a good table," said Bowler happily. "Couldn't hear most of it, of course, but I lip-read a bit. Major Geist had his back to me, so I didn't catch too much of what he said, but they were talking about the Goering Testament."

"Ah," said Ross, and he seemed pleased.

"And about Mr. Heron."

"Really? Well, well."

"You want a report for the file, sir?"

"No," said Ross. "Don't think so."

"Oh, one thing, sir."

"Yes?"

"Well," said Bowler, looking like a naughty schoolboy who had broken the rules and was not owning up, "I had somebody on tap. From the boffins. Took a chance and fitted a bug to Shilenko's car while he was in the hotel."

"Bowler!" But Ross did not seem disconcerted.

"I know, sir," said Bowler. "It won't be much use. Their transport people are so bloody thorough, they'll find it. But I thought it was worth a try."

"Well, I don't know about it, do I?" said Ross. "Nobody knows about it officially, do they?"

"Of course not, sir."

"The boffin? It wasn't Barbara, was it?"

"Yes, sir," said Bowler.

"Dressed as a traffic warden?" asked Ross incredulously.

"She looked very smart, sir."

"That will be all," said Ross severely.

So, he thought, Heron had been a subject of discussion. Idly, he wondered how much Heron's life insurance was worth and who stood to benefit.

51

The woman who opened the front door of No. 3 Knightsbridge Square was statuesque and elegant. Her ash-blonde hair was beautifully coiffured, and she wore a plain gray dress that was all the more expensive-looking for its simplicity.

"Do come in," she said, without asking Heron's name. She had a high-priced perfume on, and Heron caught a whiff. He liked it.

She led the way, and as he followed her, Heron thought she was probably in her forties but twenty years younger from the back.

The place reminded him of the flat in Mayfair. The same kind of wealth, the same taste in furnishings. Only this was lived in.

She opened a door, and Heron found himself in a library, the walls lined with books from ceiling to floor.

The woman smiled at Heron.

"I'll leave you to it," she said. Her voice was husky, intriguing.

A man stood by one of the shelves, and as Heron entered, he put a book back on it. He was handsome, despite his thinning hair, distinguished-looking, and he had very clear, unwavering blue eyes.

"Thank you, Vanessa," he said, and the woman softly closed the door. He came forward with a friendly smile. "I'm John Defoe. Make yourself at home, please."

"Thank you," Heron started to say, and then the words strangled in his throat.

The man had no hands. From each sleeve protruded a kind of combined steel hook and pincer.

Defoe saw his look. "I hope these don't worry you," he said. "I'm afraid I'm stuck with them. Sometimes I put on gloves, but they don't fool anyone."

"Of course not," Heron said, and felt stupid.

"I've got used to the shock they have on people when they see them for the first time." Defoe sat down on a couch and indicated that Heron should join him. "Actually, I'm very lucky. I can do much more with these than you can with your hands, Mr. Heron. These have a thousand uses, believe me. The German who blew them off really did me a good turn."

There was not a trace of self-pity. If anything, he seemed amused by the effect his claws had had on Heron.

"I hear you drink Scotch," he said. "Can I fix you something?"

"Not right now, thank you."

"Cigarette?"

Heron shook his head. He watched, fascinated, as Defoe picked a cigarette out of a silver box with one pincer, held a match in the other, struck a flame from an ashtray holder, and lit the cigarette. His movements were positive, sure, unhesitating.

"Well, Mr. Heron?" said Defoe. "Have you made up your mind?"

"I have a question. What exactly is the Caversham Foundation?"

Defoe looked surprised. "Didn't Shobbington tell you?"

"I'd like to hear it from you."

"Fair enough. Our object is rehabilitation."

"What exactly does that mean?"

"Good." Defoe nodded. "You're precise. Well, shall I put it this way? A lot of history people are taught is only fiction. The perpetuation of false images. Our object is to enable students, historians, teachers, opinion makers, to seek the truth."

"How?"

"By digging out the unadulterated facts before they're doctored for popular consumption. By being objective and correcting the record."

Heron said, "I think I'd rather like that Scotch now, if I may."

"But of course." Defoe poured the drink with the same skill, his claws making ordinary hands seem almost superfluous. "Soda?" The syphon presented no problems, either. "Here you are.

"You see, it's the age of double standards. Your terrorist is my freedom fighter. My patriot is your traitor." Defoe sat down again. "Our militant is their troublemaker. One man's peaceful demonstrators are another man's mob. But they can't all be right."

Heron tasted his drink. It was the same lovely ancient whiskey he had had in the Mayfair flat.

"But who's to judge?" he asked.

"That's where we can help, Heron. By researching, exploring. Helping scholars. Giving grants for studies. Organizing weekend schools. Subsidizing the work of historians." Each point was emphasized by a wave of a claw. "We shall probably rehabilitate some great men and relegate quite a few false heroes to where they belong."

His blue eyes scrutinized Heron.

"You interested?"

"These great men you want to—to rehabilitate. Who are they? Former enemies? Men like, well, men like Goering?"

Heron said it as if the name had been only a sudden afterthought.

"You're a very intelligent chap, Heron," exclaimed Defoe. "How refreshing. Yes, indeed. Take Goering. What's his popular image? A fat drug addict who wore ridiculous uniforms with too many medals and ran around playing tennis in a woman's hairnet. But that isn't the truth, is it?"

Heron kept silent.

"The truth, my dear fellow, is that Goering was a very brave and honorable man. A patriot, an air ace who won his country's highest gallantry decoration, who dedicated himself to building up Europe's finest air force from nothing, who revolutionized war in the air, and who, when they tried to hang him like a criminal, took the honorable way out. And who was about to save Europe, if they had let him."

He looked into Heron's eyes. "A great man," he repeated.

Heron raised his eyebrows.

"It was one of his blokes who did *that* to you," he said, glancing at the steel pincers.

Defoe leaned forward. "Which is why I have a right to speak like this." Then his blue eyes twinkled. "Funny you should just happen to mention Goering."

"Yes, isn't it?" said Heron.

Defoe got up and started pacing about in front of the shelves.

"Shobbington will have told you we need an image builder, a man who will make sure that we don't disappear down a hole."

"You want publicity?"

"Only of the right kind," said Defoe. "Tell me, is the money all right?"

"Very generous."

"Good. You can start in a week's time. I'll have an office for you by then."

Heron slowly stood up. "You know Commander Shayler?"

"Ex-commander," corrected Defoe. "Yes. I've met him. I know a lot of people."

"He suggested me?"

"Heron, don't read mysteries into things," said Defoe lightly. "You were, if I may say so, a big name in Fleet Street at one time. What better man to handle our business?" He peered at Heron. "It's all settled then? Excellent. You'll get a note confirming the terms."

"All right," said Heron.

Defoe went over to a desk in the corner and opened a drawer. A claw came out with an envelope and passed it to Heron.

"I nearly forgot that." He smiled, and Heron was quite convinced that he was one man who never forgot anything. "I'll see you out."

Outside, in the square whose resident parking bays were filled with Rolls-Royces, Bentleys, and Jaguars, Heron ripped open the envelope.

Inside was one thousand pounds in crisp twenty-pound notes. A slip of paper said, "On account of expenses."

The claws had a very precise, legible script.

52

In the East End parking lot, the leader stood on a lorry, surrounded by a forest of Union Jacks. His mobile platform was ringed by a line of tough, unsmiling men, most standing with their arms folded. Many wore leather jackets, and they continually watched the audience in front of them.

It was a small crowd, really, but in the street police cordons were drawn up, and the angry howls of a protesting mob could be heard in the parking lot.

The leader, puffy-faced, with a waxen complexion and cold eyes, was a good speaker, and his followers drank up his words like thirsty men.

"Look what we've got in this country today," he cried. "We've got crime on the increase. Immorality on the increase. Illegitimacy. Sodomy. Abortion. Obscenity everywhere. Old folk are afraid to go out at night for fear of muggers. Young couples can't afford a home. Small-business men are going bankrupt. And two million blacks live off the poor taxpayer, who's being squeezed of his last drop of blood.

"Well, I promise you one thing. When we win this country, and win we will, there are going to be some mighty changes. Changes in the economy, in our political life, in the arts, in the media, in immigration. Oh, yes, there are going to be a lot of changes. . . ."

He surveyed them as they cheered and stamped their feet. He raised a hand for silence.

"There's going to be a good sweep-out of the alien financiers in the city, and the political priests in the church, the Commie journalists, the mongrel legislators, the whole ragbag of them. We'll ship 'em off to where they belong, and I don't mean the South of France . . ."

They roared with laughter.

"It's time we cared for our own, for the old folk who sit alone, often without fuel, without warmth, many of them dying from the cold and lack of food, while the blacks fornicate with the street women at our expense."

The shouts of the hostile demonstrators outside the parking lot drifted to him.

"And that lot out there," he yelled, "we'll deal with them, too. Let me make this promise. Tear gas and rubber bullets will soon be the order of the day for that lot. When we get in, the police will have the means to deal with them. We will give the police the equipment, the money—above all, the power they need to rid us of those thugs out there. We'll back them to the hilt to do what we all know has to be done . . .

"My friends, the tide runs for us. History is on our side. We march in the shadow of great men. Their spirit will soon lead us to victory!"

He smiled and waved at their applause and jumped

off the lorry with a display of agility that was not accidental. Immediately, he was surrounded by a group of unsmiling bodyguards.

In the crowd stood Charlotte Gordon. She had followed every word he said, and her eyes had never left the leader's face. To get into the parking lot, she had shown the police cordon her press card, but during the leader's speech she did not take a single note.

53

The teleprinter in the Special Branch office at London Airport stuttered its peremptory message to passport control:

URGENT ATTN TO HARRY HERON DOB 18.4.34 BRIT NAT UK PASSPORT 388129 AB RESERVATION HEATHROW LH 063 STUTTGART DEP 0940 ALPHA OMEGA ALPHA.

It was an instruction that put Heron in a special category reserved for rather interesting people. ALPHA OMEGA ALPHA indicated that he was to be kept under closest surveillance but that no unauthorized person was to be made aware of it, that the embarkation channels were not to query his departure, and that under no circumstances was he to be prevented from boarding his plane.

In a way, it gave him complete immunity, even if customs officials suspected that he was carrying something illicit, or if immigration officers thought there was anything fishy about his travel documents. It indicated that certain government departments, for reasons best known to themselves, wished him to have a trouble-free departure, but under closest scrutiny.

Sometimes such an order meant that the person was in some danger, and it was considered wise to let him slip out as quietly, unobtrusively, and rapidly as possible, for his own safety.

But ALPHA OMEGA ALPHA could also indicate that the passenger was somebody whose activities were of great concern to the security authorities, and it was considered vital, in the national interest, not to alarm him in any way or give him a hint that his every move was being watched.

Sometimes the Special Branch men standing at the passport desks, looking over the shoulders of the immigration officials, knew what it was all about. Sometimes they just had to guess. But at all times it ensured that the passenger had invisible VIP treatment of a rather sinister kind.

In Heron's case, the treatment began before he even reached the airport. Even at the West London Air Terminal in Cromwell Road, the security man already hovered near him as he checked in.

And the British Airways bus that drove him the twelve miles to London Airport was discreetly followed by a maroon saloon car whose two occupants had their radio tuned to a somewhat exclusive VHF channel.

Neither vehicle was aware of the crash-helmeted motorcyclist who kept a respectable distance behind them.

54

Ross kept his promise to Major Geist. He called him on the scrambler.

"You owe me a drink," he said somewhat smugly.

"Already?" said Geist. "So quickly?"

"I told you he wouldn't let the grass grow under his feet," said Ross. "He's on his way to Stuttgart now. On the nine-forty flight LH Oh-six-three."

Geist made a note on his pad. "Thank you very much. That is most useful."

"I'm sure your lads would spot him anyway, but it doesn't do any harm to be forewarned, does it?" Ross sounded faintly patronizing.

"Of course not," replied Geist diplomatically.

"Don't forget that drink."

"I will call you," promised Geist.

"You'd better."

It was just a throwaway, thought Geist, but with Ross you never knew. "Thank you again. It is much appreciated."

He hung up and buzzed for Ludwig, who came in carrying some newspapers.

"I thought the herr major might like to see these," he said. He laid them on Geist's desk.

One headline read: NATIONAL FRONT DEMO: 24 HELD. Another said: RIOT ENDS NF RALLY. There were front-page pictures of people fighting, a policeman with his face twisted in agony, two struggling men being bodily carried to a riot van.

"Never mind that now," said Geist. "I want you to

send a flash signal right away: 'Heron on way to Stuttgart now aboard LH Oh-six-three.' My personal cypher."

"To the Bureau?" asked Ludwig. Flash signals were rare.

"Of course."

"What about Karlsruhe and Wiesbaden?"

Geist nodded. "Yes, you'd better let them know, too."

"Right away, sir," said Ludwig. He closed the door softly.

Geist stared at the framed photograph of the major general on the wall. The general was his father, Reinhold Geist, holder of the Knights Cross with diamonds and swords, commander of the panzer division Hesse, victor of the great tank battles of Smolensk and Kiev, killed in action in the Falaise Gap, loyal to the end.

The other photographs of his father—with Field Marshal Keitel, with Rommel, and with Hitler—were never on any wall. Nor was the one taken during the weekend the general spent boar hunting with Reich Marshal Hermann Goering.

Geist sighed. Fate could be ironic.

55

Lufthansa meant boiled sweets to Heron. He liked the girl offering each passenger the basket full of multicolored, cellophane-wrapped candies. It was a little frippery staid British Airways never stooped to.

The passengers were still filing into the plane and the sweets hadn't made their rounds yet as Heron settled back in his seat. He was lucky; he had a window on the starboard side, and the seat next to him was empty.

The plane was full of the clicking of safety belts, hand luggage being shoved into overhead lockers, people squeezing into their places. Heron hadn't slept well. He rested his head and closed his eyes, shutting out the others.

"Why, Harry!" said Lotte. He opened his eyes, and there she stood, smiling down at him, clutching a vanity case and her handbag. "What are you doing here?"

"I could ask you the same thing."

"I tried to call you," she said hurriedly. "I couldn't get a reply."

The tall air hostess was at her side, trying to shepherd her farther up the aisle.

"Your seat is over there, Miss Gordon," she said, looking at Lotte's boarding card: B 3.

"Oh, couldn't I sit here?" said Lotte sweetly. "This is a friend of mine. *Please*." She gave her a dazzling smile.

"Just one moment," said the air hostess severely. She hurried along the aisle to consult another girl with a clipboard.

"You going to Stuttgart?" asked Heron vaguely. A lot of things were going through his mind.

"Unless I'm on the wrong plane," said Lotte, and sat down next to him. The tall air hostess came back and saw she had been preempted.

"It's all right," she said somewhat disapprovingly. "There is no reservation for this seat."

"Thank you," said Lotte, and flashed her another smile.

"Please fasten your seat belt," ordered the hostess, as a final shot.

Lotte looked stunningly attractive. She had her sealskin coat on, the handbag was her best, and the dress was Italian. Something nice had been done to her hair, and she was beautifully made up.

She saw his look.

"I've got my best undies on, too," she said mischievously. "I do it every time I fly. If I have to die, I want to look my best."

"Don't talk like that," said Heron. "It's safer than crossing Piccadilly Circus."

"So they say." She gave a little kittenlike sneeze and dabbed her nose with a tissue.

"*Gesundheit*," said Heron.

She eyed his new suit, the Sulka shirt, the Yves St. Laurent tie.

"You know, you look pretty smart yourself, Harry. Too busy shopping to let me know you are going off somewhere?" She couldn't hide the curiosity in her tone.

"Well, as you say, if I have to die, I want to look my best."

The plane slowly began to taxi, and neither of them said anything.

Then, at last, they were airborne, and the electric-light signal went out, absolving them from having to wear harnesses. They both unclicked.

"What's happening in Stuttgart?" asked Heron.

"Search me," said Lotte. "I think the paper's gone barmy. They want a sexy piece on INTHERM."

"On what?"

She pulled a face. "I know. The International Fair for Oil and Gas Fuels. It's on this week, and idiot-features thinks it'll fascinate our eager readers."

"I suppose, being oil . . ." said Heron weakly.

"And for good measure, they want a bit of culture while I'm over. 'Do a thing on the Stuttgart Ballet. See if the ghost of Cranko still walks.' "

Heron looked bewildered. "You're joking. Not your paper."

She shrugged. "It's their money. Boy, will I lay on the expenses."

The boiled sweets came along.

"*Bitte*," said the air hostess invitingly.

Heron took a dark one, hoping it would be black currant.

"You might meet an Arab oil sheik who wants to make you the treasure of his harem," said Heron, crunching his sweet.

"Fuck off," said Lotte, and she managed to do it charmingly, and rather ladylike. "Would you care, anyway?"

Heron grinned.

High over the Channel, she suddenly asked, "What about you, Harry? How come you're going over?"

Heron signaled to the stewardess as she passed. "Champagne, please."

Lotte arched one of her eyebrows. "Harry, what's the celebration? Have you suddenly struck it rich?"

"Maybe," he said infuriatingly.

"What's up?"

"Let's play TV commercials," said Heron. "Action. The jet setters. You and me. Beautiful girl sits in airliner next to handsome man. They can't drink anything but champagne, can they? Then I will offer you a cigarette with the brand name tastefully displayed, and there'll be a glimpse of my executive-style wristwatch—"

"Why are you going to Germany?" she asked directly, ignoring his act.

He beamed at her. "Believe it or not, I'm treating myself to a holiday. I think I deserve one, don't you? So, Black Forest, here I come."

"I don't believe you," said Lotte. "You don't take holidays."

"Cross my heart, hope to die."

The champagne came, and he raised his glass to her. *"Prosit."*

She drank, her eyes on his over the rim of her glass.

"I've got myself a job, that's all," said Heron. "How about that?"

She looked pleased. "Oh, good. I'm so glad, Harry. Who with?"

"The Caversham Foundation." He saw her puzzlement. "Haven't you heard of it?"

She shook her head. "What is it? Some kind of charity?"

"You could call it educational," he said. "And the pay's better than the *Express* in the old days."

She sipped her champagne. "But what's your job?"

"I don't exactly know." Then he corrected himself. "No, that's not really true. I think I know, but it's a secret I haven't revealed to myself."

"What does that mean?" asked Lotte.

"You do ask an awful lot of questions, love," said Heron. "Let's enjoy the champers."

She put her hand on his. "I care, Harry," she said softly. "I want to know because I care."

"Well, you'll be happy to know I've landed on my feet. Twelve thousand pounds a year and oodles of expenses."

She was impressed. "You haven't got a job like that lying around for me, have you?"

"I'll see what I can do." He smiled.

He watched three tiny dots in the distance, miles away above the clouds, flying in parallel direction. NATO jet fighters, he guessed.

"You should have gone somewhere in the sun," said Lotte. "Why on earth Germany? Who wants to eat sauerkraut on their holiday?"

"What's wrong with Germany?" asked Heron mildly. He poured her more champagne.

"Nothing," she said shortly. She had *Newsweek* on her lap and she started leafing through it, as if the conversation had ended.

"Lotte," said Heron. "This is a lovely coincidence, our flying on the same plane."

"Yes, isn't it," she replied, turning a page of the magazine.

"What better start to a holiday," said Heron.

She smiled, but she wasn't looking at him.

56

It was thirty-one years since Sterling Hodgman had taken off his uniform, but his bearing was still upright and athletic. He would stride through a hotel lobby, leaving no observer in doubt that within the expensive custom-made suit was the frame of a man who had never forgotten his military background.

"Shall I hang up your clothes, sir?" asked the porter when they got up to the suite. He hoped the distinguished-looking American would say yes; after all, it was one of the best suites in the hotel, the man was wealthy—you could tell that from his appearance and the luggage—and the extra service would boost the tip.

"No, that's all right," said Hodgman. "Just put that case on the bed, and the others over there."

He gave the porter a five-dollar bill; he hadn't yet had time to change his money since landing at Heathrow. The porter was gratified, and decided that, for the length of his stay, 812 was going to get the best attention.

"Thank *you*, sir," said the porter, and closed the door gently.

A bowl of flowers stood on the table, awaiting Hodgman's arrival. It was a welcoming token from the management to all occupiers of the expensive suite. Hodgman went over to the window and looked out across Belgravia. He liked London, and he liked this particular view, which was why he usually stayed at this hotel.

The phone rang, and Hodgman picked it up.

It was reception, and when they told him who was downstairs, he immediately said, "Send him up, please."

The tap at the door came quicker than he had expected, and when he opened it and saw the visitor, his face lit up.

"John," he said, "this is a surprise. I didn't expect to see you till later."

Defoe followed him into the room.

"Did you have a good trip?" he asked.

"Couldn't be better," said Hodgman. "Now, let's celebrate. I've got a bottle of bourbon somewhere . . ."

"If you don't mind, Scotch," said Defoe. His blue eyes followed the other man around the room as Hodgman called room service. His steel claws rested unobtrusively on his lap.

"How's Vanessa?" asked Hodgman.

"Looking forward to seeing you. And sends her congratulations. You've had some great reviews," said Defoe. "It sticks in their throat, but they have to admit it's a superb piece of work."

"You're very kind," said Hodgman modestly, but his pleasure was obvious. "Which reminds me . . ."

He went over to the suitcase on the bed, opened it, took out a book, and laid it on the table in front of Defoe. The claws picked it up and opened it. There was a dedication written inside, opposite the picture of Hitler.

Defoe read it and then looked up.

"I shall treasure this," he said simply.

The waiter came with their drinks and a small ice bucket. After he had gone, Defoe asked, "How are sales?"

"Not bad," said Hodgman. "Not bad at all. And it's coming out in paperback."

Defoe nodded. "Good. You won't believe this, but a few years ago there was a real commotion in London because some bookseller displayed a few copies of *Mein Kampf*. But now . . ."

"People are starting to read their history," said

Hodgman. "At long last, they're starting to listen to the other side of the story . . ." He paused and looked at Defoe.

"John" he said, "you've got something up your sleeve, I can tell. You're itching to tell me . . ."

"Well, I'll say this. You couldn't have come at a better time, Hodg." Defoe was enjoying himself. "After all these years—" He broke off, savoring Hodgman's curiosity.

"At long last, I think we've got the Testament."

Hodgman sat rock-still.

"At least we're just about to get our hands on it, I think."

"You're kidding."

Defoe shook his head. "I don't joke about things like this. We've got the man who knows where it is."

"What do you mean, you've got him?"

"On the payroll," said Defoe with relish.

"How on earth . . . ?"

"A lot of work, a lot of digging around, believe me," said Defoe. "And a hell of a lot of opposition. They're all after it. But I think we've got in there first."

"I can't believe it . . ."

"I'll have it in my hands before you leave this country," said Defoe. "Now you know why I wanted you especially to come."

Hodgman narrowed his eyes. "Who's this lead?" he asked.

Defoe shrugged. "A man who couldn't care less. A mercenary, you could say. He sells himself to the highest bidder."

"Does he know what it means?"

"Shouldn't think so," said Defoe. "I imagine it may not make sense to him why people should be so keen to get hold of a couple of handwritten pages."

"Good." He lowered his voice. "My God, John, you realize what this will mean?"

"A milestone toward the rebirth," said Defoe. "The

relighting of the flame. It'll make them sit up, all right."

"Are you sure it's genuine?" Hodgman looked anxious. "You sure it isn't a fake?"

"Give me a little credit," said Defoe. "A British officer stole it at Nuremburg. They couldn't prove he'd taken it when they court-martialed him. He'd been trying to hold it to ransom . . ." His eyes were cold. "Very foolish of him."

Hodgman nodded. He understood. "You know something, it's a funny feeling turning the clock back . . ."

"You're wrong." Defoe smiled. "You're quite wrong. We're turning the clock forward."

For a moment they were silent. Then Hodgman asked, "When will we know we've got it?"

Defoe leaned back in his chair, quite relaxed. "He's on his way there now," he said. "Showing a little bit of initiative. He may even try a canny bit of bargaining with us once he's got it."

"But I thought he . . ." Hodgman began nervously.

"Don't worry," said Defoe. "One doesn't need to bargain with a dead man."

57

"I've had a brilliant idea," said Lotte, her eyes sparkling. The plane was approaching Stuttgart, and a lot of passengers were beginning to tidy themselves up. But Heron was conscious only of her, how attractive she was, how much he wanted her, how he'd like to grab her and kiss her.

"Oh, yes?" was all he said, however, enjoying her nearness but not, he hoped, showing it too much.

"Why don't I come with you?" she suggested.

"Where?"

"To the Black Forest, wherever you're going. Doesn't matter where, does it, but we can be together . . ."

He felt like a man watching himself from the outside.

"Yes, that would be nice," he said.

"Well, you don't sound very enthusiastic," she complained, but there was laughter in her voice. "Maybe you'd rather shack up with some fräulein."

"*Schatzi* is the word," he corrected. "And I've made no plans."

"Well, then, how's about it?" Her eyes were teasing him.

"What about the paper?" he asked. "The big piece about oil and gas? The ballet stuff? You can't just take off . . ."

"Don't be silly," said Lotte. "They'll never know. They don't expect me to have any copy for a couple of days, anyway. And then I can always say I'm onto something and I need a bit more time."

"If they find out—"

"Have you got a booking somewhere?" she interrupted him. She had made up her mind, clearly.

"No," said Heron. "I'm taking pot luck."

"Where are we making for?" she asked, and the "we" was clear.

"Well," said Heron. He hesitated. "I had intended . . ." He stopped.

"Yes?" She was putting on a dab of lipstick.

"Well, I was going to go to Freudenstadt," he said.

"Oh, where's that?"

"It's on the Hochstrasse, right in the forest."

"Sounds good," said Lotte. "Let's make for there, then."

"It might be—sort of dull," said Heron.

Lotte smiled. "Not with you it won't," she said, putting away her lipstick.

The fasten-seat-belt light came on, and when the

plane began its touchdown and the undercarriage bumped on the tarmac, Lotte held his hand tightly.

They walked side by side down the long corridor to passport control. It all went very smoothly; the green-uniformed official merely glanced at their passports and then waved them through without even putting in a stamp.

Heron instinctively looked around for some anonymous man in a suit standing close by or a sign that their arrival had aroused interest. But they just followed the stream of passengers out to the customs.

"Well," said Lotte, putting down her case, "I think I'd better call London and check in with the office."

"I thought you were going to ignore them," said Heron.

"Yes, but I want to let them know I've arrived," replied Lotte patiently, like somebody explaining an obvious fact to a not-very-bright person. "Once they know I'm here, I can breathe again."

"Can't it wait till you get to the hotel?" he asked.

"I thought we'd push off straightaway," said Lotte. "Wasn't that the idea, Harry? What do you want to hang around Stuttgart for?"

"Okay," grunted Heron.

"Why don't you get yourself a coffee over there," said Lotte, "while I find a phone?"

"What about money?"

"I'll reverse the charges."

He watched her go across the airport concourse and then sat down in the refreshment area, the suitcases next to him.

"*Ein kenchen Kaffee, bitte,*" he asked the waitress. His German wasn't too bad, he reflected. Not considering how long it had been since he had last used it.

He wondered, sitting there, why it was that all airports were the work of the same architect, the same interior designer; these two had a monopoly from Heathrow to Charles de Gaulle, Kennedy to Frankfurt,

Rome to Stockholm. And he didn't like their work one little bit.

She was taking her time. He didn't think she'd get away with it. The news desk would want to know her hotel in Stuttgart, where to get hold of her in an emergency in case a big story broke. He could visualize a frenzied news editor going hysterical at the idea of news exploding in Stuttgart and not knowing where to contact his reporter on the spot. Heron wondered how she was going to explain it to them.

He was getting impatient. He wanted to get going. Sitting here drinking coffee and listening to disembodied arrival-and-departure announcements, he might just as well never have left London Airport.

Across the way he could see a newsstand with its array of magazines and newspapers. He signaled to the waitress.

"I'm just going to get a paper," he explained in German. "Can you look after these for a second?" He indicated the cases. "And if a lady comes looking for me, tell her I'll be right back."

He hurriedly bought the *International Herald Tribune* and *Bild Zeitung*, and then, as he turned the corner, he stopped in his tracks. What he saw took him back to sitting in a Daimler with a gun in his side and being hit across the face while handcuffed in a chair.

The two men were there, the one with a striking, rather handsome profile, clean-cut like a classical Roman, who had an American accent. And the other one, the prematurely gray-haired man with the glass eye.

They were standing behind the airport florist shop, talking animatedly to Lotte.

They knew each other well, Heron could see that. And Lotte was laughing.

58

Heron rushed back to the table and picked up his suitcase.

"The lady hasn't come yet," said the waitress.

"She will," said Heron grimly. "Tell her the bill is paid."

He gave the girl the money and walked rapidly away, leaving her with a baffled expression.

He found the Hertz counter.

"I want to hire a car," he said.

He filled in the form, showed his passport and driver's license, and paid the deposit. The girl told him where he could collect the car.

"Thank you," said Heron.

After he had gone, a man in a tweed jacket came up to the counter. Casually, he produced an identification card that opened most doors in West Germany.

"That man," he said.

"The Englishman?" asked the girl. She was impressed and curious. This secret agency of Federal Security did not often enter one's life.

"Yes," said the man. "Mr. Heron, correct?"

"Yes," said the Hertz girl.

"Did he tell you what he was doing?"

"He said he was on holiday and wanted to tour the Black Forest."

"You are very helpful," said the man. "I'd like the number of the car, please."

She gave it to him.

"He's picking it up in half an hour," she volunteered.

"Excellent," said the man, and the girl did not quite understand why he seemed so pleased.

"What is your name, fräulein?" asked the man.

He was rather nice, she thought, and a girl could do worse. Besides, what an exciting job he had.

"Inge Schoenmann."

"Well, Inge," said the man charmingly, "would you do two things, please?"

"Of course."

"Don't tell anybody that we have been making inquiries."

"Of course not."

"Good. And the other thing is very important. If anybody asks questions about Mr. Heron, play dumb. And call me at once."

He gave her his card before he left. Actually, it was a disappointing card. It did not give the organization to which he belonged or its address. Just his name and a phone number.

59

A red Porsche stood parked in the driveway outside the house called Adlerhof. It looked like a stylish hunting lodge, set in its own grounds, a formidable wilderness of twisted growth. The place, although only a few miles from Freudenstadt, seemed remote and secretive.

But the air smelled clean and fresh, spiced with the aroma of conifers. Heron stood concealed in a cluster of fir trees, but it was not the wonders of nature he was studying. The house had some interesting man-made features. There was a television aerial, but also another antenna, and Heron guessed it had something to do with receiving or transmitting high-frequency radio; it was just a guess, but an educated one. There were also a couple of small, discreet closed-circuit TV cameras surveying the approaches to the house.

A thin plume of smoke rose from one of the chimneys. From a blazing log fire, reckoned Heron. The Adlerhof was just the kind of place that would have big fireplaces, and maybe a suckling pig slowly roasting on a spit in the hearth.

The house had only two floors, and three of the windows on the upper one had steel bars. To keep people in, or out? wondered Heron. A room with steel bars on its windows always fascinated him, whether it belonged to an embassy in Kensington, an eccentric millionaire in Bel Air, an anonymous building in Whitehall, or a classy hunting lodge in the Black Forest.

Heron had been watching the place for a couple of hours. He wanted to know a lot more about it before he took the next step. If Madek was right, that's where it all was—Ursula, the Goering thing, the holy grail people were hunting and killing for.

"She has bodyguards," the little man had said, and maybe that was why he died: because he knew too much about the Adlerhof. Maybe . . .

From his vantage point, Heron hadn't seen much activity—certainly nothing of Ursula. A man came out of the house once, with a dog, a fat Basset hound. Heron had expected something fierce, an Alsatian, a Doberman. The little waddling Basset hound seemed slightly incongruous.

After a few minutes the man returned. The dog was somewhat reluctant to follow him, and the man had to whistle a couple of times. Then, half an hour later, a plain gray van drove up. A man got out and rang the bell, somebody took several large cartons of groceries inside, and the van drove off again.

The rest of the time, nothing.

Maybe I should wait till it gets dark, mused Heron. It won't be quite so easy then for those cameras to spot trespassers. Maybe I can get around the back and into the house . . .

That was one way. The other was to go boldly up to the front door, ask for Mrs. Fennerman, be as casual about it as if he had just stepped off the Central Line at Ealing Broadway.

And see what happened.

He moved a little nearer, still keeping among the trees. Suddenly he stiffened. A man came out of the house carrying a suitcase. Heron had no trouble recognizing him. Kiefer, rimless glasses, short hair, and all, hadn't changed. He opened the passenger door and put the suitcase in the car. Then he went back, leaving the door ajar.

Let's see, thought Heron, what does our hero do now? Sneak into the car, curl up in the back under a rug, and see where the baddies take him? Or break cover, rush across the drive, dash through the open door into the house, and confront them all?

Well, he said to himself, let the hero do it. I've got a good view of it all, and there are a few things I still want to find out first. Like— Then he stood rock-still.

Ursula had come out. It was she, unmistakably. The blonde hair, the tall, slim figure. The Basset hound was sniffing around her legs, and she bent down and fondled it.

She stood by the door, waiting for somebody to join her. Heron crouched forward. He could see her clearly. She wore a trouser suit again, not the green one, but a very fetching red one. The only trouble was, the red clashed slightly with the car.

Ursula called out something, apparently to whomever she was waiting for. She was getting impatient.

"Keep still, Mr. Heron," said a voice, but out of the corner of his eye Heron could see the man. Still expensively dressed, still with silver cuff links.

But this time he had a gun in his hand.

"Hello, Dieter," said Heron pleasantly. "I was wondering what had happened to you."

"Please keep your hands nicely in sight," said Dieter Langschmidt. The pistol was unwavering.

"Why don't you tell Ursula I'm here?" asked Heron.

"She knows," said Langschmidt. "And she doesn't particularly want to talk to you. As a matter of fact, since you're around she's decided she'd like to go somewhere else."

Heron glanced toward the house. Kiefer had come out and was politely opening the passenger door in front for Ursula. She got in, the Basset hound watching. Then Kiefer got into the driver's seat and started the engine.

The Porsche exploded into a ball of fire. There was one sudden flash, an ear-shattering detonation, and then just flames and a column of black smoke. Like a piano accompaniment, glass tinkled from the shattered windows of the house. The ground trembled slightly with the shock of the explosion.

And what was left of the Porsche was just a few bits of twisted steel and two of its wheels, flung fifty feet away. That was all.

60

Langschmidt was still staring at the pyre that had been the Porsche when Heron jumped him. He collected his wits only a split second sooner than the other man, but it was not enough.

Heron grabbed Langschmidt's gun and at the same

time kneed him in the testicles. Langschmidt sagged, his face contorted with pain, and Heron tried to force his hand open to release the pistol. Despite his agony, Langschmidt tried to kick him, and one hand clawed for Heron's face. It was the kind of fighting that is taught in establishments where the virtues of gouging out eyes and putting the boot into a man's groin are rated above the Marquis of Queensberry's rules.

Neither of them saw the men who ran out of the house after the explosion, heard the alarm bells that began to shrill, or saw the lights that came on in the rooms with steel bars. There was nothing anyone could do for the occupants of the Porsche; they no longer existed. The dog too was dead, caught by the full force of the blast.

The men from the house did not panic. They behaved like soldiers, one of them shouting instructions, and several others fanning out on the grounds. Some of them carried short, snub-nosed submachine guns.

But Heron and Langschmidt were entangled in their savage, brutal combat. The prize both were after was the pistol, which had fallen from Langschmidt's hand and now lay, among the needles from the fir trees, a couple of feet away.

Heron was sure his nose was broken. It hurt like the devil, and his mouth tasted of blood. But he had his hands around Langschmidt's throat, and he was trying to squeeze the life out of him. He saw a kind of red shimmer in front of his eyes, and he wanted to kill the man. But then somebody hit him on the head.

The blow didn't knock him out, but he was suddenly so dazed and weak, he couldn't even lift his arms. There were men around him, armed men, and one of them bent over Langschmidt. He heard German spoken, questions and answers, and then he was picked up, not too roughly; one man grasped him under the armpits, the other his legs, and he felt as if he were floating. His confusion was such that he did not realize he was being carried.

They took him into the house, and he had fleeting impressions of being carried upstairs, and he remembered staring up at the wooden beams in the ceiling. Then he was taken into a room, a simply furnished, bare room, almost as austere as a monk's cell, and put on a bed. Everything was swimming, and Heron felt slightly sick. The blow on the head had been a heavy one, and his brain ached in his skull.

Heron closed his eyes, and what awakened him was the sound of a door being unlocked and a man coming in . . . he didn't know how long after.

Heron blinked. His head still throbbed, but his vision began to focus again. Clearly enough to see Ross.

"Well," said Ross, looking down at him from a great height. "You're in a hell of a mess, aren't you, Heron?"

61

Ross helped him sit up.

"You half killed poor Dieter," he said.

Heron groaned.

"Tough," he managed to croak.

He squinted at Ross balefully and then glanced around the room.

"What the hell is this?" he asked. His mouth felt parched.

"You're a guest of the Verfassungsschutz," said Ross.

"The what?"

"The Office for the Protection of the Constitution."

Heron stared at him blankly.

"Oh, you are an ignorant bastard," said Ross.

"Who the hell are they?" said Heron. His head was beginning to clear.

"They do in West Germany what I do in the United Kingdom," said Ross smugly. "We're close associates."

"Oh." Heron warily touched his nose.

"You're all right," said Ross. "The doctor looked at you while you were snoozing. You'll live."

Heron swung his legs off the bed. Gingerly he stood up. The room remained level, the ceiling didn't dance.

"What the devil's going on?" he asked, facing Ross. "What is this place?"

"I've never known a man who asks so many questions," said Ross. "I suppose it's a throwback to your Fleet Street days. As for this place, it's nothing. Just a safe house."

Heron remembered the Porsche exploding.

"Not very safe for some," he said dryly.

"Yes, you're right there." Ross nodded. "Poor girl . . ."

"Ursula?" said Heron incredulously. "Poor girl. Why, she . . ."

"Was a Judas goat." Ross saw Heron's bewilderment. "Have you ever been in India?" he asked.

"No."

"Pity. You'd know all about a Judas goat if you'd been in Bengal. It's a little goat that is staked out as a bait to lure a man-eating tiger. The hunters lie in wait in ambush. The goat's bleating attracts the tiger, and then—boom." Ross smiled encouragingly. "Now you're in the picture."

"The hell I am."

"The tiger is too smart to be deceived by all the ordinary ruses," Ross went on patiently. "He knows all the tricks. But a live Judas goat is too big a temptation. He simply can't resist it."

"For God's sake, stop lecturing me about bloody

goats and tigers!" snapped Heron. "What's your game?"

Ross looked sad. "You'll never make a really good intelligence man, Harry," he said ruefully.

62

They sat in the back room of a little inn, two thousand feet up, overlooking a panorama of dark evergreens stretching into the distance. Behind them they had left a hive of activity at the Adlerhof. Explosives experts, forensic scientists, searching the grounds, examining the scene of the blast, taking photographs, measurements. The men had one thing in common: none of them were police. They all belonged to the same anonymous organization that was a law unto itself.

Ross had driven him to the inn, about four miles south of Freudenstadt, because, as he said, "There's somebody I'd like you to meet." He corrected himself. "Or maybe I'd like him to meet you."

"Glen here is one of our friends," he said, introducing Seltzer.

We've already had tiger hunting in India and "our friends," thought Heron. All we need is "the firm," "the organization," "the company."

"You look exactly as I imagined, Harry," said Seltzer cordially. What he meant was that Heron could be recognized from the somewhat fuzzy surveillance photos.

They ordered *Badisches Ochsenfleisch*, which, decided Heron, was a kind of Aryan boiled beef. It came with a delicious horseradish sauce and a salad in which

Heron identified cheese, pickles, bits of melon, cherries, plums, and then gave up.

With it they drank kirschwasser. "NATO vodka," Seltzer called it.

"They told you?" asked Ross.

"Yes," said Seltzer. "Tough luck. How the hell did they manage it, right under everybody's nose?"

Ursula they didn't even mention. They might have been discussing an opponent's chess move.

"I thought we might . . ." Ross began, and stopped. He was studying Heron pensively.

"Put Harry wise to a few things?" suggested Seltzer.

It was getting darker outside. The Black Forest began looking more ominous in the dusk, and Heron shivered slightly. He still felt fragile.

"Let me put it this way," said Ross slowly. "Everybody's got to have a piece of paper."

Seltzer smiled. "Not bad," he said. He relit the King Edward he had started smoking, his eyes never leaving Heron's face.

Ross ignored him.

"Doesn't matter what you call it, but they have to have it. Everybody needs their holy writ, whether it's called *Das Kapital*, *Mein Kampf*, or the New Testament." Seltzer frowned but said nothing. "There wouldn't be a United States without a Declaration of Independence, an Israel without a Balfour Declaration, but it all boils down to the same thing—something written on paper that inspires them to do or die . . ."

"Who's they?" asked Heron. The kirschwasser was beginning to glow at him.

Ross shrugged. "Patriots, fanatics, martyrs, revolutionaries, nut cases, idealists—you name it."

"Friend, you're a cynic," said Seltzer.

"Tell me about Ursula being blown to pieces," suggested Heron. "Tell me about Fennerman."

Ross didn't appear to hear him. "Suppose somebody was trying to revive a religion that's fallen into disuse? What the faithful few would need to wake up the masses is a sign from heaven. A new word from the prophet. You follow?"

"You can guess the religion, Harry," said Seltzer.

"I think I can," murmured Heron.

Ross smiled sourly. "I wonder what made you guess. They're doing all right, too. People are beginning to sit up and listen. It's almost getting respectable again. All that's needed to light the flame is that piece of paper.

"The last thing Goering wrote. His prophecy for the future, his call for revival, his message for now, the greatest sales gimmick ever—if they could get their hands on it.

"You see, when he sat in that cell, Goering was thinking of the future, of two, three generations ahead, of now and tomorrow." Ross had suddenly come alive, almost enthusiastic. "And when he sat down to write his dying statement, his final testament, he knew he was lighting a fuse that . . ."

He faltered and stopped.

"You sound as if you admire him," commented Heron sourly.

"Well, he wasn't a Himmler or a Streicher, or a Goebbels. He . . ." Again Ross paused. "He was different from the rest of the gang. He had integrity. That's what makes him so dangerous."

The waitress came and cleared their table. She was a buxom Bavarian girl, and she smiled at them.

"*Hat es gut geschmeckt?*" she asked them.

"*Sehr gut,*" said Seltzer. "*Ich muss wieder kommen.*"

His German was perfect, his accent faultless, and Heron thought, I don't know what you were doing in other countries, but, by God, here in Germany you fit perfectly. You could pass as one of them. The girl winked at Seltzer and carried the plates away.

"It's irresistible to *them*," said Ross, as if there had been no interruption. "Unfortunately, the tiger got to our Judas goat first." His eyes glinted. "He wasn't fooled."

In the distance, hundreds of feet below, little lights began to twinkle like glowworms in the darkness of the forest, in the windows of cabins and houses.

It was fairyland, and if there were monsters, they were well hidden.

"Now you know it all, Harry," interrupted Seltzer, and Heron thought that was the most ironic remark he had heard. "We're trying to smoke out the big 'uns. The respectable ones. The ones we haven't got listed. And the one honey pot they can't resist is that little scrap of paper."

"But where is it?" asked Heron. "Who's got it?"

"You," said Ross very quietly.

And for the first time Heron knew what it was like to be a Judas goat. The trouble was, he didn't know which was the man-eating tiger.

63

"Police block," said the Roman centurion with the American accent.

The man with the glass eye, sitting beside him in the Taunus, nodded. He could see it, too, ahead of them, on the road to Baden-Baden. The traffic narrowed to a single lane, and the police vehicles were drawn up across the road, their blue lights flashing. There was a small line of cars, each waiting its turn to be checked.

"Let me do the talking," said the Roman centurion. Again the glass-eyed man nodded, without saying a word. Obediently, the Taunus took its place in the line.

They were fifteen miles from Freudenstadt, with a breathtaking view of the Rhine plain stretched beneath them, but they had little interest in the scenic beauty.

They drew up to the control point, and a green-uniformed policeman, with a submachine gun slung over his shoulder, came up to the driver's window.

"*Ihre Papiere, bitte,*" he said.

The centurion smiled. "*Wir sind Amerikaner.*"

.."*Ach,*" said the policeman, and lapsed into quite good English. "Your ID, please."

"What's all this for?" asked the young man, reaching inside his coat.

"There has been some trouble. A bomb. Terrorists."

"Gee, how awful." The centurion handed over a small identity card. "I'm with the Air Force, at Lindsey. Wiesbaden."

The policeman examined the card with its thumbnail photo, then stood in front of the car and looked at the license number.

"You have no American armed forces plate," he said. "This is a civilian car . . ."

"Sure," said the centurion. "I hired it. This is my uncle. He's over here on vacation, and I've taken a few days' leave to show him the sights."

"*Ach so,*" said the policeman, but he did not relax. "Where are you going?"

"Baden-Baden."

"From?"

"Freiburg."

"Your uncle's papers, please, Lieutenant."

"Of course," said the man with the glass eye. He produced a U.S. passport.

The policeman started leafing through it.

"Anybody hurt in that bomb business?" asked the centurion.

"Two people were killed," replied the policeman, still examining the passport.

A Jeep pulled up, and two American military policemen walked over to them. For a second the glass-eyed man and his companion exchanged looks.

"You're just in time, Sergeant," said the policeman. "These are your people. The lieutenant and his uncle."

He passed the documents over to the NCO.

"That's a Twenty-fourth Division patch you got there, son," said the glass-eyed man.

"Yes, sir."

"Well, shake," said the glass-eyed man. "It's my old outfit. In the war."

The MP smiled. "Is that so, sir? Guess you wouldn't recognize it now."

He handed the papers back to them.

"That's fine," he said. "Have a good trip, Lieutenant. And you, too, sir."

He gave them a quick, informal salute, and the Taunus swept through the roadblock.

The Roman centurion and the glass-eyed man smiled at each other. It hadn't been too difficult.

Of course, what had helped was the fact that their papers had been forged by the best man in the business. His passports, it was always said, were more genuine than the real thing.

It was just as well. They hadn't been to Freiburg. It would have been of considerable interest to the police to learn where they had really been and who was the passenger they had had aboard.

64

Ross dropped Heron in the Lauterbadstrasse, in the center of Freudenstadt.

"Is that where you're staying?" he asked, looking at a small hotel across the way.

"As if you didn't know."

"My dear chap, I had no idea. It's simply that it looks cheap. I thought you'd be staying at a cheap hotel. No offense meant."

"I'm not on government expenses," said Heron.

Ross snorted. "Count yourself lucky. I'm really crossing another department's preserves by being here, and the bureaucratic tangle when I want my per diem will be unbelievable."

"What is DI Five doing, anyway, operating on DI Six territory?" asked Heron. "You're not allowed abroad, are you?"

"Something like that. We're all as jealous of each other as six spinsters after the same man."

"So what are you doing here?" asked Heron.

"Call it a labor of love," said Ross, and Heron knew he didn't expect to be believed. "Man does not live by bread alone."

Heron put his hand on the door handle.

"The idiot who said that ought to try it," he said.

"I suppose you speak from experience."

Ross seems to like needling me, he thought.

"If there's anything urgent, contact the consulate in Stuttgart. Ask for Mr. Johnson. You can talk reasonably freely to him."

"Only reasonably?"

"Does it matter?" asked Ross. "I don't expect you'll be here much longer."

Heron got out of the car.

"Good night," he said.

"Sweet dreams," said Ross, unsmiling.

You sarcastic bastard, thought Heron. He had almost entered the hotel before he heard Ross start his car and drive off.

The old porter at the reception desk got off his stool as Heron came in.

"Good evening, Herr Heron," he wheezed. "Did you enjoy yourself?"

"My key, please."

"Freudenstadt is beautiful, no? Completely rebuilt after nineteen forty-five. Beautiful, no?"

"My key," repeated Heron. But he saw his slot was empty.

"I forgot," said the old man, coughing. "Your wife has arrived."

"Really?" said Heron.

"Yes, Frau Heron is upstairs. She took the key." He stroked his white walrus moustache. "So happy for you now, to have her with you, no?"

Heron started to go up the stairs, but the porter called after him, "Sorry, there is only one towel. You did not tell us she was coming. Tomorrow there will be two towels."

There was a light under his door. Slowly he started to turn the handle. The door was unlocked.

"You're late, Harry," said Lotte. "Where on earth have you been?"

She was lying, fully dressed, on the bed. Only her shoes had been kicked off, and lay on the floor. Her suitcase stood nearby.

She smiled. "Surprise?"

"No," he said, "I had been expecting you."

"You're a real son of a bitch," she said affably,

"running out on me like that. I looked all over for you. What happened?"

He sat down on the edge of the bed.

"How are your friends?" he asked.

"Who?"

"The guy with the glass eye. And the fellow you say didn't go to the London School of Economics."

"You're crazy," said Lotte.

"I saw you with them. At the airport."

Her face cleared. "Oh, those people. I met them once at a press conference. They're here for the trade fair. I just bumped into them. What's wrong with them?"

"I think you're lying," said Heron.

"Thank you," she said coldly. "Harry, if you want to pick a fight, there are easier ways." She bit her lip. "I thought you'd be glad to see me. I had a hell of a job finding you . . ."

"Those men," said Heron, "nearly killed me."

Her eyes opened wide, but Heron didn't wait.

"No, Lotte," he said. "No playacting. Not any more. You know what you're after. So do I."

She reached for her bag and lit a cigarette. Her hand didn't shake.

"Yes, Harry," she said. "We're both after the same thing. You and I. The Goering Testament."

He felt as if somebody had struck him. She was telling him what he had not wanted to tell himself. He didn't matter. He was just an incident along the way.

"Who are you working for?" he asked quietly.

She blew out some smoke. "Who do you think? The paper." She leaned closer to him. "Don't you realize what a fantastic story this is? If we find the piece of paper everybody's been trying to keep secret for thirty years?"

"No," he said dully. "You're not working for the paper. I called them, in London. They said you were on holiday. You're not on any assignment for them. You're working for somebody else."

She looked at him pityingly.

"My god, Harry, what the hell has happened to you? Have you been out of it for so long? Don't you even remember that when a paper assigns somebody to a red-hot exclusive that they're trying to keep secret, nobody knows? It's not on the diary. The office isn't told. The reporter is officially on leave or sick. Only the editor and a couple of others know anything." Her lips trembled. "And who the hell do you think I work for anyway? The fucking Nazis? Is that what you think of me?"

She stubbed out the cigarette furiously in the bedside ashtray.

"How do you know about it?" he asked.

"Harry, be your age. I've got contacts. Friends. Even in Special Branch. I heard whispers. About you. That's why I wondered if you are something in security. Maybe in intelligence." She gave a lopsided smile. "I still wonder."

"Just what did you hear?" He was pale.

"That Goering's last testament, which everybody thought had been under lock and key since Nuremberg, had in fact been stolen and was being offered to the highest bidder, and that you were involved."

He looked at her silently.

"I even heard that there was that D-notice out on you. There seemed to be something funny about that junk shop and your pal Fennerman getting killed. Rumors said he had double-crossed somebody and that you now have it. Is that true?"

"Is that why you go to bed with me?" he asked.

Her eyes smoldered. "You bastard," she hissed.

"Oh, come on," said Heron. "I'm just being realistic. You think I can lead you to the scoop that'll make your name, and you're feeding me a little kickback now and then. To keep me sweet."

She hit him across the face, and it hurt so much

that he felt tears in his eyes. She was shaking slightly.

"I hate you," she said in a low voice.

"No need. Now we both know what we are," he replied.

"You think so?"

He suddenly felt desperately weary. He stood up, took off his jacket, started undoing his tie.

"Listen," he said brutally, "I'm catching the first plane back to London in the morning, and I need my sleep. I'm going to sleep in that bed, and if you want to take your clothes off and come in with me, I'll fuck you and then go to sleep. If you want to sleep on the floor, that's all right with me, too. And if you want to piss off, I couldn't care less."

She stared at him in disbelief.

Then, trying to keep her voice steady, she said, "Go to hell."

She got into her shoes, grabbed her bag and the suitcase, and slammed the door.

A great sadness came over him, and he felt like a man who had hacked off one of his own limbs. He wanted to rush after her, take her in his arms, tell her he had said it only because he had to, beg her forgiveness, and love her. The look she had on her face cut into him like a knife.

But he couldn't forget the men at the airport. And before he put the light out, he opened the drawers of the dressing table and the wardrobe, checked his suitcase, looked through all his things. One of the two cotton threads had been broken and some carefully placed cigarette ash disturbed.

There was no doubt about it. She had searched everywhere very thoroughly. Like an expert.

65

Rognov, the chief of station in Bonn, reread the signal he had drafted:

MOST URGENT SECRET EYES DIRECTOR ONLY: CRAYFISH IDENTIFIED NOW PROCEEDING LONDON BY COURIER NAMED HERON LANDING HEATHROW URGE IMMEDIATE ACTION TO INTERCEPT.

He initialed it, put it in an envelope, and took it to the code room himself. Normally, he only informed Moscow and left them to make the decisions. It would be foolhardy, in the usual course of events, to suggest specific courses of action to the Director. But Rognov felt that in this case he was onto a winner. He knew how much they cared about CRAYFISH.

Since there wasn't that much time, it couldn't do any harm to suggest somewhat drastic action, he thought.

It was also one in the eye for Shilenko at the London station. Shilenko had had most of the operation under his jurisdiction, but it would not escape the Director that it was the Bonn Station that had come up with the goods.

Rognov did not like Shilenko, and he would much rather take over the London post, with all its attractions, than stay stuck in this glorified provincial village the West Germans insisted on calling their federal capital.

Maybe putting the finger on CRAYFISH might, with luck, be a big step along the road.

66

They drifted into the country almost unnoticed. They landed at Heathrow and Gatwick and Luton. Some flew into Manchester from Dublin because, despite checks on Irish terrorists, the passport situation was a little easier. Others stepped ashore at Harwich and Dover. Some were picked up by friends as they passed through customs; others made their own way to London aboard buses and trains.

They took care to draw little attention to themselves. Their papers were in order, their appearance was neat, they were polite, and they had plenty of traveler's checks. Few of the men had long hair or wore sandals or faded denims.

And usually they got through, because most of them weren't known. There were some who sported little lapel badges, rather daringly, with flaming swords or crosses in a circle or stylized eagles; but no one really knew what these insignias meant.

It was a multinational crowd—Frenchmen, Swedes, Germans, Spaniards, Belgians, Italians, Austrians. They were schoolteachers, shop owners, students, truck drivers, doctors, businessmen.

Sometimes, one of them had bad luck. Something about him would arouse the interest of the immigration officer, and he'd open up his thick black book. And if he found certain codes beside the name, he'd very politely inform the man that he had been refused permission to land. But that was rare; the majority were European Community citizens, and their entry into the United Kingdom was a formality.

Once clear of the barriers, they often shared train compartments or taxis. They had traveled separately until now, but they knew one another and greeted their pals joyfully.

In their suitcases, concealed from superficial customs check, they carried magazines and newssheets with titles like *Kampfruf* and *Croix de Feu*, *White Power* and *Christian Advocate*, *Soldaten Zeitung*, and *Front Nationale*. They eagerly exchanged them away from prying eyes.

A few concealed other things. Bundles of leaflets, posters with ugly caricatures, adhesive stickers they hoped would soon grace London lamp standards. But they were careful not to carry guns or knives; the checks were too thorough, so they left them behind.

When the immigration man asked what they were coming to Britain for, they'd say, "A holiday," or "To meet friends." And if anybody asked how long they planned to stay, they'd say, "Only a few days."

Which was true. They were coming for a special purpose, and they didn't propose to remain long after that. There'd be too much to do back home.

They were all, in a roundabout way, making for the same place, for the same reason.

They tried not to show it, but they were excited. They were looking forward to wearing the black and brown and blue shirts they had packed alongside the belts with special buckles. In Britain, they had been warned, there was a law against wearing political uniforms, but you couldn't really stop a man from wearing a shirt of his favorite color, could you? Especially not in rather private surroundings.

The clans were gathering.

67

The Stuttgart plane had landed ten minutes previously, and Bowler stood outside the customs hall in the European building at Heathrow, waiting for the arrivals to emerge.

Bowler had a knack of merging with his background, and he was typecast for the man who sits in a hotel lobby reading a newspaper and isn't noticed by anyone. As a matter of fact, on a shadowing job he always carried a neatly folded copy of the *Times*. He believed it was an essential prop to have handy. And in any case, he hadn't done the crossword yet.

The order was clear: tail Heron from the airport. See what he does. Who he talks to. Where he goes. Above all, don't lose him.

The Stuttgart passengers started to straggle out, carrying their plastic bags with the duty-free booze and cigarettes. They were an uninspiring lot, thought Bowler. But then, Stuttgart was an uninspiring place.

After a quarter of an hour, Bowler wore a slight frown. There was no sign of Heron. The rear guard of the passengers had appeared, and most of the flight had now been cleared through.

He waited another ten minutes, his eyes never leaving the exit doors. But Heron did not appear.

Bowler put his paper under his arm and went to the Special Branch office. His pass impressed them there.

"The Stuttgart flight that's just come in," said Bowler. "Was there a man called Heron on it? This man?"

He showed the detective sergeant Heron's photograph.

"Just one moment, sir," said the detective sergeant respectfully. He didn't know exactly what Bowler's rank might be, but people from his outfit had to be handled with kid gloves. Bowler smiled inwardly; if the man only knew that he was listed as a civilian driver with the Ministry of Defence. The pass he had shown was only revealed in an emergency.

Like now.

"No, he wasn't on the plane," said the detective sergeant after he had made several phone calls and checked with the immigration desk at passport control.

"He was listed?"

"Yes. But he never checked in." The detective sergeant suddenly seemed to remember something. "Heron? Isn't there a special instruction about him?"

"Yes," replied Bowler, but he was already thinking about other things.

"Anything wrong?" asked the Special Branch man.

"Maybe," said Bowler. "Have you got a scrambler line?"

"In there," said the detective sergeant. He indicated a door. "The green phone. It's secure."

"Thank you," said Bowler.

When he got through, he told them that Heron never made the plane.

"No," they said. "We've just heard from Stuttgart. He checked out from his hotel in Freudenstadt first thing this morning and disappeared. He gave Johnson the slip . . ."

"Christ," Bowler said. "What's he playing at?"

"It might be," they said, "that Mr. Heron is not what we thought."

68

Major Geist, whose English was as fluent as his German, never quite knew how to translate *Schadenfreude*. On paper it meant "malicious joy," but a better way of putting it might be "delighted malice." Whatever the right phrase, he could not resist having a touch of it at this moment.

"Ludwig," he chuckled, "the British have lost Mr. Heron."

"Sir?" said his aide.

"I just had them onto me in a panic. Their surveillance has broken down. They were watching his flight at both ends, and they've mislaid him."

"Mr. Ross will be mad, won't he?"

Geist's expression clouded over momentarily. "Ah, yes, Mr. Ross . . ."

He looked thoughtful for a while, but then he had to smile again. It was all too piquant.

"What do you think has happened to Heron?" asked Ludwig. He was neatly stacking into a pile various reports and memoranda Geist would have to read when less urgent matters were on his mind.

"Ah," said Geist mysteriously.

"Is he in danger?"

"My dear Ludwig," said Geist expansively, "a man like that, doing what he does, is always in danger. But it so happens that we know all about Mr. Heron. And where he is."

"But, sir, you just said . . ."

Geist stretched himself comfortably in his leather-upholstered chair.

"I said the British have lost him. We haven't." He beamed. "They should really stick to their own territory. I am sure they do very well in Yorkshire."

Ludwig grinned. The major certainly was in a good mood.

"You want to know where Mr. Heron has been? In Heidelberg. You know what he has been doing? Something very interesting. Drinking beer. First at the Goldener Hecht. Then at the Roter Ochse in the Haupstrasse. Lots of beer."

The major chuckled again, at the sight of Ludwig's face.

"You see, we know our job, don't we, *Junge?*"

"But, herr Major, is that all he's been doing, drinking beer?"

"Oh, there was one other small thing. A man sat down at the same table in the Roter Ochse with a briefcase. He had a stein and left. Now Mr. Heron has that briefcase. Interesting, no?"

He glanced at the clock on his desk, a farewell present from his colleagues at NATO headquarters in Brussels when he finished his tour there.

"I think Mr. Heron will soon be leaving for Frankfurt, where he has booked himself a flight to London. On Pan American, curiously enough. He is avoiding European airlines." He chuckled. "He is entering the house by a different door."

"Are we going to tip off the British?" asked Ludwig, reaching for his note pad.

Geist raised a cautionary hand.

"The good Lord will provide, I'm sure. Have you ever thought, in any case, that perhaps they're not telling us everything, either?"

Ludwig thought it was wiser not to comment. But he asked one more question. "What do you think is in that briefcase, sir?"

The major was no longer smiling.

"His death warrant," he said.

69

Ross's boss was still in an expansive mood when they came out of the National Liberal Club. As they walked past the old War Office Building, he continued his thesis.

"It is like a mathematical formula, don't you see?" he declared. "Extremes will always meet in a neat circle. Take your right and your left. Those sworn enemies, revolutionary Marxists and Nazis, apparently so opposed to one another, actually end up on common ground. For example, who's more anti-Semitic than those two put together? Israel, for one, is a hate word to both. They sneer at the same things, they believe in the same methods of silencing opponents, their style is the same: slogans, flags, marches."

"Yes," said Ross. Experience had taught him that when the Director was in one of his tutorial phases, nothing stopped him from expounding his theories.

"It is no accident, Ross, that Hitler called himself a National Socialist. It was the National Socialist Workers' Party, remember. Mark that well. If you've seen our gentry who call themselves International Socialists or Revolutionary Workers, you'll know it's only fitting that their names are so similar."

"Quite so," said Ross. He had a memo on his mind that he had to dictate to Miss Foley.

They crossed the road, but the Director was still lecturing.

"I always thought that Hitler's pact with Stalin was the most logical alliance imaginable. It was inevitable, Ross. Just as revolution, in the name of freedom and liberty, invariably disintegrates into the worst tyranny. Or can you think of worse racists than the Afro-Asian bigots who preach hatred of apartheid? The circle always meets."

"Doesn't make our job any easier, does it?" said Ross. He really needed to get going.

"On the contrary," replied the Director, "perhaps it makes it all the more simple. How is CRAYFISH, by the way?" It was one of his quirks; he liked using the opposition's code words for the department's own operations. And he liked changing subjects in midstream.

"Biting, sir," said Ross. "Biting, I think."

"Glad to hear it," said the Director, and gave him a nod as he went through the archway into Admiralty House.

Ross buzzed Miss Foley when he was back in his office. She came in, prim as ever, clutching her notebook.

"Sit down," said Ross. "I want to do a classified memo. Top copy only, eyes of Director, classification most secret."

"Yes, sir," said Miss Foley impassively. She poised her ever-sharpened pencil. "Any subject heading?"

"Departmental Infiltration," said Ross.

She put down the shorthand outlines and waited.

Ross lit one of his Turkish cigarettes. Miss Foley, disinterested, stared out of the window, ready to go on.

Ross came to a sudden decision.

"No, scrub that," he said.

She drew a line across the page and waited to start once more.

"That'll be all for the moment," said Ross.

Miss Foley got up and went to the door. "Anything else you want me to do, Mr. Ross?"

"No." He looked at some papers on his desk. "Not just now."

Miss Foley took a daring step.

"Is anything wrong, sir?" she asked.

"Why should anything be wrong?"

"I wondered if we've some kind of security problem . . ."

"What makes you think that?"

"What you started dictating," said Miss Foley.
" 'Departmental Infiltration.' Does that mean—"

"It means nothing at all, Miss Foley," said Ross.
"That's why I changed my mind. That's why we're not
sending it."

"I see," said Miss Foley. "Thank you, sir."

She closed the door. Ross stubbed out his cigarette.
Then he opened his right-hand drawer, took out a
sheet of note paper, and began to write the memo by
hand.

70

Because the Pan American jet Heron took from
Frankfurt's Rhein-Main airport was on the final lap of
a flight from the Far East, the Boeing 747 did not
unload its passengers at Heathrow's European terminal.
Instead, Heron passed through passport control at the
International Building.

Special Branch did not expect him to land there,
and there was a delay before they realized that the
man they had cleared was on the List.

Bowler, who had been hanging around all day in
the other building watching European arrivals, was
out of breath after sprinting across to the Overseas
terminal as soon as he got word that Heron had been
spotted.

He was in time to see Heron walk over to the cab

rank, carrying his travel bag in one hand and a black leather briefcase in the other.

There was a line, and Bowler joined it behind Heron. This was where the *Times* was worth its weight in gold to him. Bowler held it in front of him, studiously reading it.

They didn't have long to wait. A cab pulled up, then another one, and suddenly it was Heron's turn.

"Ashfield Gardens," he said as he jumped inside, and at that moment yet another cab appeared. Bowler grabbed it.

"Follow that taxi," he said. The driver hesitated, and Bowler, who looked it, said sharply, "I'm a police officer."

It was much easier than explaining, in a couple of words, what he really was.

They were passing the disused shoe-polish factory, halfway into London, when Bowler noticed the motorcyclist behind his cab. If it had been a car, he might not even have become aware of it. But suddenly he was conscious that that motorbike had been following them since the airport.

At first Bowler wondered if he was being foolish. But every time he turned and looked out of the rear window, the motorcyclist, hunched over his handlebars, face hidden by a space helmet, was still there.

And he made no attempt to overtake them.

Bowler felt pretty sure the shadow was really interested in Heron and was keeping behind Bowler because he was sticking so closely to the prime target. He wished he had some means of contacting his people; they could whistle up a police car to wave down the motorcyclist . . . they could do a lot of things.

But he had no walkie-talkie, nothing. Then he saw the driver's mike. Of course, most cabs had a radio. Bowler slid the glass partition aside.

"I say," he called to the cabby through the window. "This is an emergency. Can you send a message to my headquarters? Ask them to relay it?"

"Sorry, mate," said the driver. "The bloody thing's out of order. Hasn't worked since I came on."

Bowler cursed. The whole operation was going wrong. And in the mirror he could see the motorcycle still following . . .

Take it easy, he said to himself. Those hours waiting at the airport have made you jumpy. All you're supposed to do is to see where Heron goes. Once he's indoors, you contact the office.

And if Mr. Space Helmet is still hanging around, they'll deal with him, too. You just worry about not losing Heron.

He sat back, trying to feel relaxed. Heron's cab was still in front. He could even see the back of Heron's head.

They had long passed Hammersmith, and Bowler realized he had heard right. Heron was going to his bed-sitter. It was going to be Ashfield Gardens.

Heron lived in a seedy neighborhood, but at the corner of Ashfield Gardens was a welcome sight he had forgotten about: a phone booth.

"Stop!" he shouted. "By that phone."

He jumped out, almost throwing a five-pound note at the cabdriver. "Keep the change," he yelled. Instantly the taxi drove off.

Bowler dived into the call box and began to dial the security number. Ahead, Heron's cab had stopped outside his front door. Heron was paying the driver. The holdall stood on the sidewalk, but the briefcase was in Heron's hand.

Bowler's number answered, and he gave the code word. Then he saw the motorcyclist. The man was sitting astride his high-powered eight hundred pounds of gleaming steel, its engine still throbbing, and he was aiming a small, compact, snub-nosed machine gun at Heron.

Bowler did several things as one. He dropped the receiver, pushed open the door of the phone booth,

pulled out his pistol, and yelled at the motorcyclist:
  "Drop it!"

Heron's cab was pulling away, and he was picking
up his travel bag when he heard the yell. He saw the
gun in the motorcyclist's hand and flung himself flat
on the sidewalk.

The motorcyclist swung around and fired at Bowler.
It was a short, sharp burst from the magazine, and the
bullets struck Bowler in several places. He was only
able to fire one shot from his pistol, and that went wide
as he collapsed.

The heavy motorbike roared, and its space-helmeted
rider raced it around the corner at full speed.

Bowler lay sprawled in a pool of his own blood beside the phone booth, his pistol just out of reach of
his lifeless fingers. He had survived the back-street
war in Belfast, storming a hijacked plane alongside
German commandos in Mogadishu, a Marxist bomb in
Rome, and an IRA shoot-out in Liverpool, but this
time his luck had evaporated.

So had somebody else's. By the time the first police
cars arrived, Heron had gone.

71

A platoon of SAS men was drilling outside, jumping
to the commands of a hard-bitten, suntanned lieutenant. In their berets, camouflage smocks, and jump
boots, they looked as tough as hell.

Heron watched them through the window from the
room with the photographs on the wall.

"So," said Ross, "been doing a bit of freelancing,
have we?"

Heron was tired. Four hours ago he'd been standing in the Kaiserstrasse in Frankfurt. A lot had happened since then.

"I'm sorry about Bowler," he said quietly.

Ross ignored that. "What were you doing in Heidelberg? Playing the Third Man?"

"Doing my little bit as your pet Judas goat," said Heron. "Making it look good."

"The bloke with the briefcase, who the hell was he?"

"Maybe you ought to ask your American pals," said Heron. "Aren't they in on it? Seltzer laid it on. He thought it was rather neat, for the benefit of anyone who might be gawping."

"He never told me," grumbled Ross. "You led us a hell of a dance." He looked at the briefcase lying on the desk. "What was in it, anyway?"

"This," said Heron. He snapped it open and took out a folder. From that he extracted a blank sheet of paper.

"The Goering Testament," he said.

"Oh, very clever," snarled Ross.

Heron glanced over to the table where Bowler had been doing his crossword the last time he had been at the barracks. Now the chair was empty.

"Who was after me?" he asked.

"We'll know soon enough," grunted Ross. "Any number of people seem to have you marked down. What happened to your girl friend, by the way?"

Of course, they'd been watching that little hotel. Heron wondered how they had reacted when Lotte swept out in the middle of the night.

"Lovers' tiff, was it?" said Ross, as if he had read his thoughts.

"Tell me," asked Heron slowly, "is she one of your people?"

"Sometimes you aggravate me, Harry," said Ross. "What's the point of asking me? If she was, I wouldn't tell you. If I say she isn't, you won't believe me.

Supposing she's just Miss Ace Girl Reporter after a big story?"

"I wouldn't believe that, either," said Heron.

"Exactly," purred Ross. Suddenly he became quite friendly. "I'm sorry, old chap. We *are* taking a bit of a liberty with you, aren't we? I think we really ought to put you on the payroll, don't you?"

"I thought I was," said Heron.

Ross stiffened.

"You ever considered that? Maybe I know more about you than you know about me. Maybe it's you who's being set up. Maybe we're working for the same boss."

The worried look in Ross's eyes was enough reward for Heron. God, he thought, they're so bloody insecure in their double-dealings and counterbluffs that they're really afraid of their own shadow. Supposing I was right, eh?

"Very amusing," said Ross, composed again. The sudden anxiety had passed. "But now let's talk business."

Outside, on the parade ground, a sharp command rang out, and the SAS troop marched off, their jump boots crunching on the concrete in unison.

"I want you to deliver the Goering Testament to them," announced Ross.

"You what?"

"You are to give it to them, understand?"

Heron suddenly felt curiously relaxed. At last he was going over the top, into no man's land.

"You've got it, then?"

"Of course."

"I see." He reached over to Ross's cigarette case. "May I?"

"Please."

Heron lit the Turkish cigarette. "And then?"

"That's all. The rest is our business."

Heron exhaled. "Back in Korea, one of our blokes was ordered by an intelligence bod to nip over to the other side, surrender, pose as a defector, and then return with any information he had picked up. It was so secret nobody else knew. Nothing on paper, of course. Well, my pal did as he was ordered. On his way back he was caught by one of our patrols and charged with being a traitor. He said, 'Don't be silly, I'm acting on orders from so-and-so. He will bear out that I was on an undercover mission.' The only trouble was that so-and-so had in the meantime stepped on a land mine and got blown to bits."

"Really? What happened?"

"My pal got executed by a firing squad."

"How very unfortunate for him," said Ross. "But I can assure you that you'll be perfectly safe. We'll look after you. We won't let anything happen to you, I promise."

Heron shook his head. "No. I want to know what the object of the exercise is."

"What was the object of the Trojan horse, Harry?" asked Ross.

"To get inside."

"And once inside, the soldiers took over."

Heron shook his head. "You know what you ought to do, Ross? Open a bloody zoo. Full of Judas goats and Trojan horses. You'd have a place all to yourself. In the reptile house."

Ross's expression didn't flicker. "Bring them the Goering Testament, Harry, and they'll open their doors to you. And that will help us find out . . ." He was silent.

"Yes?" prompted Heron.

"What you want to find out, too," added Ross quietly.

"All right," said Heron at last. "Where is it?"

Ross went over to a safe in the corner. He fiddled with the combination and then swung the door open. He produced a small envelope from a shelf in the safe. He held it up.

"Here it is, Harry."

"*That?*" said Heron. "The hell it is."

"Open it," said Ross, and gave him the envelope.

It wasn't even sealed. Heron opened the flap and pulled out a small ticket. A cloakroom ticket for the Dorchester Hotel.

"*That's* what you'll give them," said Ross. "When they collect that, they've got the Goering Testament."

Heron was still holding the ticket.

"Gives you a chance to become rich, Harry. Gives us a chance to stick with whoever collects it, and to get you out if things go wrong at your end. It'll lead us to them, and wherever you are you'll be safe."

"Sounds so pat," said Heron. "Like Dunkirk."

"You have no choice," purred Ross. "If you don't do this, you know we'll put you inside."

Heron started to say something, but Ross went on. "Somebody can always dig up the past, can't they? Bribery, corruption. Something like that." His tone was very mild.

"Your connections with Shayler, for instance. The way you sometimes got big scoops. I dare say the Director of Public Prosecutions could always be persuaded to blow the dust off the file. Or even start a new one." Ross beamed at him. "No, Harry, you really have no get-out at all."

Ross had two phones on his desk, a black one and a green one. Now he reached over and pushed the black one in front of Heron.

"Go on," he instructed. "Call Defoe. Tell him you've brought it back from Germany. Tell him."

Put your neck in the noose, an inner voice said to Heron. Do it, because you know you have to, said another. Do it, because if you don't, you know you're dead, anyway.

"That's right, I told you you've got no choice, Harry," said Ross softly. "You're in it too deep."

Heron dialed the number while Ross, across the desk, sat there smiling.

"Yes, I've just come back," said Heron on the

phone, and Ross hung on his every word. "And I think I've got something that will interest you very much." He paused. "Yes, indeed. Thank you." He listened for a moment. "Surely. I'd like that."

Slowly he put down the receiver.

"Well?" asked Ross.

"He knew I'd been over to Germany. I never told him, but he knew."

"Of course."

"You heard me. I told him I've got it."

"And what did he say?"

Heron stared at the phone thoughtfully. "He invited me to dinner."

Ross smiled. "Excellent. Don't forget your cloakroom ticket."

"What exactly is the cloakroom?" asked Heron, and he knew the answer was the one he wouldn't expect.

72

"Seamus Corrigan?" said Ross incredulously. "The motorcyclist? An IRA hit man?" He read the paragraph in the police report again, as if he didn't trust his eyes. "IRA. Are you sure?"

Hood, sitting opposite him, nodded. He relished the fact that Ross couldn't deny the plodders were one up on his lot.

"Provos. Definitely. One of their assassination experts. Now safely back in Dublin."

"And he's the man who shot Bowler?"

"He was after Heron, of course. Or, rather, what Heron carried."

"Nonsense. The IRA couldn't care less."

"They were simply paying back some interest on a debt," said Hood. "You know who supplies their best firepower. Their guns and bombs."

"Colonel Qaddafi," said Ross bitterly.

"But he's not the only one, is he?" said Hood smugly. "There's the Russians. They do their share. Sometimes they want something in return. Like having somebody dealt with. Makes it more convenient, anyway, if it's an IRA job. Doesn't put the finger on them."

Not bad, Hood, thought Ross, but he kept it to himself.

"You remember the bomb that went off in the hotel? In Mayfair?" Hood went on. "Everybody thought it was the Irish. Well, maybe it was, but it was a guy who was having a meet with one of our people in the lobby they were after. At the request of their Soviet suppliers."

Ross put down the thin folder. He was unhappy.

"Shilenko wouldn't do such a thing," he said. "He's in on it with us, up to a point."

Hood smiled, but kept it discreet.

"Maybe it wasn't Shilenko. Maybe somebody went over his head," mused Ross.

"Eh?"

"Their station in Bonn has been rather busy lately."

"And?"

"Rognov, their man there, had a tail on Heron . . ."

"There you are," said Hood. "Anyway, it was a Provo job, and I bet you a month's salary those are the people who asked them to do it."

"Maybe you're right." Ross's department never admitted anybody else could be correct in his deductions. The "maybe" was as far as he would go.

"And how's Heron?" asked Hood. His tone indicated his hostility.

"It's all going nicely," said Ross. "I think," he added as an afterthought.

"How can you people rely on such a man?" Hood seemed perplexed. "How can you trust him?"

"We don't rely on people and we don't trust them," said Ross softly. "We use them."

"Well," sighed Hood, "all I can say is that the gulf between Special Branch and your service . . ."

". . . is sometimes very wide. I know."

There was a knock, and a mousy little girl in thick patterned stockings entered. They made her legs even more unattractive than they really were.

"You're not forgetting the deputy director's meeting, are you, sir?" she reminded Ross.

"I'll be there right away," said Ross.

Hood was curious. "New secretary?"

"Just a stand-in. Miss Foley's taken a few days' leave. A sick aunt or something."

Ross smiled to himself.

73

"The memory," said Defoe, holding the crystal wineglass upright in his steel claw.

The others in the sitting room rose with him. So did Heron. He knew he was expected to, like a stranger in a foreign country who is required to stand for the local anthem.

As they all drank, Heron's eyes moved from one to the other: Vanessa, soignée in a black Dior dress, with just one sparkling diamond brooch on her left shoulder; the American, Sterling Hodgman. "I'm sure you've come across his work," Defoe had said, introducing him.

And the German, Klaus Mahler. Laugh lines around the mouth, a receding forehead, penetrating gray eyes, a wedding ring on one finger. "An old friend," explained Defoe. "In shipbuilding."

Then he introduced Heron to them:

"There you have him. In the flesh. My new right hand."

Heron glanced at Vanessa, but her husband's choice of phrase did not seem to have been noted.

Heron felt nervous. He had been ever since he arrived for the dinner. Nobody had said anything about the Testament. They didn't even ask him why he had come empty-handed, no briefcase, no envelope, no folder.

It had been a good meal, well cooked and beautifully served on a tastefully laid table. The centerpiece in the dining room had not surprised him: a large white ceramic bowl. Allach porcelain, with the clean, pure lines that was the stamp of the SS china. Its display there in front of him this time had seemed to be a more sinister statement. Only those high up ever got their hands on it: we have the connection, Heron.

"You were in the services, of course, after the war, weren't you?" Defoe suddenly asked. "Korea?"

It was no question, really, for the answer was already supplied. Defoe was well informed.

"What outfit were you in?" asked the leathery American. They were all looking at him.

"Intelligence," said Heron. "Sort of."

"So," said Defoe, glancing around the company. "We have all got something in common. We've all been in the military in our time."

"On different sides, of course," said Mahler, and smiled.

Still they hadn't shown any curiosity about the Testament. How he had acquired it, where it was, when he'd produce it, who had had it . . .

"We particularly thought you'd be interested to meet our two friends," said Vanessa, pouring coffee out of a silver Georgian pot. She had dismissed the house-boy. "They both knew Hermann Goering. They've come over specially."

"Hodg was a colonel in the Seventh Army," said Defoe, like a relay runner picking up the baton from her. "And Herr Mahler—"

"I was only a major," said the German.

"In the army?"

"Not quite, Mr. Heron. A Sturmbannfuehrer in the Waffen SS. We were all very involved with Goering."

"Which is why they were rather keen to meet you, too," said Vanessa gently. "Face to face."

Defoe's right steel claw rested on the arm of his chair, by the coffee cup. His eyes were like a spectator's at Wimbledon, switching from player to player.

"I got to know him very well," said Hodgman. "Very well, indeed. Everything about him. Even his handwriting."

The light signal in Heron's brain was flashing caution. He turned to Mahler. "And you? How well did you know him?"

"I was going to shoot him," said Mahler. "You sometimes get to know a lot about a man you're going to execute."

"Execute Goering? *You?*"

"Sure. It was *Götterdämmerung* in the bunker. Berlin stood in flames. Goering had invoked the decree of nineteen forty-one, making him Fuehrer if Hitler was out of action. The deadline was midnight on April twenty-third, nineteen forty-five. We were the nearest SS unit in Bavaria. Martin Bormann ordered us by radio to arrest Goering, strip him of his rank, and execute him." He shook his head. "For high treason, would you believe it?"

"When all the while he was trying to save Germany," cut in Hodgman. "The Reich Marshal was already communicating with Truman, with Churchill, with Eisenhower. He was thinking of the future. Of today. The great alliance. The West against the East.

Civilization against barbarism. Christianity against the heathen."

Heron raised his eyebrows.

"But they didn't want to know," he suggested, sipping his coffee.

"Oh, yes, they did." Defoe was sitting upright, his blue eyes shining. "That's where you're so wrong. I told you, we have to take a new look at history."

"There was already an intermediary who had made contact. Who was the go-between. A hot line from that little toy village in Bavaria to the top. The very top." He looked across at Hodgman. "Wasn't there?"

The American smiled, and there was no need for him to say anything else.

"Hodg was a G-Two bird in the Seventh Army," said Defoe. "He's very modest, but he nearly saved Europe. He had the vision his superiors lacked. He smoothed the way."

"Instead of putting him in front of a firing squad, I got Goering through to the American lines. To him." Mahler smiled at Hodgman. "Berlin was finished. Goering convinced me Germany's only hope lay with him. And you know what happened? He was absolutely right. They welcomed him like an ally, as he knew they would."

"He was treated like the head of state, the full red-carpet bit," recalled Hodgman. "VIP treatment. Champagne. Guard of Honor. The groundwork had paid off. They were ready for him."

"I don't believe it," said Heron.

"Those generals knew where our future lay, Harry," declared Defoe. "They were men of vision. But they were betrayed. If only the military had been allowed its way. If only the generals . . ."

"What generals?"

"The big brass, Harry. Yes, even the four stars." Hodgman banged his knee. "Almost to the goddamn top, it was all set. The great alliance. The linkup of the West. Oh, sure, Germany was beaten, but she had millions of fighting men left, still armed, and, combined with the Allies, she would have been unbeatable. We could have finished the Russians. That's what Goering offered us. If we hadn't all been stabbed in the back. You realize what that would have meant? No East Germany. No divided Berlin. No Warsaw Pact. No Red invasion of Hungary and Czechoslovakia. The map of Europe would have looked quite different."

"Why are you telling me this?" asked Heron. "Why all this?"

"Because we want the world to know." Defoe's voice was intense. "Because Europe has a right to know how it was betrayed. Because somebody has to tell the truth . . ."

"The traitor was Eisenhower," Hodgman almost spat. "Goering was arrested. I couldn't believe it. He couldn't. None of us could. The man was offering us a unted Europe, an invincible alliance of the West, and instead, they carted him off to the ashcan. He was put in solitary in the Palace Hotel in Monsdorf. Over in Luxembourg. Out of the way, a prisoner, incommunicado."

"And that's where Colin Fennerman first met him," added Heron.

"Exactly," said Defoe. And they all seemed to relax suddenly.

"He wasn't the first British officer to purloin something that didn't belong to him, Mr. Heron," said Vanessa. Until now she had sat quietly, listening to them.

" 'Steal,' you mean, my dear. 'Purloin' is far too genteel." Defoe reached over, smiling, and brushed her cheek gently with what should have been his hand. She did not flinch, and a grisly thought crossed Heron's mind. She was an attractive woman, a woman with all the attributes of sensuality—a firm body, well-formed breasts, inviting hips—a woman who would be good in bed and would desire a man to be the same. He suddenly had a hideous vision of Defoe and her, both naked, his steel claws moving along her body . . .

Or did he unscrew his pincers and try to feel her with . . . what? His stumps.

There she sat across from him, elegant, desirable, and for a moment Heron was nauseated, almost ashamed of his thoughts as he visualized her body under that chic, expensive dress.

". . . if a field marshal can do it, why not a captain, eh, Mr. Heron?" came Mahler's voice.

"Oh?" said Heron vaguely.

"He means Montgomery, Harry," said Defoe. "After all, he set the example. He pinched the German army's surrender document, didn't he? Spirited it away at Lüneburg Heath under everybody's nose."

"I think there were those who thought he might have a few other interesting documents hidden away," added Vanessa. "Perhaps that's why burglars were so interested in Monty's house in the sixties."

Defoe tapped the coffee table impatiently. "What we're trying to say, Harry, is that Fennerman stole the Testament the night of the executions at Nuremberg. He'd been one of the official interrogators, and he was there as a witness."

"No." Heron's voice was firm. "You're wrong," he said. "You're all wrong."

Later, reflecting on it, he recalled that Vanessa had a faint smile on her face. The others just stared at him.

"That wasn't Goering's Testament," said Heron.

"Go on, Harry." Defoe's tone was silky, but the eyes of the three men were as cold as those of the man-eaters he had seen in the zoo.

"Everybody's been chasing the wrong ghost," said Heron. "You all made a big mistake."

"That sounds intriguing," murmured Vanessa. She looked at the others, slightly amused. "Mr. Heron is a character, wouldn't you say?"

"Tell us our mistake," demanded Mahler.

"It's not a piece of paper you're after. It's a tape recording. Made by Goering."

Heron picked up his cup and started to take a sip of the coffee that was left. He had drunk most of it, but the last mouthful had turned cold.

They all started to say something, but Defoe silenced them with a wave of his steel claw.

"That's not very clever," he said. "In fact, it's slovenly. Your staff work is bad, my friend. Tape recordings in the war? There were no tape recorders. Not then."

"You tell them," said Heron, and looked at Mahler.

Mahler nodded, eyeing Heron. "Maybe his staff work is very good. You see, *we* had tape recorders. We had perfected them. They were called—"

"Magnetofon," interrupted Heron. "And they were already being used by German government agencies."

They were silent. Then Defoe asked, "And when did Goering record this, this Testament?"

"In May nineteen forty-five. In the ashcan. Fennerman used a German recorder. He was supposed to interrogate Goering. He taped most of it. This was one reel he kept. Goering's call to the future. Goering's message for today."

"In his own voice?" Mahler leaned forward.

"In his own voice. The voice you know. The voice no one can forge."

"And you have that tape?" asked Vanessa.

"I have that tape," said Heron.

"Ah," exploded Defoe. "So. We were right all along. You knew where Fennerman had it. He tried to double-deal everybody, but you knew where it was."

Heron's grin was twisted. "You could say I sort of inherited it."

"One might almost think you killed him," said Vanessa.

"The perfect motive, definitely," said Defoe. "Perhaps he also dealt with Madek. One partner less to share with." He waited expectantly. "Well, Harry?"

You bastards, thought Heron. Who are you trying to play games with?

"I can only quote a friend of mine," he said aloud instead. "You wouldn't expect me to say yes if I had, and if I said I hadn't, you wouldn't believe me. Would you?"

Defoe's face was blank.

"Mr. Heron," said Mahler quietly, "I would like to hear this tape."

"Naturally," said Heron.

"Well?"

Heron cleared his throat. "First, we have a little business to discuss."

"Of course," said Defoe. "If you'll excuse us." He rose. "This way, Harry."

The other three were left sitting as Defoe opened the door for Heron. They did not say a word, but Heron knew their cold eyes followed him all the way.

74

Defoe took Heron to the library where they had first met, and indicated the same armchair. By its side stood a suitcase.

"What do you make of us, Harry?" he asked conversationally.

Heron shrugged. "Does it matter? We both want something from each other, that's what counts."

"Of course," replied Defoe. "But you could be on the winning side, you know. The future belongs to people who think like us."

" 'Tomorrow the world,' " said Heron dryly.

"Well, something's got to be done. Look at what's happened to the world. To this country. To London. Sleazy. Porn shops. Dirty films. Eastern bazaars. Riots. Human dungheaps. Drugs and prostitution. The very air smells dirty. Is that what I fought for, what I gave these for?" He held up his claws.

"There are other things," said Heron.

"Oh, yes. The brave new world. Human computers, walking automatons, with no control over or consciousness for their actions. Terrorists holding nations to ransom. The cult of the illiterate. Cynical politicians manipulating the mockery they call democracy. Subversives undermining our culture, our heritage. Mob rule. Trade Union blackmail. Can you deny it?"

"I thought we were going to talk business," said Heron.

Defoe smiled coldly. "Practical as always. All right. Open that." He indicated the suitcase.

Heron got up, laid the suitcase flat, snapped the lock. The lid swung back. The contents were covered with a sheet of newspaper. Underneath, neatly laid out in rows, were bundles of banknotes.

"You can count 'em if you want to," said Defoe. "You'll find there are two layers. Each bundle is fifty twenty-pound notes. Do count them, please."

"I'll take your word," said Heron.

"Forty thousand pounds," said Defoe. "All for you." Heron whistled.

"Well, you didn't think we imagined you were doing all this for love?" said Defoe a little bitterly. "We know we have to pay the right price for the right things."

Unexpectedly, Heron yawned. He was tired.

"Of course, if you prefer, you can have it in dollars, or Swiss francs, or any other currency you care for."

"Or gold?" asked Heron.

"Certainly."

Heron sat down in the armchair. He had left the

suitcase open, and now he stared at its contents. He had never seen so much money.

"Now, your turn," said Defoe.

Heron took out his wallet, extracted the cloakroom ticket, and handed it over.

"It's at the Dorchester," he said. "You can collect it with this."

He felt very peaceful, almost languid.

Defoe's claw was holding the ticket.

"Really?" he said. "The Dorchester? Just like that?"

"It's a little package." Heron was very comfortable in the armchair. "The tape's inside. Just give it to the attendant."

"I see." The blue eyes were staring at him.

"Well," said Heron, "you didn't bloody well expect me to bring it along, did you? Not without first having my money?"

"No," said Defoe. "I didn't expect that."

"So there you are." He was growing uneasy. "It's all fixed."

"Absolutely." Defoe nodded amiably. "But, of course, you don't expect us to let you disappear until we have the goods, either, do you?"

"If I have an . . . an accident, a friend of mine has a letter," said Heron. "It gets posted to Scotland Yard. You follow?"

Defoe put down the cloakroom ticket. On top of it he placed a glass ashtray.

"Please, Harry," he said, pained. "Nobody's going to have an accident. You simply will enjoy some more of Vanessa's hospitality until we have the tape. Then you take the suitcase and enjoy yourself."

Heron got to his feet. He looked at the curtains, heavy damask, from ceiling to floor.

"Do you mind if I open a window?" he asked wearily. "It's rather hot in here."

"I wouldn't worry," said Defoe. He was smiling at Heron. "And don't be nervous. Chlorpromazine will do you no harm at all. You'll just have a good night's rest."

Heron stood rock-still.

"A little addition to your coffee . . ."

Heron screwed up his eyes.

"It'll just loosen you up. We pick up the package in the morning, and then off you go."

Heron held on to the armchair.

"What's that stuff?" he asked, and yawned again.

"The specialists used to give something like it to important POWs. During interrogation. It used to be chloral hydrate. The other side believed in potassium bromide. You've had the aristocrat of them all. It simply destroys the desire to be aggressive. Makes you very cooperative."

Defoe was beside him now. "Relax, Harry. We never double-cross anybody, unlike some people. You're quite safe."

But Heron slid back into the armchair, his head lolling.

"They will know . . ." he mumbled. ". . . letter . . . Scotland Yard . . ."

"Don't worry about Scotland Yard," said Defoe. His pincer snapped up the ticket. "Don't worry about anything."

He closed the door gently, but Heron never heard him.

75

The man with the rolled umbrella entered the lobby of the Dorchester Hotel through the swinging doors and strolled toward the tea lounge. If he was due to meet somebody, he didn't appear to find them, and if they were already there, no one got up to greet him.

He turned right, walked over to the news agency teleprinter near the bank of telephones, and began reading its screeds hanging at the side. Then he strolled slowly past the reception desk, over to the newsstand, where he looked at the books on display.

The man certainly wasn't in a hurry, but his eyes—trained, alert eyes—scrutinized everyone and everything.

He crossed to the little flower shop and sniffed the roses appreciatively.

"Beautiful," he said to the girl florist. She was busily making up a corsage. "I grow my own, but these are almost as beautiful as mine."

"Would you like some?" she asked.

"Some other time, my dear," said the man. He took one more glance around the entrance hall and then walked into the cloakroom.

"I've come for my package," he said, handing the attendant a ticket.

"Thank you, sir," said the attendant, and then, looking at the ticket, muttered to himself, as if he were in danger of forgetting, "One-nine-four."

He emerged with a small, square packet wrapped in brown paper.

"Here you are, sir. One-nine-four. Been here since yesterday."

"Yes," said Shayler. "Somebody left it here for me. Thank you."

He took the package, handing the attendant a pound note.

"Thank you, sir," said the attendant gratefully. His tone indicated that there were at least a few gentlemen left.

Shayler walked out of the cloakroom, and the attendant made sure no one else was around. Then he produced a small walkie-talkie.

"Oscar to Zulu," he said.

"Zulu receiving," crackled the walkie-talkie back at him.

"Your party leaving now with package".

"Thank you, Oscar."

The attendant switched off his walkie-talkie. In his years with Special Branch he had been a milkman, a plumber, a Mormon missionary canvassing door-to-door, and even a uniformed traffic cop, but this was the first time he had ever had to look after the cloakroom of the Dorchester.

In the radio car parked across from the main entrance of the hotel, Hood watched the man come out and walk down the front steps toward Park Lane.

"Shayler!" he cried. "You see him? Shayler!"

"Of course," said Ross unemotionally. He was sitting beside Hood, smoking one of his Turkish cigarettes.

Hood spoke into his walkie-talkie. "Zulu to all units."

In various parts of Park Lane, half a dozen walkie-talkies received the alert.

"Party has left the hotel, is now proceeding south along Park Lane. Proceed to follow."

"Forget that," said Ross sharply.

Hood stared at him, baffled.

"I said, call them off," snarled Ross.

"But . . ."

"Damn it, Hood, you're under our orders," snapped Ross.

Frowning, Hood called into his walkie-talkie:

"Zulu to all units. Cancel. Repeat, cancel."

Then he turned to Ross, furious. "What the hell is going on? He'll lead us to Heron."

"Who cares about Heron?" said Ross.

"The instructions are—"

"Forget the instructions," said Ross. "We've got what we want."

"And Heron?"

Ross shrugged.

"If we don't get to him . . ." Hood began.

"Damn it," said Ross, "I thought you didn't like the son of a bitch. What are you getting so worked up for?"

"I don't know what you lot are up to, but if he's stuck with that bunch, he's had it." Hood was worried. "We don't even know where they've taken him."

"That's tough," said Ross.

"I'll have to make a report."

"And I'll tear it up."

Hood glowered at him. "Where now?"

The driver in front, an impassive Special Branch constable, waited for instructions.

"Nowhere," said Ross, and got out of the car. He slammed the door and didn't look back once at Hood.

"Funny people, that lot, aren't they, sir?" volunteered the driver, greatly daring.

"There's nothing funny about them," grated Hood. "Nothing funny at all, I assure you."

He never thought the day would come when he'd feel sorry for Heron.

But it had.

76

"Are you sure the line is working?" Lotte asked the operator.

"Yes," said the operator patiently. "The phone's in order. Why don't you try later?"

But she had already tried to call Heron three times. At the Soho number. And at his bed-sitter. Each time the phone rang but no one picked up the receiver at the other end.

As a woman, she had sworn to herself that she would never call that bastard again. Not after what he had said to her in that lousy German hotel room. That night she had finished it between them, she told herself, and almost believed it.

But there was the other Lotte, the professional. Feelings came second. Heron wasn't around, and that was what mattered. He had faded into thin air, and she had to know what had happened to him. It was her job, after all.

Previously, of course, there had been days, weeks, when they had no contact, but that was when he hadn't been so important. If a pawn could be important . . .

She had taken a taxi around to Ashfield Gardens and rung his bell, but he wasn't there. She had climbed the steps of the pied-à-terre in the cul-de-sac off Wardour Street, but this door, newly repaired, was locked. The girl who had taken Kelly's place upstairs didn't know anything.

"Never seen him," she told Lotte, wondering what

this female wanted. Well-dressed women didn't visit the premises much.

Lotte phoned again later, but again there was no reply. He still wasn't around. Maybe it was her conditioning, or just feminine intuition, but she knew something was wrong. Heron was in danger.

And although she hated herself for it, Lotte cared.

77

He stared up at the wooden ceiling. It puzzled him. He couldn't place it. It could belong to a Russian dacha, a hunting cabin in the woods of East Prussia, a crofter's hut in the Highlands, a tree feller's shack in a forest . . .

"You've had a good sleep, Mr. Heron," said Vanessa.

His eyes swung around. She was sitting on a stool, contemplating him. She wore no chic Dior dress, but a sweater and slacks. She was smoking a cigarette, and her hair, usually so carefully coiffured, hung loose. It made her look wilder, almost rapacious.

Heron felt stiff; he was lying on a blanket on the floor, and his back ached.

"Sorry it's so primitive," said Vanessa. "We haven't had this place properly furnished so far."

Slowly he got to his feet. His mouth was dry, and his hand felt the stubble of his unshaven chin.

Now he was aware of his surroundings. They were bare, wooden walls, wooden floors, a window through which he could see trees, a kitchen table, a couple of stools.

"Are you cold?" she asked. "I suppose we could put

a paraffin heater in here, but they're so dangerous, I always think."

"What is this?" he asked. "What the hell am I doing here?"

"You're on the estate," she replied.

"What estate?"

"In the country," she said, as if that explained it.

"And I suppose this is the manor house?" he said, gesturing at the bare walls.

"As a matter of fact, I think it was a gamekeeper's hut once. It's fallen into disuse, I'm afraid."

"Why am I here?" he demanded.

She dropped her cigarette and crushed it with her booted foot.

"We're a little tight for space up at the house," she said coolly. "But then, you've got privacy."

Heron stretched his arms. "Thanks a lot," he said dryly.

She stood up. "You're free to come and go," she said.

"How kind." His tone was acid.

"As long as you stay within the grounds," she added. She came closer. "It won't be for long, Mr. Heron. As soon as everything is . . . is in order, you can be on your way."

I wish it were going to be that simple, thought Heron. I only hope Ross can get his Judas goat out of this little situation before the tiger feels hungry.

"Mrs. Defoe—" Heron began, but she cut him short.

"My name is Vanessa," she said, "and I think I'm going to call you Harry." She put a hand on his arm. "You don't mind, do you, Harry?"

She was very close to him now, and her eyes stared into his, unblinking.

"I don't mind," said Heron.

"Good."

Suddenly she was kissing him, full on the lips. She didn't seem to mind the stubble on his chin. Her eyes were shut, and she kissed him long and hard. Then she stepped back.

"You're not very demonstrative, Harry," she said, "are you? That was rather one-sided, wasn't it?" She looked at him mockingly. "What's the matter? Have you taken a vow or something?"

He grabbed her and kissed her savagely. The desire was rising in him, pure, raw desire to have this haughty bitch, to take her and make use of her. She responded in the same animal way, arching her body against his, pressing herself to him, fueling his physical demand.

"There," she said a little breathlessly when they broke. "That's better."

Defoe's stumps flashed through his mind, a sudden return of the vision of the steel claws groping, searching, feeling.

"Didn't know you played Lady Chatterley," said Heron brutally. "Gamekeeper's hut and all, eh?"

She struck him across the face, a hard, vicious blow, intended to hurt. And it did. It stung.

Heron hit her, his right palm slapping her cheek. She laughed wildly and flung her arms around him, and kissed him fiercely. He felt her teeth on his lips, and she clung to him. Then, almost violently, she pushed him away. In a quick movement she tore off the sweater and stood facing him, her breasts bare.

"Take your things off," she commanded, and started to unzip her slacks.

They lay on the blanket on the floor, and she hissed, "Stroke me, seek me . . . hands . . . your hands."

Impatiently she grabbed his hand and led it down her body, guiding it, making it explore where she wanted him to feel. Suddenly the desire drained out of Heron, and he felt as if he were indulging in some ugly ritual act. She took hold of his other hand and pressed it to her breast.

"Please," she moaned. "Please. Feel me. Feel me everywhere. Please."

Afterward they lay silently, and then Vanessa got

to her feet. Without a look at him, she dressed, slipped on her sweater. He still lay on the rug, watching her.

"You needn't stay here," she said coldly. "Why don't you go for a walk? Take a look around. You might see some interesting things."

"I already have," said Heron. "Right here."

Her lips curled.

"As far as I am concerned, Mr. Heron, your useful functions are very limited. When you've finished your business with my husband, you won't even be remembered." Her eyes dismissed him. "But please make yourself at home, meanwhile."

She opened the door of the hut and went out without another glance at him.

78

Heron found the path among the trees and started following it. He had been wandering around in the woods for some time, trying to find his directions, seeking a way that would lead to the outside. The time was near, he knew, when he would have to get out, fast.

Already it was growing dark, and all that he had found out so far was that it was a huge estate, most of is still unexplored by him. In the woods the rest of the world seemed remote and cut off. He hadn't even heard the sound of a distant train. He was in a sprawling, isolated place that seemed to stretch endlessly to every point of the compass.

But somewhere there must be a frontier. A wall. A fence. A gateway to the outside. What worried him was how confident they were that he couldn't get out. He had left the hut and started roaming, and no one seemed to care. He had been left to himself, to walk where he wanted, and so far he hadn't seen a soul.

He had tried to figure out the geographical location. But he had no clues to help him. He had been out cold during the journey here. He had no idea how long the drive from London had taken. He had never had the chance to see a signpost, a landmark that might help him pinpoint this place.

It stretched for hundreds of acres, that was for sure, but where were they? Somewhere in East Anglia? Or Oxfordshire? North? South? It was a private kingdom, he reckoned, on which trespassers were not welcome.

The path was narrow, and a couple of times he had to duck overhanging branches, but something must lie at the end of it.

Suddenly, in front of him, stood three men. Two—youngish, fair-haired fellows—wore incongruously short pants and military-style shirts. They were in their twenties, athletic-looking types, and one of them was carrying a shotgun.

The third figure was familiar to Heron. He had last seen the man with the glass eye at the Stuttgart airport.

"You're going the wrong way," said the fellow with the shotgun. He was courteous, like someone trying to help a lost pedestrian.

"Hello, friend," said Heron to the man with the glass eye, ignoring the others.

"You heard him," said glass eye. "This isn't the way."

"Where are your pals?" asked Heron.

"If you go back the way you came, you'll be okay," said the man with the shotgun.

"We'll show you, if you like," said glass eye.

They all had badges. The man with the glass eye had his fastened to his leather jacket; the other two had them pinned on their ties. Black ties on gray shirts.

The badges were round, a white arrowhead on a red background.

The trio formed up around Heron like an escort, and he found himself going back the way he had come.

They trudged through the woods, and the man with the shotgun walked behind Heron. Unexpectedly, the other fair-haired one in shorts said to Heron, "It's so easy to get lost in this place, isn't it?"

It was said in a friendly, conversational way, with no hostility at all.

"It's pretty big," said Heron.

"You can say that again. I'd love to own it."

They crossed a glade, and Heron realized they had branched off somewhere. He was sure he hadn't come this way. Leaning against a tree was another man, in riding boots. He had his arms folded, and out of the top pocket of his shirt peeked a walkie-talkie. When he saw them approach, he gave a nod.

Of course, it had all been deceptive, thought Heron. They had allowed him to roam around because they knew he couldn't get anywhere. Security was tight.

The glass-eyed man had shown no sign of recognition.

"You staying for the whole thing?" he suddenly asked, as if he had read Heron's mind.

"Depends on what's the whole thing," said Heron. He thought he could hear sounds in the distance, like people singing. Then the trees thinned out, and he could see tents. Campfires were burning. People were sitting in circles around the fires, and here and there flags fluttered from poles stuck in the ground.

Then Heron knew that this was the summit.

"You'll be all right now, won't you?" said the man with the shotgun.

They left him standing, and vanished among the trees as silently as they had appeared.

No one took any notice of Heron. He sat down on a tree stump.

He heard singing, stirring songs, not openly heard in Europe any more, coming from the throats of many nationalities. Songs that had once been the marching tunes of millions.

So, he thought, here they are. In this private, secluded corner of England, hidden from outsiders, on a vast estate where strangers were not welcome.

Most of the people around him wore uniforms, all kinds of uniforms. Some had scarlet armbands with white circles and twisted black crosses. Others sported black shirts, Sam Browne belts, and smartly creased trousers. There were young men in shorts, like the ones who had picked him up, and many leather jackets, like the glass-eyed man wore.

People passed Heron, ignoring him, speaking in French and Italian, German and Flemish. He heard the dialect of Yorkshire and the drawl of Georgia. They were enjoying themselves. It's like a sick Boy Scout camp, thought Heron. Jolly open-air fun.

There were plenty of women, young and middle-aged, in sensible skirts and plain blouses. Some of them had berets. They strode about confidently in their flat-heeled shoes, and many hummed the catchy tunes. The Horst Wessel song. Even "Lili Marlene" and "Rule Britannia" were on the song sheet.

"Your attention, please," commanded a tinny, disembodied voice. It came from loudspeakers rigged up among the trees. "Supper will be served in the mess tent at nine."

In the center of the camp stood a small wooden platform with a microphone.

"One, two, three," a man tested, and many of the campers laughed.

Heron saw Defoe coming toward him. He was smiling.

"Ah, there you are," he said. "Enjoying yourself?" He clapped him on the back with one of his steel claws. "Vanessa tells me you had a good rest." He followed the direction of Heron's look. "It's a great gathering, isn't it? Good company, fresh air, good food, companionship."

A man in a pince-nez was at the microphone making some kind of speech, and in between listening to Defoe, Heron caught snatches of it:

". . . they say we will bring in a police state. Let me tell the world, there will be no witch hunts in our Britain—because the climate of our Britain will not be suitable for witches . . ."

There was a roar of applause, and Defoe smiled tolerantly.

". . . we will take a message from here that will help to set the world alight. They will not be able to silence us, and we will not give an inch . . ."

"He's a good speaker," commented Defoe. "Bit of a demagogue, but very effective."

". . . six million Jews is a lie. Our enemies invented genocide. You can't show me a single document with Hitler's signature authorizing it . . ."

"That's historical fact, Harry," said Defoe.

"Yes, I know. All the newsreels are faked," said Heron, but his voice was drowned by more cheering.

Defoe looked at his watch.

"I suppose we ought to be getting back," he said.

"I'd like to wait for the fireworks," said Heron. The speech had finished, and he was looking at a big mound of wood, like a pyre, around which people were gathering.

Another man was at the microphone, and his voice echoed from the loudspeakers:

"Ladies and gentlemen, Ingrid has come all the way from Sweden with her group." He smiled down at a pretty blonde, her hair in plaits, who was holding a torch. "Give her a big hand."

They cheered, and Ingrid smiled. She ran forward and put the blazing torch to the pyre. Flames began to lick the wood.

"Right," said the man at the microphone. "Make sure it's well alight, and then it's all yours."

Out of the loudspeakers came military music, and in front of the pyre a big crowd had collected. It took Heron a second or two to become aware that most of them were carrying books. Some had two or three volumes, but nearly everybody had at least one book.

The blaze had taken hold of the wood, and the heat was so intense that the throng moved back a little. Then somebody tossed a book into the flames, and soon they were all doing it.

"Pornography, Harry," said Defoe. "Filth. It's a symbolic protest against the poison in our schools and universities and libraries."

People were lining up, patiently waiting their turn, clutching the offerings they were about to throw into the flames.

"You disapprove." Defoe frowned. "You don't have to say anything. I can see it in your expression. But you forget the times we live in. Drastic surgery is needed if the body is to survive."

The blaze was consuming the books with a roar.

"Isn't the written word the most dangerous thing in the world, Harry? Aren't there words that need to be destroyed?"

Heron turned away. "I think you're right. I think you're absolutely right."

Defoe looked surprised. "I thought the mere idea of doing such a thing repelled you."

"Well, maybe it depends on what it is you're destroying."

They started walking away from the camp, back through the trees.

Defoe smiled. "You know, perhaps there's hope for you yet. Perhaps you could one day be one of us." He frowned. "One of us. Or a Marxist."

"Is there any difference?" said Heron.

They passed a clearing where some archery targets were set up on tripods.

"Outdoor games?" asked Heron.

"We have a crossbow championship. It's become a

very popular sport in recent times," said Defoe, and Heron shivered slightly. "You'd be surprised what good shots some of us are now."

They strode on in silence, and then, almost casually, Defoe broke the news.

"By the way, everything's gone splendidly, Harry. We've picked up the package. It's on its way. Aren't you pleased?"

But Heron kept thinking, They're going to make sure I don't leave this place alive. They'd never allow me to see all this, to hear it all, to remember it all, if they thought I'd ever get out. They've already seen to it.

And then he wondered if that was exactly what Ross intended.

79

The film flickered across the screen in short, jerky takes. It showed them arriving at the village railway station, stepping off the trains from London. Driving along the country road to the estate. Sweeping through its entrance. It showed a bus load of them, station wagons filled with them. It showed them walking and driving, all on their way to the same place. It recorded all of them.

Faces, faces, and more faces.

Ross sat in the viewing theater of the guarded building that D-notices made it a security offense to mention. Beside him sat Seltzer; next to him, Geist. They all watched the parade on the screen.

Now and then one of them would call out.

"Jesus," said Seltzer when one face flashed in front of their eyes. "*Him*."

Ross pressed a button and the film froze.

"The Grand Dragon. Big mouth of the Klan. How the hell did he slip through your immigration?" In the dark, Seltzer scrawled a note on his pad. "Spreading his empire, eh?"

The film started again.

"Interesting," murmured Geist at the sight of a man getting off the local train. "He defended one of the Bader-Meinhoff gang. Now look where he is."

It took nearly an hour for the clips to be screened, and at the end of it they had seen scores of faces.

"We've indexed all those we can identify," said Ross when the lights came up, "and believe me, we've come up with some beauties. This time the big ones really came out of the rat holes. They took the bait."

"You got some great camera work there," declared Seltzer approvingly.

"We have good equipment," said Ross modestly. "We rigged up concealed surveillance right down the line. Cameras, the lot. Everybody going in and out of the place had his mug photographed. And look what we've collected."

He glanced at a typewritten list.

"So far, we've identified one Member of Parliament, a TV news commentator, three senior civil servants, a bishop, two City bankers, four trade union bosses, several lawyers, teachers, a serving general." He paused. "Even a member of my own department."

Ross let that sink in.

"What did you say?" gasped Seltzer. "One of your own people?"

"That'll be taken care of," Ross assured him. "In our own time. The point is, they've shown themselves. They never gathered with the rank and file like this before, all together. This time they came like the proverbial bees to honey, as we hoped."

"We got a few there, too," said Seltzer. "Wait till our people see these."

Geist just smiled. He'd already telexed Bonn that a load of dynamite was coming their way.

"I guess history repeats itself," Seltzer said reflectively. "It's a new twist on the Apalachin Caper."

"Apalachin?" repeated Geist, puzzled. Ross smiled smugly.

"Back in fifty-seven," explained Seltzer for Geist's benefit. "The FBI wanted a record of all the East Coast Mafioso top brass, but these guys never showed themselves under one roof. So the Bureau rigged a special situation that called for an Extraordinary Mafia Summit. The big shots all gathered at this one country house in upstate New York, and we just kept out of sight, filming each one and taking car numbers. Did we find some surprises! At the end of the day, we had the whole goddamn list."

Ross sniffed. "Really?"

Geist scratched his chin thoughtfully. "Tell me. Are you going to raid the place now that they're all there? Why don't you pull them all in?"

Ross looked shocked. "My dear chap, this is Britain. We can't just walk in on private property. They're not doing anything illegal, are they?" He got out his Turkish cigarettes.

"So," said Geist. "You're going to do nothing."

"We don't need to," said Ross quietly. "From now on, their cards are marked. That's what it's all about."

Geist grunted.

"We have missed a few here and there, but it's a rich harvest, gentlemen," declared Ross. "By the time we've identified the lot, all of us are going to know a hell of a sight more about these characters. The computers will have a busy time."

"And Heron?"

There was dead silence. Seltzer waited for his answer.

"What about Heron?" asked Ross coldly.

"He was your bait, wasn't he? The guy who got them together. Is he still in there?"

"Well?" Ross was expressionless.

"How are you going to get him out? Once they find out the whole darn thing was rigged by you . . ."

Ross shrugged. "That's his problem."

"Christ." Even Seltzer looked shaken.

"Look here," said Ross, "how the hell do I get him out? Order in the troops? I told you, we've got no rights on private property. I'm not going to start making waves. Neither is the department."

"Prevention of Terrorism Act . . ."

"What terrorism?" snarled Ross. "Damn it, man, they're using their democratic rights. It's we who'll get our fingers burned if we burst in there officially. It's a private party, that's all."

"So Heron . . ."

"Heron's on his own," said Ross.

"You mean, he's expendable," murmured Seltzer. Inwardly he thought, Remind me never to turn my back on this lot.

Ross shrugged. "He's been in tough spots before."

"Not, I would venture, as tough as this one," said Geist.

The projectionist, a Royal Signal Corps NCO especially cleared to run such material, had emerged from his booth.

Ross stood up. "I think we'd better get out of here, gentlemen. They need the facilities."

Upstairs in Ross's office, after Geist had gone, Seltzer said, "Hell, it's none of my business, but haven't you just put paid to Heron?"

"Who's Heron?" said Ross. "I never heard of him."

It had become his favorite line. He might even use it to the Director if awkward questions began to be asked.

80

On his way back to Grosvenor Square, Seltzer wondered if Ross was a double-crossing son of a bitch or really hadn't noticed the face on the screen. The camera, concealed near the gates to the estate, had captured him briefly as he drove through. He was alone in the car, and the lodge keeper passed him right in. Then the camera could see no more.

But Seltzer recognized the man with a start, and it put a new angle to the whole setup. Ross had made no comment at all, no indication that he knew who the man was.

"Maybe the bastard hopes I didn't spot the guy," said Seltzer to himself. Then he began to wonder why Ross didn't draw attention to him. After all, he was ready enough with other little choice pieces of information about the people who had been caught by the cameras.

It made Seltzer feel once more how unfair life was. They had thrown all that dirt at the agency, accusing it of being devious, dishonest, cheating, lying, corrupting, and here was Ross's outfit, doing it in spades, and even more nastily. When it came to being devious, the British service's tradition was hard to beat.

By the time his diplomatic car slid to a halt in front of the embassy, Seltzer knew one thing for sure. He had better let Washington know at once that the man with the glass eye was in the middle of that unholy gathering in the fair English countryside.

81

It was a beautiful, stately eighteenth-century mansion, and the big room in which Heron found himself lived up to its grand style. Beyond the French windows stretched the lawn and, in the distance, the woods.

But it was the people in the room who made Heron feel cold. They all looked at him, and none of them smiled.

They're like a hanging jury, he thought, and he knew who the condemned man was. They sat around in chairs, and he knew who they were. Even Miss Foley, whom he had seen so briefly at the Ministry of Defence.

Defoe sat, grim-faced, next to Hodgman. Mahler was smoking from a long cigarette holder, and if he had had jackboots on his crossed legs, the typecasting would have been perfect.

Vanessa stood by the wall, surveying the scene. And next to her was Shayler.

There was also a treasure in the room. A unique, priceless, irreplaceable treasure. The finest collection of Allach porcelain Heron had ever seen. There were commemorative vases of the Nuremberg rallies, ornamental bowls dedicated to the glory of the SS, ceramic statuettes of storm troopers and Wagnerian maidens, helmeted soldiers and Aryan heroes. All handmade by concentration-camp inmates.

On a table in the center was a tape recorder, its cord trailing across the parquet floor to a wall outlet. Already spooled into it was a reel of tape.

"You're a very stupid man, Harry," said Shayler without rancor.

He switched on the tape recorder. Slowly the spool began to revolve. But from the tape there was no sound. Just the faint hiss of blank magnetic tape passing through the pickup.

Shayler switched it off. "We've played it through completely. That's all there is. Nothing. Nothing at all."

"Well, Harry?" said Defoe.

We'll get you out, Ross had promised. Once they've swallowed the bait and been flushed out, we'll get you away from there. All we want is their faces, their identities, their connections. But you'll be all right, Harry, we'll see to that.

The hell you will, thought Heron.

Shayler frowned. "I don't understand what you hoped you'd gain by this. You stood to make a lot of money . . ."

"That was it," said Heron. "I thought I could try a ripoff. I never had the bloody thing, but you were all so convinced and you seemed ready to pay the moon for it, so I thought I'd try it on—"

"Forty thousand pounds for a blank tape?" interrupted Vanessa. "How did you think you'd get away with it, Mr. Heron?"

"It all went wrong," said Heron, thinking, So this is what the Judas goat feels like when the tiger comes in for the kill and the hunter isn't around to shoot him.

"You're quite right," said Defoe. "It's gone very wrong for you. The joke is, we'll find what we're looking for. It'll just take us a little longer."

Mahler uncrossed his legs. "Meanwhile, what do we do with you, Mr. Heron?" he asked genially.

"What you intended all along," snarled Heron, and his hand swept out, knocking the Allach pieces off their stands. Several of them crashed to the parquet floor and smashed.

"No!" cried Vanessa, but Heron again lashed out, and other pieces tumbled down, cracking and breaking, the fragments scattering on the floor. The collection was in ruins.

They stared, disbelieving, rising out of their chairs, coming toward him, but Heron shoved an armchair straight at them. It zoomed across the polished floor on its casters, straight into Shayler and the American, who were rushing toward him, faces twisted.

He had noticed, when he came in, that the French windows were ajar, and now he flung them open and ran onto the lawn, not even looking back. He could hear shouts behind him, but he ran as only a scared man can run who knows that if he's caught . . .

In the room, Defoe was already on the phone.

"He can't get away," he said. "I've told the gate. And as long as he's on the grounds, we'll have him."

He smiled at the others.

"I think we might have some sport now."

82

Deep in the woods, Heron could hear distant sounds of the hunt. Men shouting and even, he thought, the barking of a dog.

Blindly he rushed on, trying to keep hidden, his mouth dry, panting, wildly looking from side to side, trying to work out which way to go.

He did not know how long he had run, but the sounds of pursuit died away, and he began to feel he might yet make it. Perhaps they had lost him. Perhaps they had given up.

He leaned against a tree, gulping in air, recharging himself, trying to think logically. Maybe he shouldn't try to run now. Perhaps the best thing would be to lie doggo, wait until the middle of the night, then creep through the woods in the darkness. That way he might find the outer limits of the estate. A wall, a fence, over which he could escape.

But, for no reason, a growing sense of panic began to overtake him. He glanced around, but the only noise was the rustling of a light wind among the leaves. He felt danger closing in on him, although he could see nothing.

He began to run again, blindly, to shake off a sense of menace he knew was actually a sign of his own panic.

He kept trying to organize his thoughts, to make a plan. But his fear kept telling him, Move, move, don't stand still or they'll catch up with you.

He could continue rushing ahead, hoping it was in a straight direction, praying that he wasn't going around in circles. If only I can keep going straight on, he kept telling himself, I must eventually reach the borders of the estate.

He stood still for a moment, trying to catch a glimpse of the sky through the thick branches, and then something whistled past his head. He heard a thud and stood paralyzed, staring at the crossbow bolt in the tree trunk four inches from him.

From behind some bushes emerged Defoe. He had a crossbow pointed at Heron, and another bolt was already in place. The steel claws clutched the weapon, and the right pincer was around the trigger.

"The trouble is, Harry, that I rather like you," said Defoe. "I just couldn't bring myself to kill you like that. For God's sake, run. Keep running. I don't like shooting sitting ducks." He laughed. "Make a fight of it, man. Give us a bit of a chase."

Another bolt flew through the air. It hit the tree.

"Go on, run, or I'll finish you now!"

Heron swung around and began fleeing into the thick undergrowth. Any moment he expected to feel the impact between his shoulder blades.

He was completely lost now, blundering through the woods, listening for the sounds of pursuit that didn't come, mistaking shadows for enemies.

Then the man with the glass eye stepped in front of him. In his hand, a gun with a silencer.

"All right, Heron," he said. "It's all over."

Heron was breathless, his mind in a whirl. He mouthed something, but no words came out of his dry throat.

"This way," said the man with the glass eye.

"Damn you, finish it," croaked Heron.

"Just follow me," said the man. "We've got to get out of here."

Heron stood rooted to the spot. His mind was going in circles. He wiped blood from his cheek where a branch had ripped it.

"We're friends," said the man. "Mossad."

Major Asher Ben David, of Israeli Intelligence special operations, did not talk a great deal at best. He felt too many words had already been wasted.

"Come on," he ordered.

As Heron stumbled along beside him, trying to fit the pieces together, the glass-eyed man kept looking straight ahead.

They ran through the woods, the major leading and Heron following blindly.

"Only half a mile," said the major.

But at that moment, crackling in the distance like dry twigs, came shots. Three, four, in quick succession.

"Damn," said the major. "Hurry."

They ran faster and then, through the trees, came Lotte, a pistol in her hand. At that moment Heron was too dazed to react. That came later. She was wearing a track suit, her hair tangled, and she called to them, "This way."

"What happened?" asked the major when they caught up with her. "Where are the others?"

"Waiting."

"What was the shooting?"

"A couple of them found us. Rather, we found them." She looked at Heron.

"Are you all right?"

He nodded.

"Come on, then."

Again he heard the sound of men shouting to each other in the distance.

"I'm going ahead," said the major. "You bring him . . ."

He disappeared ahead of them into the bushes.

"You, too?" said Heron. "Mossad?"

"Later," she said.

He hurt all over. Somewhere, he seemed to have done something to his left ankle, and it was agony when he stepped on that foot.

"You go on," he called to Lotte. "I'll catch you up."

"No. There's no time."

"I can't run much," he said. "My foot . . ."

She bit her lip.

"I'll fetch the others," she said. "They'll help you. Try to keep up with me."

She ran ahead and he hobbled on, but soon she was among some thick trees, and he lost sight of her.

"Put your hands up, Mr. Heron," said Vanessa, from behind him. "Turn around and let me look at you."

She too had a crossbow aimed at him, but she also had a thin, ghastly smile, like a beast of prey enjoying the dispatch of its victim.

"Pitiful," she said. "A hunted animal. Wide-eyed. Terrified. And clumsy. It was so easy to trail you. You and that Jewish bitch. I could have finished you both off, but I thought I'd get you alone."

"Runs in the family, doesn't it? Little chats with

the condemned man." He looked at her with loathing.

"The chats are over," Vanessa said, and raised the crossbow. But she never fired it. There was a shot, her mouth dropped open, her eyes widened, and the blood spread across her sweater. She collapsed and lay still.

Lotte looked down at her with contempt.

"The poor man's Valkyrie," she spat. She had emerged from the trees at the back, and there was no pity on her face for the woman she had killed.

The man with the Roman centurion's profile was with her.

"Come on, Ricky," she ordered. "Help him. Let's get out of this Nazi Berchtesgaden."

Ricky said nothing but put his arms around Heron, taking the weight, and supporting him as they staggered the next quarter of a mile.

The glass-eyed major and another man were waiting by a wall, slumped against which was Shayler. Shayler's eyes were blank, and he didn't react when Heron appeared. There was a good reason. A bullet had gone into his forehead.

"He wanted to be awkward," grunted the major. "Now let's go."

And they started to help Heron get up the rope that had been tossed over the wall.

83

"So your Israeli friends got you out," said Ross.

"They did your dirty work for you," grunted Heron. "I'd still be waiting for your lot."

Ross shrugged. "They can bend the rules. They're

quite useful at that sort of thing. They're not really gentlemen, you see."

He poured Heron some more tea. You're a fine one to talk, thought Heron. You really know all about being a gentleman.

"I found it quite piquant, your having a girl friend who's a Mossad agent," said Ross, dipping a digestive biscuit into his tea. "Filthy habit, I'm sorry, but I do like the taste."

You would, reflected Heron.

"The Americans and Bonn knew what it was all about. That we were using the idea of a Goering Testament as a kind of bait to flush out the top *Kameraden*. To get them to the rally. But the Israelis got wind of it and thought it was the real thing. Even got that major of theirs to infiltrate the movement. Beat you up, too, didn't they? No sense of humor, the Jews." Ross shook his head.

"Not about the Nazis," said Heron.

"Oh, I'm sorry. You like the girl. I mustn't say anything nasty about her friends, must I?" Ross could be supercilious at times. "Anyway, isn't it funny? All these years, ever since forty-six, the real article has been safely in the vaults in the U.S., marked 'Top Secret.'"

The sound of a drill hammered through the office.

"God," said Ross, "those workmen. We're getting extra space, you know, but it's chaos at the moment."

"Fennerman was your man the whole time, wasn't he?" said Heron. "The court-martial was set up to launch him into the postwar world and establish contact with the Nazi survivors."

Ross smiled. "You weren't the only Judas goat, Harry. Anyway, they all bit when he dropped the bait. Everybody wanted it. The Russians for propaganda, and quite prepared to kill for it, too. They disposed of your little Soho tart."

"And Ursula?"

He nodded. "German security sugared the bait by

spiriting her away. The Russians blew her up when they couldn't get at her. No sense of humor, either, you see."

He stared at Heron. "You look terribly disapproving, Harry. What's the matter?"

"You don't care, do you?" said Heron. "Not about anybody. It's just a complicated chess game to you."

"Oh, my gawd." Ross sighed in mock agony. "Sermon time. You know, I told you before. You're really not cut out for this sort of thing. It took the KGB forty years to set up the Lonsdale operation. They're planting the seeds now of things that won't even come to fruition before the year two thousand. We have to do our little things, too."

"And now?" asked Heron.

"We've got all we want, thank you. It's all in the files."

Heron pushed aside his teacup. "Well, I'm going to blow the lid off it," he said. "I'm going to sell the story. The whole story. I'm going to expose this crowd, believe me. I'll get them on the front page, I'll . . ."

Ross shook his head. "That's what you think, old boy. Now let me tell you the facts of life. You're discredited. A washed-out Fleet Street man. Who'll believe you?"

"They will," said Heron grimly.

Ross sighed again. "And there'll be the little matter of a D-notice. You can't win, Harry. We've got you to rights. Go away. Leave it to us. Don't make more trouble for yourself."

"I like trouble," said Heron.

84

They were having dinner in a little dimly lit eating place behind King's Road, but they weren't really interested in eating.

"You know your phone doesn't work?" said Lotte.

He smiled. "That's right," he said happily. "They've cut it off."

"Congratulations," she said. "At least they're no longer interested in you."

"I wouldn't be so sure."

It was over the coffee that she said it.

"Harry, one thing he didn't tell you, did he?"

"What?"

"Why it's still secret. Why, after all these years, when all the files have been opened and all the archives are available and everything can be read by historians and students, Goering's real testament is still kept secret."

"I suppose they think it wouldn't do any good to release it," said Heron, but he didn't sound convinced.

"I don't believe that," said Lotte. "They haven't worried about the rest of the Nazi muck. What is it Goering wrote down that they're so frightened about? What are they afraid of?"

"I don't know."

"Or maybe . . ." She stopped.

He felt cold suddenly.

"Or maybe Ross told you a lie. Maybe they *can't* release it. Because they haven't got it. Because it *has* been stolen."

They stared at each other.

Later that night, she asked him sleepily, "Harry, what are you going to do now?"

"I've got big plans," he said, and yawned. "I'm going to spend a lot of time being very busy doing nothing." He paused. "At first. Then I've got unfinished business."

She snuggled up to him. "Can I do that with you?"

"Yes," said Heron. "Why don't we start now?"

85

"What's the matter, Glen?" asked Wurtzberg, straightening the new official photograph of President Carter that he had just hung on the wall next to the one of Nixon. "Something bothering you?"

"Ross just called," said Seltzer. He had entered looking unhappy.

"So?"

"That guy Heron and the girl flew off half an hour ago on the noon flight to New York. They'll arrive at Kennedy in six hours." Seltzer pressed his digital watch. "Two thirty-five New York time."

Wurtzberg had straightened the picture to his satisfaction. He sat down behind his desk.

"How kind of Ross to keep us posted," he said, shifting some papers to one side. He was in a tidying-up mood.

"Ross wants us to turn them back at Kennedy." Seltzer studied his boss warily. "He doesn't want them out of his little grasp. He says it shouldn't be a problem for immigration to find some excuse."

Wurtzberg shook his head. "No way. If their passports are in order, if they've got their visas, they can do what they like."

Seltzer stared at the statue of Roosevelt through the window. Wurtzberg's rank gave him a good view of Grosvenor Square.

"You know what's worrying Ross," said Seltzer.

Wurtzberg smiled. "He's not worried, Glen. He's shitting himself. Once Heron's in the States, he can find friendly ears. He can start letting this out of the bag . . ."

Seltzer sat down. "Right. That's what's bugging the British. No D-notices. No Official Secrets Act, not in God's country. Heron will find somebody to listen. Maybe even some eager beaver on *The Washington Post*. Or the *Times*—"

"Or *Screw* magazine, for all I care," interrupted Wurtzberg. He reached for his Havanas. "Relax. I don't think anybody will buy it."

"Ross says some guy might invoke the Freedom of Information Act. Resurrect the Goering document. And then . . ."

Wurtzberg lit his cigar with relish.

"It'll be too late, Glen," he announced happily. "Much too late. You see, next week we're releasing it."

Seltzer sat upright. "You what!"

"That's right. Too many people in on the act now, so Langley says let's release it. Give the text to the public. Then who cares? It'll be staler than the Duke of Windsor."

"They must be crazy." Seltzer blinked. "Not the text. The real text."

"Ah," said Wurtzberg. "Good man. You guessed."

Seltzer kept staring at him.

"You hit it on the nail. We're going to release a text. We're going to say, 'That, fellows, is the Goering Testament.'" Wurtzberg beamed. "Got it?"

Slowly Seltzer stood up.

"And the real thing—" he began, but Wurtzberg stopped him.

"The real thing, Glen, well, that's another story, isn't it?" He pressed his office intercom.

"Jean, call Mr. Ross at the Ministry of Defence. Tell him Mr. Seltzer and I are taking him to lunch." He looked at Seltzer. "The Ivy, okay? Say, one o'clock?"

"Jesus Christ," said Seltzer. "And what about Heron?"

Wurtzberg looked up at the array of Presidents on his wall. Kennedy, Johnson, Nixon, Ford, Carter. They made a neat line next to his framed official commendations.

"Heron?" he said. "Oh, that's all taken care of, too."

The Prophecy

"In fifty or sixty years' time, there will be statues of Hermann Goering all over Germany. Little statues, maybe, but one in every German home."

—Goering, before he committed suicide

"If those papers ever come to light, they would cause a third world war. . . ."

—Field Marshal Lord Montgomery

About the Author

George Markstein began his wide-ranging writing career as a Fleet Street crime reporter. He has been story consultant and feature writer in British television; his screenplay for the feature film *Robbery* won the British Writers Guild award. Two of George Markstein's credits in particular have made his name a familiar one in the U.S.: he wrote the screenplay for *The Odessa File* and created the popular TV series *The Prisoner*. His novels include *The Cooler* and *Chance Awakening*.

The most fascinating people and events of World War II

Available at your bookstore or use this coupon.

___**ADOLF HITLER, John Toland**   27533 3.95
Pulitzer Prize-winning author John Toland's bestselling biography of Hitler based on over 150 interviews with the numerous survivors of his circle of friends, servants and associates.

___**A MAN CALLED INTREPID, William Stevenson**   28124 2.50
The authentic account of the most decisive intelligence operations of World War II - and the superspy who controlled them.

___**CYNTHIA, H. Montgomery Hyde**   28197 1.95
The incredible, but fully-documented true story of a brave, shrewd sensual woman's contribution to the allied victory — in World War II's most unusual battlefield.

___**PIERCING THE REICH, Joseph E. Persico**   28280 2.50
After 35 years of silence, top-secret files have been opened to reveal the stupendous drama of the most perilous and heroic chapter of intelligence history.

**BB   BALLANTINE MAIL SALES
      Dept. NE, 201 E. 50th St., New York, N.Y. 10022**

Please send me the BALLANTINE or DEL REY BOOKS I have checked above. I am enclosing $. . . . . (add 50¢ per copy to cover postage and handling). Send check or money order — no cash or C.O.D.'s please. Prices and numbers are subject to change without notice.

Name_____

Address_____

City_____State_____Zip Code_____

06   Allow at least 4 weeks for delivery.   NE-13

The best
in modern fiction from
BALLANTINE

Available at your bookstore or use this coupon.

____ SOMETHING HAPPENED by Joseph Heller   29353 2.95
By the author of **Good As Gold**, about greed, ambition, love, lust, hate,
fear, marriage, adultery—the life we all lead today. "Brilliant."—Saturday
Review/World.

____ ORDINARY PEOPLE by Judith Guest   29132 2.75
The remarkable novel about an ordinary family coming together—and
apart.

____ ANOTHER ROADSIDE ATTRACTION by Tom Robbins   29245 2.95
An extravagant, wonderful novel by the author of **Even Cowgirls Get the
Blues**. "Written with a style and humor that haven't been seen since Mark
Twain . . . it is a prize."—Los Angeles Times.

____ FALCONER by John Cheever   28589 2.75
The unforgettable story of a substantial, middle-class man and the pas-
sions that propel him into murder, prison and an undreamed of liberation.
"Cheever's triumph . . . a great American novel."—Newsweek.

____ BLOOD TIE by Mary Lee Settle   28154 2.50
National Book Award Winner. A powerful novel of strangers on an idyllic
island, whose common needs in the face of destruction bind them together.

____ THE KILLER ANGELS by Michael Shaara   29535 2.75
The Pulitzer Prize-winning novel about the Battle of Gettysburg. Chilling,
compelling, factual.

____ A CLOCKWORK ORANGE by Anthony Burgess   28411 2.25
The most terrifying vision of the future since 1984. "A brilliant novel
. . . inventive."—The New York Times.

BB BALLANTINE MAIL SALES
Dept. LG, 201 E. 50th St., New York, N.Y. 10022

Please send me the BALLANTINE or DEL REY. BOOKS I have
checked above. I am enclosing $. . . . . (add 50¢ per copy to
cover postage and handling). Send check or money order — no
cash or C.O.D.'s please. Prices and numbers are subject to change
without notice.

Name_____

Address_____

City_____State_____Zip Code_____

Allow at least 4 weeks for delivery.

G-3

Military works by
MARTIN CAIDIN

One of the best known and most respected writers of true-life war adventures.

Available at your bookstore or use this coupon.

___**FLYING FORTS**   28308 2.25
The extraordinary story of the B-17 in World War Two. With 32 pages of photos.

___**FORK-TAILED DEVIL: THE P-38**   28301 2.25
More wartime excitement, in the air and on land.

___**THE NIGHT HAMBURG DIED**   28303 1.95
The bomber raid that turned Hamburg into a roaring inferno of flame. With 8 pages of photos.

___**THUNDERBOLT**   28307 1.95
Flying the deadly P-47 with the 56th fighter group in World War II. 8 pages of photos.

___**A TORCH TO THE ENEMY**   28304 1.95
The complete story of U.S. air power and the fire raids that destroyed Japan. With 16 pages of photos.

___**ZERO**   28305 2.25
The first overall account—from the enemy viewpoint—of Japan's air war in the Pacific. With 8 pages of photos.

BB **BALLANTINE MAIL SALES**
Dept. AL, 201 E. 50th St., New York, N.Y. 10022

Please send me the BALLANTINE or DEL REY BOOKS I have checked above. I am enclosing $.......... (add 50¢ per copy to cover postage and handling). Send check or money order — no cash or C.O.D.'s please. Prices and numbers are subject to change without notice.

Name_____

Address_____

City_____State_____Zip Code_____

06   Allow at least 4 weeks for delivery.   AL-26